PRAISE FOR ALYSSA RICHARDS

THE HAUNTING OF ALCOTT MANOR is a fascinating tale of tragedy, ghosts, and soulmates. Mystery fans will enjoy this heroine's efforts to track down clues -- both tangible and ghostly -- while trying to find the truth about a woman's death. Romance fans will adore this match-up of a strong heroine and an enigmatic yet endearingly charming and earnest hero. I look forward to reading the next book in this tantalizing ALCOTT MANOR series." Fresh Fiction Review, THE HAUNTING OF ALCOTT MANOR

"Having read Alyssa Richards other books, I knew I was in for a treat, even though this was a slightly different genre. And gothic suspense being one of my absolute favorites, I was extremely psyched to read this book. Fortunately, everything that I anticipated about how good this book would be, and how much I would enjoy it, came true.

At first glance, this might appear to be your average haunted house story. But in the hands of this very capable, and highly readable author, it becomes so much more. The haunting was unique and the story revolving around the haunting was very intriguing. I totally did not anticipate the way the story was going or how it was going to end up. This was a great first entry in a new genre that I hope the author will continue. This book, as well as everything else this author has written, comes highly recommended." — DT Chantel, book reviewer, THE HAUNTING OF ALCOTT MANOR

"Man oh man! Alyssa Richards has seriously outdone herself with this trilogy. It encompasses love, passion, deception, heartache, reality and alternate reality. Just stunning from start to finish. This trilogy is awesome. If you're looking for a paranormal romance that's focused around psychics and time travel, definitely grab this trilogy. It's simply amazing!" —*Nay's Pink Bookshelf, THE FINE ART OF DECEPTION SERIES*

5.0 out of 5 stars "Now this is what I'm talking about...absofreakingamazing!

"It's authors like Ms. Richards that really opened up the portals to my world, and instilled/nurtured within me a love for reading. Hook, line and sinker you are pulled fast and hard into her storylines and are wrecked when you've reached the end...you just don't want it to be over. The Haunting of Alcott Manor is no different and has a wonderful mix of gothic suspense/mystery with a titter of romance that will captivate you..and the end...omg I so didn't see that coming. What a stunning conclusion!" —*Amazon Reviewer, THE HAUNTING OF ALCOTT MANOR*

5.0 out of 5 stars That ending...!? Are you kidding me?!

"Like others, I'm sure, I've read hundred(s) of

these types of books. This was a great read, great twists and turns. ...and the end...? WOW! What's really getting me right now though? Henry and Gemma at still with me....days after I've finished the book! I cried with them, I loved with them, and they touched me deeply! Great job! (This is the first time I have been inspired enough to write a review, too!)" *Amazon Book Reviewer, THE HAUNTING OF ALCOTT MANOR*

"A MURDER AT ALCOTT MANOR is very definitely a thrill-a-minute tale of evil trying to keep a stranglehold on the living. This is a perfect book for readers who enjoy non- stop action and suspense with a dash of sexy. ...This story will appeal to readers who love suspense, the paranormal, and everyday people who become unexpected heroes. Hope to read more gothic tales of love and paranormal peril by Alyssa Richards in the future." Fresh Fiction Review, A MURDER AT ALCOTT MANOR

A STRANGER AT ALCOTT MANOR

ALYSSA RICHARDS

Ebook ISBN-13: 978-0-9991555-5-4
Paperback ISBN-13: 978-0-9991555-7-8
Editing by Peter Senftleben
Proofreading by Charity Chimni

**Sign up for Alyssa's newsletter at to receive special offers and news
about her latest releases.**

You can follow her on:
Instagram

Contact Alyssa at:
authoralyssarichards@protonmail.com

1

Ancient water oaks swayed in the warm, salty breezes and threw their inky shadows against the front pillars of Alcott Manor. Peyton Alcott stood next to the passenger side door of the rental and dropped the car keys onto the seat. She stared at the front of the house, tracing the outline of the bottle of Xanax bulging in her small soft-sided purse.

The manor's first floor windows were warped with age, and the darkness inside was deep and cold and formless. The home's secrets were palpable, but unseen. They shifted like forgotten spirits, hidden memories and old nightmares.

This visit to her family's ancestral estate was her first alone in twenty years. The prescription bottle lid flicked open with a pop. Just one dose would cushion whatever memories came to light. She glanced at her overstuffed computer bag in the backseat. Remembering the mountain of work she had to do, she reluctantly recapped the bottle.

She lifted her work satchel, filled well beyond its unzipped brim with a laptop, client files and instructions from her mother. Rounded oyster shells crunched beneath her Jimmy Choos.

At a long squeal of brakes, she spun, squinting at the black car with its round headlights and narrow front grill. She lowered her bag to the ground, her stomach clenched. The car's white-haired driver was a ghost from her past she'd hoped to outrun.

An oceanic updraft caught her work papers and they scattered. She snatched at them, catching only one. The rest danced and twirled down the stark white drive and away from Alcott Manor. She envied their ability to escape.

She cursed the wind and the lost papers, the manor and the land it was built on, and her own attendance at this godforsaken place.

The old Plymouth rattled to a rolling stop behind her rental car with another long screech of brakes. The elderly woman exited with a slowness that made Peyton wonder if it was wise for her to be driving.

"Mrs. Miller?"

"Hope those papers weren't important." Her smile was broad and welcoming, a gesture Peyton knew better than to trust. Her eyes were moist, more from age than emotion. One was glassy.

"My goodness, it's been years." Peyton leaned down to hug her. Mrs. Miller was frailer than she remembered, but her perfume was the same. The delicate scent of roses infused with Mentholatum.

"Well, let me take a look at you." Mrs. Miller cocked her head to the side. She raked her good eye in a slow survey from the top of Peyton's jeweled hair combs to the tip toes of her polished heels.

Peyton stood trying to hold her smile, feeling like the

blue-ribboned pig at the county fair where winning made you the blue plate special.

"Still have your daddy's good looks, I see. Let's hope you kept his temperament. Your mother says you're a big city girl now, but coming home to get married?"

"Yes, ma'am. I live in Boston, and the wedding is in four days." Peyton wished she had remembered to spin her large diamond engagement ring to the inside of her hand. But Mrs. Miller caught sight of it and Peyton saw her lips tighten.

"You still take all those pictures like you used to?" Mrs. Miller asked.

"No, I haven't had the time for much photography these days."

"I thought as much." She patted Peyton's shoulders twice. "I've got just the thing for you. Carry these inside." The rear car door groaned when she pulled it open. Mrs. Miller pointed to two large gray containers and instructed Peyton to be careful.

"These are more of the estate's cameras and tintypes that we had at the museum. We're bringing much of it here, now that you're organizing the house for tours. You'll need them for exhibits and whatnot. Jayne Ella insisted I bring these. You know how your mother is." She raised one eyebrow.

Yes. She knew exactly how her mother was.

"Are you still working at the museum?" Peyton hoisted the first plastic carton from the back seat and directed the small talk away from herself.

"Lord, yes, honey. I'll probably die in the place. No one else in Charleston knows as much about the city's history. Or Alcott Manor's history. Except for you, of course. I taught you especially well."

"Yes ma'am." She put the container near the double

front door, and the tintypes shuddered with a metallic clat-
ter. She stared at a sign that was pasted to one of the front
pillars, and her stomach dropped to the floor.

Beau Spencer
Missing
Last Seen at Alcott Manor
REWARD

Beau was in his early twenties, with bed-head-sexy
blond hair and light blue eyes that were striking enough for
a double take. The camera had caught him with his devil-
may-care smile that won him a free pass whenever he
wanted. Too many emotions knocked at the back door of
her memory bank.

"Sad about Beau, isn't it?" Mrs. Miller said.

Peyton started at the closeness of Mrs. Miller's voice that
squeaked like an old chair.

"He was such a wild child. Lord only knows if he's really
missing or if he just hopped a plane and left. Did y'all ever
speak after he stood you up at the church?"

The question hit her like a slap, Peyton squeezed her
eyes shut to stem the angry tide of memories: Waiting for an
hour in the church parlor in her full-skirted wedding dress,
her mother ultimately telling her they had waited long
enough, that Beau obviously wasn't coming. Her father
saying he would make the announcement to the guests.

"No," she finally said. "Do you know who posted this
here?"

"His daddy, I'm sure. Austin Spencer has them posted all
over town. He stuck one right on the museum's front
window."

Beau had been gone for nine years, long enough to be

declared legally dead. His parents had even held a funeral for him and erected a gravestone with his name on the front as if he were buried there.

Peyton peeled the tape from the white paint, folded the flyer in half, and half again.

Mrs. Miller's phone rang like an old telephone bell. She retrieved it from one of the patch pockets of her cotton dress and tilted her head to look through the bottom half of her glasses. "Just a minute, honey. I have to take this." She walked to the far end of the wide porch, her low-heeled shoes scuffling along the painted wood.

Mrs. Miller looked and moved like a woman far older than she actually was. She used to be a vibrant and beautiful woman, not much older than Peyton's own mother, Jayne Ella. But when Mrs. Miller's daughter went missing over twenty years ago, her hair turned stark white and everything about her physique withered and slowed and sagged.

Peyton loaded the other container to the front porch to keep herself distracted. Mrs. Miller was still talking on the phone. Peyton's directions for the combination lock were gone with the wind, so she decided to wait. Maybe Mrs. Miller would have the access code.

She opened one of the containers and found seven neat rows of dusty tintype photographs. She hadn't touched a tintype since college. The first captured memory—several Alcott family members posed in front of the grand staircase —sent a pang of anxiety from her head to her heart and back again. The threat of an old nightmare.

"Stop it," she whispered to the fear like she was the one in charge. She licked her dry lips and held a different glass plate to the light.

This tintype was a traditional wedding photo from the

1850s, and Peyton recognized the bride. She was a niece of the original owners of the manor, Benjamin and Bertha Mae Alcott. The wedding party had gathered in the ballroom and Peyton scanned the faces one by one. She knew them all, and their stories, thanks to her internship with Mrs. Miller at the museum.

One man at the side of the gathering sent a shiver of cold dancing across her back. His hair was shorter in length, though the layers had grown out. His light-colored eyes fixed straight ahead as if he looked right at her. The charm-filled smile he had often used as his ticket to get what he wanted was gone, but his lips were the same full shape she remembered.

It was impossible, though undeniable. The guest in the 1850s tintype was the man she almost married. He was the man who was missing, Beau Spencer.

2

M rs. Miller's shuffling footsteps echoed in the black hallways of Alcott Manor.

Peyton waited on the front porch, one of the manor's 500 pound doors was open. She was uninterested in crossing the threshold, unable to offer Mrs. Miller any assistance in finding a light switch. She knew the renovations had been completed. But she couldn't forget the manor as it looked from the inside when she was ten: dark and dank, holes in the floor, windows boarded and barred.

She studied the darkening sky, dotted with gray clouds that hung still. Even with all the wind blowing off the ocean, the clouds didn't move. Nothing moved or changed in this town. Not the manor or her family, certainly not the past. Which was why she had left.

She tapped her left foot three times, then her right foot, a brain and energy balancing exercise they taught in her yoga class. "What we do to one side, we must do to the other," the teacher said before a movement.

She liked the idea of balance. The practice calmed her, made her think there might be some universal formula that governed the insanities of life, offered her a way to be safe. If only she did things right.

In the years since Beau disappeared she had built a good life for herself. She was up for a big promotion, and her fiancé was as handsome as he was successful. Her life was brand new again and her future was waiting for her in Boston. A different life, a much busier life, filled with anthills of traffic and people, following agendas that seemingly held the utmost importance.

She had a few things to wrap up first. For her family. Mostly for her mother who stood ready and willing to become the next matron of Alcott Manor.

Peyton agreed to have her wedding on the great lawn of the manor. Her mother had convinced her that her wedding would help launch a new line of business at the manor. Once those glorious wedding photos hit the paper, every girl within 100 miles would want to have her wedding at Alcott Manor, too. Renting the property out for weddings and other events would be a hefty revenue stream for the family. She acquiesced to her mother's insistence, because the sooner the manor was financially stable, the more freedom Peyton would have.

She had also promised to get the tours and exhibits set up, for the manor's other source of income. After those three things had been checked off her list, then she would begin her new life in Boston with Ira.

Mrs. Miller's trailing footsteps moved in the opposite direction of the front doors. She muttered something about how a fuse must have blown.

Peyton reopened the plastic container and searched for the tintype of the wedding party she had seen earlier. She had been so convinced that Beau Spencer, her first love, her former fiancé and a man who had been missing for nine years, was in the photo. Of course she must have been mistaken. Seeing his face again after all this time, and pasted to the front of the manor where she least expected it, had thrown her.

It concerned her that his image still had that effect on her, mostly because she never wanted to despair like that again. She ran her fingers over the folded image she had placed in her pants pocket. Memories danced across her heart. Nerves stirred in the pit of her stomach.

Her phone rang—her boss. "Amanda."

"Peyton, just wanted to check in and see when you're going to have the proposal for The Sweet Chocolate Company."

"I'm working on it tonight. I'll have it to you before morning."

"You have all the ideas ironed out between your ears?"

Amanda knew that Peyton had to see the plan in her own head first, then she typed it out. She was the only Account Director who prepared a proposal by pacing and talking to herself before she put anything on paper. Then she wrote a perfect proposal on the first draft. She could remember every detail, that's how her near perfect memory worked.

"First thing we'll do is change their slogan. It has to come off of their website, their to-go bags, napkins, advertisements, everything. 'By hand' is not the right slogan considering the founder was accused of sexual misconduct."

"Excellent idea. By the way, his daughter called this morning. Lily said she needs to make a decision by Wednesday as to which PR firm to go with."

"As in two days from now? I thought we had until next week on this?"

"Apparently someone leaked the lawsuit to the news and

they're getting bad press. Former employee, I think. Did you talk with Lily before you left?"

"I did. She was great. Very open about everything that happened." Peyton exhaled relief. That first step with any client always made her nervous. They had to be honest with her about what they did, or what someone did in their company that screwed things up. Once she knew the real story, she could go about fixing their image.

"Confess the truth," Peyton remembered her grand-mother's words. "It will set you free, sweetheart. Confess it, stand on it, cling to it. The truth will always give you a way forward." She believed that. She also believed that honesty was necessary for her clients. It gave her projects momen-tum, started a measure of healing. Nothing could be truly fixed without honesty.

"I'll definitely send it tonight."

"Great. I'll pitch it for you tomorrow."

Peyton stopped talking. Last thing she wanted was for this account to go to someone else in the firm. Amanda had a reputation for letting other people do the creative, while she took the client for herself.

"I'm just going to pitch it for you," Amanda said like she had read Peyton's mind.

"And our agreement is the same, that I'm promoted to Senior Vice President when I land this client?"

"Well, technically, I guess I would be landing the client since—"

Amanda seemed to catch herself. The Sweet Chocolate Company was a prize account and Peyton didn't think Amanda could get it without Peyton's creative.

"Not that that matters. Of course, stakes are the same. Senior Vice President when this client comes in."

"Great. Let's make sure we have that in writing and I'll get the creative to you tonight."

"Oh—I'll, um—"

"I do better when everything is in writing."

"Yeah, I'll email something to you today," Amanda said quickly. "Now, hurry back. I don't want to lose my best person to the plantations of Charleston."

Peyton glanced at the house that seemed to watch her. "You don't need to be concerned about that"

They said their goodbyes and Peyton flipped her hair behind her shoulders. She stared at the house like a challenge. She walked toward the front door. Each step reminded her of a different time when boards fell from the front of the house, revealing its darkened insides.

Her phone rang. Like grabbing for a lifeline, she answered it quickly. "Ira. Hey." She walked back down the stairs and into the driveway.

"Hi, hon. I'm at the hospital, only have a minute. Wanted to make sure you're okay." The sound of Ira's voice calmed her, brought her back to the person she was in Boston—confident, strong, accomplished.

"Thanks, I'm fine. I'm at the manor. I guess my Mom will be here shortly." The thought of seeing her mother filled her with dread. Her mother was too controlling, too selfish, too...everything. Being at the manor again was bad enough. But being there with her mother made her want to drink shots of hard liquor. For breakfast.

"Alright, well, call me if you need me. My flight arrives tomorrow morning."

"I thought you were coming in tonight?"

"Got called into a surgery for tomorrow morning. After that I'm on the first plane out. You sure you're alright? You sound, I don't know. Not quite yourself."

Peyton twisted the oversized diamond solitaire around her ring finger. "I'm fine. Just—this woman is here. She's always been odd." She didn't tell him the real reason she felt uncomfortable around Mrs. Miller.

"I thought the South took pride in their odd family members."

Peyton laughed. "I guess under normal circumstances we do sort of put them on the proverbial front porch and show them off. Mrs. Miller isn't family, though. Our families were friends when I was younger. I interned with her at the museum when I was in high school."

"If you've known her all your life, then she's probably close to family."

"I don't remember exactly when we met." Peyton did know exactly but she didn't want to think about it. She didn't want to think of most things concerning the manor.

"You—not remember something? You should see a doctor. I'll be down immediately."

"Stop. Be serious."

"I am serious. I miss you. Too much. And now you're forgetting things, which isn't like you."

"I haven't been gone long enough to be missed. I've always had a few blank spots around that time in my life." No one besides Beau and her family knew that she had missing memories. She was surprised she mentioned it to Ira.

She glanced at the doorway, remembering the only snippet she could from that night when she was ten—sitting on the bottom step of the grand staircase inside the manor, smoothing her torn and bloody white dress.

An oily chill slid through her insides. It had been so long since that happened, she tried to tell herself she didn't actually know if it had happened. Maybe her mother was right that it had been a dream, a nightmare that she had inadvertently held onto as truth. Children did that sort of thing.

A stiff breeze shot across her back, like the manor tapped her on the shoulder, correcting her. Still she argued her point. Actually, they were her mother's points. First, she didn't forget things. Ever. Her memory was nearly photogenic. Second, why would she have been in the manor at age ten? The house was mostly dilapidated then. Some parts were completely restored, but no one had been allowed near the grand staircase. So it would have been impossible for a child of ten years to wander in and sit on the bottom step of that area of the house.

Her mother had been insistent that it was only a bad dream. But even as an adult, Peyton occasionally woke up in the middle of the night, crying, gasping, dreaming that she was ten again and sitting on the bottom step of the grand staircase inside Alcott Manor. Alone, frightened, the front of her dress splotched with blood and sticking to her skin.

Then, a hand reached up from beneath the floorboards and snatched her, dragged her below ground where she suffocated to death. Her mother told her she had been reading too much Greek Mythology back then. The teacher made them read about Persephone and how she became Queen of the Underworld. Jayne Ella said she never should have let her read those colorful stories when she was so young and her imagination was so wide open.

No other details came to light about that flash of a memory. Not while she slept and not after she awoke. In fact, the entire last half of her fourth-grade year had disappeared from her otherwise perfect memory.

Peyton didn't want to remember. She liked not knowing.

She looked at the tintype still in her hand, her gaze sunk into the expression in his eyes. The others in the photo appeared to look at the photographer. He looked through the lens and right at her.

"It's not the time you've been gone. It's more just the knowing that you're gone that makes me miss you. That's more than enough. Have you gotten any of our registering done?" Ira asked.

"Registering?"

"For our china and silver, the everyday and the flatware..."

"Oh, right."

"You know, typically it's not the groom who remembers these things. I thought you loved china?"

"I do. It's just—there's too much going on with work and the manor."

"Well, you're only getting married once. So, you might want to think about it, soon. Also, Mother is asking about the patterns we've chosen. I need to let her know."

Her heart tightened. His mother had been involved in the wedding planning from the beginning. Carol Byrne adored her son, and by default, Peyton. But she was strong to the point of domineering and Ira defaulted to his mother's opinion more frequently than Peyton liked.

Their family was unlike Peyton's in every way and she struggled with the very public arena where their family thrived. Ira's father was a high profile attorney who was often in the news for his latest case. Ira's mother was a society queen, also featured in the paper and magazines but more so for the events she either organized or attended. Their world revolved around money, image and prestige.

Peyton attended the fundraisers and the society events that were important to Ira and she enjoyed the dresses and the limos and the fancy dinners. Unlike Ira she felt she was pretending, an outsider visiting a foreign world. With time she would adjust and her discomfort would dissipate.

The smile in Ira's voice gave her new motivation. "You're right. I'll go online and get that done."

They said their I love yous and she ended the call. She looked again at the image in the tintype that resembled Beau.

When she'd first met Beau she'd had no idea that her heart could love someone as much as she loved him. When he left her at the altar, she hadn't known it was possible to feel that much pain.

She left the church on what should have been her wedding day in faded jeans and a blue t-shirt, hairpins still holding her bridal updo in place, and she'd overheard Beau's parents arguing. His mother stood on one side of their car, blaming his father for insisting that Beau work at the bank. "You pushed him so hard he left!" his mother yelled.

"He left because he came to his senses and decided not to marry that girl. He'll be back, and it's a good thing we won't be connected to that family," his father said. "The lot of them, they're all trash."

Peyton aimed her phone flashlight on the tintype to see the photo more clearly. Her stomach clenched. She snapped a photo of him and enlarged it on the screen. Maybe it was an ancestor of Beau's. His family had been in Charleston as long as hers had.

She replaced the tintype in the box, pulled her shoulders back and narrowed her focus on the job ahead: get her proposal done for work, map out a publicity and tour plan for the manor, organize the manor's artifacts into exhibits. Wrap up last minute wedding details. Marry Ira.

Beau's doppelganger stared at her from her phone screen.

She turned her screen to black.

She stepped inside the house.

She shivered even though the weather was warm.

The gold chandelier in the foyer shined bright, its light reflecting on highly polished, black and white marble floors. Mahogany wainscoting and marble walls ensconced the space in regal warmth and comfort. Heavy crown molding in a gold leaf and floral theme accented the ceilings and arched doorways in good taste, and she saw the appeal she had often spotted in long ago photographs.

The small bust of a woman was carved into the center of every arch molding in sight and Peyton recognized her immediately. With her hair piled into high pinned curls, her high neck lace collar, and poised expression, Peyton knew that was Bertha Mae, the original matriarch of Alcott Manor. A woman who was known as much for her beauty as she was for surviving the tragic mysteries that filled her life.

She was a legend in Alcott family lore and a heroine of Peyton's. She had already planned to build an exhibit dedicated to Bertha Mae Alcott. She could include Bertha Mae's diary as a testament to her ability to overcome. Her ancestor had documented her trials in detail, her strength rising off of every page. She forgave those who wronged her and acted with compassion when life and luck turned against many of them. Her daughter Rachel was sick for most of her short life, and there were quite a few tintypes of Bertha Mae caring for her sick daughter, giving her spoonfuls of medicine and holding her on her lap. Tragically, Rachel drowned at an early age.

Mrs. Miller appeared from a side door at the end of the hallway, holding a lit candle. "It was a fuse." Her heels dragged along the hardwoods with each step in an even, lazy rhythm. She blew the flame from the candle, a wisp of smoke curled next to her.

When she reached the foyer, she craned her neck to look where Peyton had been studying the crown molding. "I see you found Bertha Mae." Her smile was broad and knowing, as if she had just introduced an old friend. Her uneven teeth appeared gray in the low light.

"The original Mrs. Alcott still watches every person who has ever walked through those double doors. This is still her house. She owned it first, she owned it best. Probably always will, I think." Mrs. Miller kept an eye on the carving. "If you listen closely you'll find that she's here—her memories, the way she ran the house. It's all here."

Peyton felt it, Bertha Mae's presence. It was palpable, even though they had long been in their grave. The sensation bled through the walls like a dark stare, an angry mood, a thickness that clung too close.

The past needed to be put to rest.

The exhibits would do just that. They would be a salute to the first Alcott family, and especially, Bertha Mae. That would bring the manor the peace it needed.

She could have sworn she felt the house notice her plan.

It could have been the lush period furniture or the architecture or the entire picture-perfect presentation. But it seemed that the house was more than a structure full of relics.

Life shifted beneath the seen.

Like the combination of the furniture, the fixtures, and the life inside the walls, set the stage for something to occur.

A shiver ran through her body. Like the wiggle of a live wire.

"This house has seen it all," Mrs. Miller said. "And it

forgets nothing. It shares its secrets when it wants and exacts a measure of justice in the process."

Whatever Mrs. Miller was referring to, Peyton didn't want to know the manor's secrets. She didn't want its justice. She knew enough about the manor's past to know that some stories shouldn't be told.

"Of all the Alcotts, I've always related to Bertha Mae the most, because she lost a child, you know. A beautiful child," Mrs. Miller said. "Oh, put the containers in there with the rest of them. Now that the fuse is fixed, I'm going to make a pot of coffee." Her voice bounced off the wide hallways like she was in a vacant castle.

Peyton hadn't always been afraid of the manor. When she and her younger sister, Layla, were little, they would run along the beach and stop where the great lawn met the sand. They would challenge one another to see who would run closest to the house. Peyton always won.

But after one brisk night when Peyton was ten, that all changed.

Peyton watched Mrs. Miller muddle her way to the kitchen, feet scuffling, her hand touching the wall now and then for balance. She griped under her breath; Peyton couldn't hear what she said but it didn't sound good.

Peyton glanced toward the foyer, ornate with gold and marble, a pre-Civil War version of an English castle entry. She tried to focus on that aspect and to get into a work frame of mind. But memories of her and Beau in the manor played too clear, like they were really there: sneaking in the front door as teenagers, his smile and eyes gentle and wide, encouraging her to follow him. He said he could get her over her fears. He said that he wanted to, that he loved her so much he didn't want her to be afraid of anything.

She pressed her fingers against the pain in her chest, turned away, tried to focus her attention on something else. Her therapist in Boston prescribed Xanax for her time at the manor, she wondered if she should take it.

"Treat your anxiety like a headache," she had said. "First sign of any symptoms of anxiousness, take a pill. Or at least half of a pill. Some memories just aren't meant to be recovered, the brain insulates us for a reason." Peyton agreed and swore she would take at least a half of one when she needed it. She put her hand in her purse and felt the smooth outline of the bottle.

Long before he left, she had told Beau how she remembered being at the manor one night. Alone, cold, scared. Bloody.

"Oh, darlin'. You're safe now." He held her close, his voice was smooth and sweet like warm caramel. Her fears relaxed when she was in his arms, as if that night at the manor had never even happened.

That was when he talked her into visiting the manor with him, once when they were in high school, and again when they were in college. The manor was fairly well restored then, at least for a little while. "Revisiting will help you get over that nightmare," he'd said.

He walked them into the ballroom, played waltz music on his phone and offered her his hand. "Miss Peyton, may I have the honor of a dance?" He strengthened his already southern accent with the longer vowels used only in days gone by.

They waltzed together under the windowed ceiling, it was the same waltz they had learned in cotillion classes years before. Peyton wondered if she could recover enough from that night when she was ten, if they could have their wedding and reception at the manor. Just like so many other Alcott family members had.

But she never recovered.

Mrs. Miller whistled from the kitchen and the scent of coffee wafted through the hallways. Peyton followed orders and brought the other container into the foyer. On her way to the ballroom she passed through the main living room. It was an area long enough to boast three small chandeliers—one over the sitting areas at each end of the room, and a larger one in the middle that was centered over a round table.

Alcott Manor's past was shadowed with murder, disappearances and a century of ghostly hauntings. Thanks to the last restoration, it had once again become a beautiful home with patterned silk wall coverings, gold-framed portraits and exquisite furniture, but there was still a darkness beneath it all, threatening to haunt.

Was it just because she knew the home's history?

Maybe the anxiety was getting to be too much. Alcott stories, memories of Beau. They swirled faster through her head, competing for center stage. She felt it on her skin, the manor pushed its story from all around her, like it could own her, make her a part of its sad history.

She felt that if she spent too much time in the house, she might never leave. As if one day in the manor might turn into another and then another, and then one day, there wouldn't be a way out.

She breathed deeply to center herself, tried not to take the prescription. Finishing the job at hand was her ticket out, so she shifted into work mode. Several crystals on the chandelier moved as though someone had touched them, and she chose to ignore that. She figured she might have to ignore several more things in the manor before her time here was done. Her left hand tapped five times, then the right hand did the same. She focused on the rhythm, breathed in the calm.

Getting tourists into the house was all about connections with tourism outlets and branding. The house would need a tagline, a positioning statement, something they could put in advertisements, on brochures and specialty items like coffee cups and drinking glasses.

She stood still. She could almost see and hear a band playing from the alcove in the middle of the room that jutted outward into the side garden. She could almost smell the scent of cigar smoke and hear the tinkling of champagne glasses that were raised in toasts. The house was a captive, not just to its history, but to its long-ago owners.

The empty rooms felt crowded. Noisy.

"Come on, Pey!" She jumped.

Beau's voice from two days before their wedding rang through the space. He jogged ahead of her, only now in slow motion, waving her forward. Too real. He stopped, doubled back and took her hand. His endless strength surged through her, lifted her up.

Life was a brilliant force coursing through him, a bright light that commanded whichever space he happened to occupy. People were drawn to that light, like moths, like worshippers who couldn't get enough.

Peyton never tired of watching the effect he had on people. Even so, she often felt his flame might consume her altogether, if she stood too close. She shook her head, turned away yet again.

She closed her eyes, tried to shut him out. But it was as if he reached for her through the walls. The memory of him wasn't going to leave her alone.

These rooms exuded a power, a draw and a pull into its past that tourists were going to love. She couldn't deny that there was some energy about the house that was alive, movement she couldn't see. She felt it on her skin. Like someone brushed her sleeve as they passed by. She examined the entirety of the room, half expecting to see someone turn the corner or come into view.

She thought of:

Alcott Manor ~ Where History Comes Alive

She made a note of it in her phone.

The juxtaposition of the splendor of the manor's design and the tragedy of the lives that had been lost there was something she would have to embrace. There was no denying Anna Alcott's murder or her husband Benjamin Alcott's hanging, or all the current day people who had either disappeared or lost their lives within the old manse.

She would have to decide if the darker information needed to be reserved for special midnight ghost tours, or would they simply blend a few plaques around the home describing the more tragic histories of certain family members?

She walked across the room, feeling watched.

Like if she peeled back the walls, she would find her Alcott ancestors living there, alive and well.

Silver framed photos were set up on a wide table and she studied them closely. Peyton hadn't seen them since she interned under Mrs. Miller in the Charleston History Museum. Alcott Manor history had occupied a significant amount of space and multiple exhibits.

When Peyton and Layla were old enough, their grandmother had insisted that both girls intern at the museum. "They should represent their own family history," her grandmother had said. "There may be dark spots in our past, but we'll overcome it one day. The girls need to be a part of that process of moving the manor forward."

Layla refused, opting instead to volunteer at the regional hospital as a candy striper. Peyton reluctantly accepted the job, knowing that her grandmother's insistence was something that had to be accommodated. The emotional price for refusing her was too steep.

There was no job training necessary, since she had long ago memorized all the stories and speeches from her grandmother.

The selection of furniture that the museum allowed occupied a suite of rooms: bedroom furniture, a couch and two chairs from the parlor, the dining room set along with its china and crystal settings, and some statuary from the ballroom. The rest was kept safely in climate-controlled storage until the manor was restored enough to once again house it on its own.

As a tour guide, Peyton described the exact history of each piece of furniture, where it was made, its style, how it had come to be in the family and its current worth. And, of course, the family stories that went along with each piece. For example, how the children piled onto the Queen Anne style couch near the fireplace each week to hear their much-loved father read Grimm's Fairy Tales to them.

Peyton's grandmother knew all sorts of stories about the original 1800s Alcott family as well and she flavored her museum tours with them. Like how the family gathered for a weekly croquet match on the back lawn, how the mother, Bertha Mae carried a skeleton key tied to her waist because she was obsessed about locking certain doors and cabinets. Or how Rachel, one of the Alcott children, loved the color blue, and her favorite place to play was in the side yard under the old magnolia tree.

She studied the three furniture settings grouped together in the long room. The stories about the Alcott family exuded from the walls, ready to spring to life. She wondered if she repeated these stories aloud if the memories might do just that—spring to life.

She went into the ballroom, a long rectangular room, painted robin's egg blue and topped from end to end with a glass ceiling. Tables along the far wall were stacked with photo albums, old newspapers, framed pictures and foam-mounted, poster-sized photos.

She recognized many of the pieces when they had either been on display or in storage at the Charleston Museum. Now that the manor was restored, Jayne Ella had negotiated for their return. It was Peyton's job to select and organize the Alcott family memorabilia into exhibits for the tour.

Her text alarm dinged. Her mother:

He's at it again. More bad press for the manor. Can you do something to offset this?

There was a document attached and she tapped the screen.

She adjusted the picture size so she could read the caption, and gasped when she saw yet another picture of Beau:

Beau Spencer, hired by the Alcott family organization to document the progress of one of the family's many restoration attempts, disappeared nine years ago today. His father, Austin Spencer, President of First Charleston Bank, has renewed his campaign for information regarding his son's disappearance. "He was last seen at Alcott Manor, then he disappeared," Austin Spencer said. "He told me not long before his disappearance that he was breaking the engagement. The two are obviously related."

"That's low even for you, Austin." She shoved her phone into her purse and wished she had dirt on Beau's father. Something, anything she could threaten him with and get him to shut up about the manor. But she didn't. She had looked.

"My Dad has spent years trying to talk me out of the photography thing, as he calls it." Beau's voice from their first date was so loud and too clear. She pressed her hands to either side of her head.

Her first date with Beau, simple, romantic, the beach for swimming and a picnic lunch. He brought his 35 mm camera and took pictures of her, which he later developed by hand. Normally she was critical of herself in photos. But he had captured a soft and pretty side of her. Unguarded, open.

"It's easy to see the beauty in you," he told her when he took her photos that day.

She still kept several of the photos tucked in the bottom of her lingerie drawer.

After they graduated from college, they were going to travel the world together. They had each complained about their respective home lives. Beau said, "We'll be homeless together. Completely free. At one with the world."

"Ira, Ira, Ira." She whispered her fiance's name to remind herself where things were in the here and now. She walked to the female mannequins, each one donned in a long period-specific dress. Peyton paused briefly in front of an ivory brocade wedding dress.

She exhaled deep and long and texted her mother that she would think about what to do. Austin Spencer had long blamed the Alcotts and the manor for his son's death, saying there was something strange about the home. That it ought to be condemned. Unfortunately, he had a very loud voice in Charleston, one that people tended to listen to. That was a problem for their grand opening. They couldn't have the tide of public opinion turning against them now. Last time that happened, the community nearly shut the manor down forever.

Austin would never stop grieving the loss of his son, but she couldn't bring Beau back, and her entire family was counting on the income that the manor would generate.

There were a surprising number of photos, several boxes full. Peyton made a note to organize them into groups by event. Some of the photos wouldn't make the cut for exhibition because the sheer quantity was overwhelming. Guests would get fatigued and lose interest if too many items were on display. She needed enough to show highlights of the Alcott story, no more, no less.

She walked to the tables of Alcott memorabilia and lifted one of the antique cameras. It was a wet plate camera from the mid-1800s.

Her college photography professor taught his class how to take photos with wet plate cameras and dry plate cameras, then they had to develop the photos. The process wasn't that difficult once they figured out what they were doing, although the dry plate process was far easier.

It had been fascinating for the students to see that the century-old cameras still worked. Their class even set up an exhibit of all the tintypes that they produced for their assignments. The exhibit had been so impressive that it made the local paper.

She stared at the mountain of old cameras, newspapers and memory books stacked on tables against the wall and made notes on how she wanted to display them. She moved a few of the items around on the table; it was a massive amount of information to organize. The muscles in her chest tightened.

One photo had been left on the table. It had captured a party in the ballroom. Women in full, ankle-length ball-gowns danced with men, some of whom wore Confederate army uniforms, others wore long-tailed tuxedos. Six grand chandeliers hung from either side of the domed glass in the ceiling. She glanced up, where only two of those fixtures remained today.

The ballroom displays would need to focus on the celebrations that had taken place there, she decided. She would pull all of the photographs and tintypes of the wedding receptions and galas and sort them for the displays. The plastic containers held rows upon rows of tintype photographs and she popped open the lid of one of them. She filed through them, their firm structures clapped against one another. People and places looked so different in tintypes. Black and white photos appeared as though the camera had only visited a minuscule space of time and preserved a memory. Tintypes were heavier, denser. Looking at them was like looking at captured lives beneath solid glass-paned windows. It was hard to imagine the people or anything else moving beyond that very moment.

Her text alarm dinged. It was her mother:

Meet me at the back door, if you would, please.
Need help bringing a few things in.

Peyton's heels echoed in the vacuous room. She left the ballroom through the doors on the opposite side of the room. From all the trips she had made through the manor with her father when she was young, she remembered cutting through the great hall. It was a large room toward the back of the house that featured a grand staircase. She had seen it many times in photos, where the original Alcott family members often posed with dignitaries.

When she stepped into the great hall, a chill swept over her. It blew across her face strongly enough that her bangs moved off of her forehead. Goosebumps spread down her arms and legs. Her heart thrummed.

Someone was there. A presence.

Peyton tried to move. She couldn't.

The presence swirled around her, stalking her, screaming in a soundless voice that made her chest hurt. She couldn't quite hear the noise but someone was there. Yelling. Threatening. Peyton closed her eyes, put her fingers over her ears.

There was a realm where things were said spiritually—angels gave guidance, departed souls spoke to their loved ones, earthbound spirits spoke to mediums or whomever they wanted—Peyton didn't hear any of that.

"Go away!" she said.

The presence faded. The chill dissipated.

She opened her eyes and lowered her hands from her ears.

The lowest step of the grand staircase was right in front of her.

The memory snatched her quick and cold: She was ten, sitting on that bottom stair. She shook from the inside out, the damp cold deep in her bones. Memories flashed like lightning: a scream, the sickly sweet scent of blood, the rotting smell of sick.

Peyton's heart jumped to her throat, made her gasp for air.

"Are you okay, sweetheart?" Mrs. Miller stood in the doorway, twisting a round locket between her fingers.

"Yes." She pressed her hand against her chest, tried to catch her breath.

"I'm sorry to have startled you. We'll have to put bells on my shoes," Mrs. Miller said, her tone smooth and slithering.

4

———

"Peyton?" her mother called from somewhere near the back of the house.

She tried to call to her mother but her throat was dry and tight.

"What's the matter, dear?" Mrs. Miller whispered, her stare clinging to Peyton.

She saw the room as it used to be, dark and cold, the sound of water dripping.

The distant sound of keys jingled and high heels clomped on hardwoods in a hurry. "Peyton?"

She dashed to the ballroom and grabbed her purse. The Xanax was in the side pocket. Her hand shook when she tipped the bottle, and several pills bounced onto the floor and under the table.

She kneeled, grabbed at the pills as if they were tiny bits of gold and dropped them into the bottle. She stopped herself from throwing several of them into her mouth.

"Peyton!"

She lifted her head too quickly and hit it on the underside of the table. Hundreds of tintypes rattled above her.

She pressed her hand to her head.

Peyton looked up and saw her mother and her sister, Layla, standing over her. Layla held Peyton's wedding dress.

"Hey, Layla-pop."

"Hey, yourself. Let me see your head."

Peyton tilted her head toward her younger sister, who was still dressed in her nurse's scrubs from work. With a delicate touch, she rubbed her fingers over the painful spot.

"You're gonna have a goose egg. Let me see your eyes. Look at me." Layla searched her sister's eyes, held up one finger and asked her to follow it. "No concussion. But you could use some ice."

"What are these?" Jayne Ella took the wedding dress from Layla, laid it over the table and picked up one of the pills.

"Something for a headache."

Her mother held the tablet to the light. "This is prescription. Are you getting migraines these days?"

Layla took the bottle. "Xanax?"

"When did you start taking anxiety meds?" Jayne Ella's tone pitched high.

Peyton snatched the bottle from her sister and dropped several of the pills into the container. "My doctor gave me a prescription for them before I came down. I didn't know how I would handle being here for such a long period of time."

Layla ran her hand across Peyton's back as if to comfort, as if she understood.

"Oh, Peyton, don't—" Her mother checked to see where Mrs. Miller was behind her. "You and I both know that you don't have anything to worry about." Jayne Ella's tone was low and scolding.

Peyton had always been the strong one, the smart one,

the organized one. She was the one who made good on her college education by leaving town and building a highly paid career. She was the one her mother loved to brag about. That Peyton might have to rely on medication probably didn't sit well with her mother.

Layla pushed a piece of blond hair from her face and leaned toward their mother. "There are very strange things that have happened in this place. I can personally testify to that fact. Peyton, if you don't want to stay, I strongly urge you to honor that—"

"Are you feeling alright, dear?" Mrs. Miller asked from across the room.

Jayne Ella straightened and flashed her PR-perfect smile. "I think she must be having a reaction to some airplane food."

"Mmm. I thought it might have been that she was remembering something." Mrs. Miller smiled at Jayne Ella with an air of satisfaction.

Jayne Ella helped gather the rest of the pills and returned them to the container. Then she walked to where Mrs. Miller stood in the doorway. Her steps were determined and her arms were crossed in front of her.

Peyton leaned against the table and held her hand to her head. A knot was forming.

"Why does it strike me that Mrs. Miller has some sort of hold over our mother?" Layla whispered.

"I noticed the same thing," Peyton said.

"Hey." Layla patted Peyton's arm twice. "Do not let our mother twist your arm into staying here to do this work if you don't want to." Layla raised one eyebrow to emphasize her point.

Peyton didn't know what Layla's experiences in the

manor had been, since they hadn't had much of a chance to talk lately, but she knew something strange had happened because Layla didn't want to spend any time there.

Layla squeezed her knee gently. "I'll get you some ice for that bump."

"Did you bring the rest of the Alcott family items from the museum?" Jayne Ella said to Mrs. Miller.

"Yes, everything is here now. Peyton helped me bring the tintypes inside. Those are the last two boxes there on the floor." Mrs. Miller pointed toward Peyton. "It's strange to see them like this, boxed up and not at my fingertips. I've grown so attached to seeing them every day at the museum, they're like old friends." Her voice echoed and carried across the nearly empty room.

"I can imagine." Jayne Ella rested her hands on her hips. Peyton recognized that move as the You Can Leave Now signal her mother gave when she had no more use for you.

Mrs. Miller's lips pressed together. She returned Jayne Ella's stare and tipped her chin. Apparently she wasn't leaving.

Jayne Ella took in Mrs. Miller's loose-fitting dress and low, fat heels.

Mrs. Miller let out her cackling laugh. It danced through the vacuous room too loud and too free. "But after taking care of these Alcott possessions for so many years, these tintypes are more mine than yours. Aren't they?"

Jayne Ella dropped her hands from her hips. Her sense of control seemed to deflate.

"Peyton, I have sandwiches and drinks in the refrigerator. I stocked the kitchen for you when your mother said you were going to help us with our PR. I have plenty of chips. I thought you might still like those." Mrs. Miller's smile was softer but still without any trace of empathy. "How about some lunch?"

"I think that's a good idea. You look pale." Her mother walked across the room and stood next to her as if she were her ally.

Peyton nodded. Her vision of her young self in the manor was still too vivid, too prevalent in her mind. She placed her hand against her own forehead, her skin was clammy.

She watched Mrs. Miller pass the bottom steps of the grand staircase in the distance and anxiety shot through her chest like a spray of fireworks. Her chest hurt from the adrenaline. Wave after wave, it peaked.

"Oh, she's a menace. I don't know why she doesn't just hurry up and die," Jayne Ella said and launched into a tirade on all things Mrs. Miller.

"Why do you keep her around if she bothers you so much?"

"It's just easier that way." Her mother looked away.

When her mother was lying or even thinking about lying, she had a specific tell. She chewed the inside of her cheek, the area just to the left side of her lips. Occasionally she used the knuckle of her index finger and pushed her cheek so her teeth could get a better grip. Around the time of her divorce she chewed a hole in her mouth and Peyton often found her spitting blood into the bathroom sink. The doctor prescribed a medical rinse that cleaned and anesthetized the area. But it also numbed her mouth and caused Jayne Ella to drool slightly.

"How is that easier?"

"Because. She's lost her husband and her daughter and she's taken care of our ancestors' belongings for decades. It's the right thing to do." Jayne Ella's knuckle pushed against her cheek twice.

Peyton thought yet again about chewing a Xanax. She looked at her wedding dress draped over the long table. The bottom hem hung out of its plastic cover.

She had wanted to shop for her dress in Boston, but Jayne Ella had insisted that they shop together in Charleston. She ended up buying a chic crepe gown with a halter bodice, a high neckline and a t-strap racerback to make it ultra-contemporary. Exactly the opposite of the full-skirted satin dress with the long train she had purchased for her wedding with Beau.

Strange how both dresses suited her, and yet there wasn't one similarity between them.

For a quick moment she thought about grabbing the dress, leaving the manor and eloping. Ira would do it, too. He had already told her that he would marry her wherever and whenever she wanted. "As long as we get to be together for a lifetime," he said. "The wedding is all yours."

Maybe she could design the tours and the publicity plan from Boston. Surely there would be another bride nearby who would kill to have her wedding on an oceanfront property. Jayne Ella could have the photographer take pictures of *that* wedding for the website.

"Anyway." Her mother dug through her shoulder bag. "You *have* to help us."

"I'm here, aren't I?"

Layla returned with a plastic bag filled halfway with ice cubes. She handed it to Peyton.

"You have that look on your face that says you're calculating a way out of the situation."

"Don't push her, Jayne Ella. If she doesn't want to be here, let her go," Layla said.

Peyton put the bag to her head and wondered what her own tell was. "I could make some notes while I'm here, then I could send directions from Boston. You and Aunt Laura and Mrs. Miller could set everything up."

Her mother scoffed. She started pacing. When she moved, the grand staircase reappeared just beyond the door. A chill covered Peyton's arms, the same chill she'd felt when she had first entered the manor.

"You're so secretive," Jayne Ella whispered. "Secrets are destroyers. I've been completely open with you. You need to be more vulnerable, more open with me. What's the real reason that you don't want to do this?"

Peyton studied her mother, watched her lips twist to the side. She imagined Jayne Ella's canines gnashing against the soft insides of her mouth, blood mixing with her spit. Her mother had a secret, and it was eating her up inside.

Peyton knew her mother didn't believe what she was saying. It was just the right thing to say at the moment. Jayne Ella rattled on about how honesty was everything and that's what relationships required in order to succeed. Then she laughed into how her daughters took for granted the close family they had. They didn't know what it was like to have a difficult mother. Unlike her. She had had a very difficult mother.

Layla let out one loud, "Ha!"

Jayne Ella fussed at Layla.

Peyton questioned whether she agreed with this practiced advice on openness and vulnerability. Sometimes keeping a secret was what kept the relationship together. Not all secrets needed to be shared. That was the advice she had gotten from a relationship book she had read recently: *The Clean Slate Theory*. Especially if sharing the secret only made *you* feel better, the need to confess wasn't always the best reason. So the book said.

Peyton was torn on the idea. Half of her landing on one side of the issue, half of her positioned on the other.

"The manor isn't an easy place to be." She hoped she redirected the topic.

"The manor is all cleaned up and I know you, Peyton. Now, our entire family is depending on you to set this up for us. We're all gathering around to celebrate your wedding, this is only a few days of work."

"I've never asked for anything special for my wedding. I just wanted a very small, very casual—"

"Then you should have spoken to Ira and his mother about that. They keep adding names to the guest list."

"What?"

Jayne Ella waved Peyton off. "What's most important, what we really need, is our Fixer."

Peyton wished she had never told her mother about the nickname she had earned at the office. She also wished she had never bragged about her unique talent for taking corporations with image problems and repositioning them in the public eye for a fresh start.

An internet expert, a goodwill campaign, a new slogan and she could erase a company's poor image from the public's memory. Her mother wasn't wrong, this was exactly what Alcott Manor needed.

"The truth is I'm having a hard time being here. I know we don't agree on this, but I do have this very realistic memory that I was here, alone, when I was young. It's coming back to me in bits and pieces, and honestly, it's terrifying. Maybe it would be best if you hired someone else to do this."

"We've been over this. You're remembering some sort of

dream. I would never have allowed you to be here alone when you were younger. Obviously. Peyton. Let it go. You have to do this because we don't have enough funds left to hire someone else. How long have you been taking those?" Jayne Ella pointed to the prescription bottle.

"I said I could help you remotely. Just as soon as we get back from our honeymoon." She shoved the bottle into the side pocket of her purse and decided to take one as soon as Jayne Ella was out of sight. It hadn't been a dream.

"Don't be selfish." Her mother stepped in front of her.

"*I'm* selfish?" She was suddenly overwhelmed with an extraordinary need to get back to Boston, to her work and to her life that waited to reward her. "That's rich."

She tried to walk around her mother but Jayne Ella stepped to the side and blocked her again.

Layla took one step back.

"I get it, Peyton. You finally have everything—a wonderful man, the prestige of a great career, money. I really do get it. But what about family? We were there for you before you had any of those other things," her mother said.

"That's hardly it, Jayne Ella. I was just open with you about what was bothering me, then you discounted me. You make a better case for secrets than you do for vulnerability."

Her mother waved her off again. She pulled a letter from her purse and handed it to her. "We just got this today."

Peyton unfolded the paper, with the letterhead of First Bank of Charleston. Her eyes dropped to the signature and she recognized the name immediately: Austin Spencer. Beau's father.

"How did Beau's dad become affiliated with First Bank of Charleston?"

"Read on." Her mother popped a piece of cinnamon gum in her mouth.

The letter detailed how River City Bank had merged with First Bank of Charleston. They had chosen to keep the First Bank of Charleston name. Austin Spencer, former President of River City Bank, was now the President of the newly formed conglomerate.

As a result of the merger, they were evaluating the bank's loans and assets, among them, the loan for Alcott Manor.

"They've asked for a face-to-face meeting in order to re-evaluate the family's ability to pay back the loan. They say they want to better understand the Alcott Manor business model.

"So, essentially you have to show Mr. Spencer how the manor is making money, otherwise he calls the loan."

"Essentially. Yes," Jayne Ella said.

"But this is really about Beau," Peyton said.

Her mother's lips pulled to the side. Her teeth were working on the inside of her cheek. "He still blames you for Beau's disappearance."

Peyton squeezed her eyes shut. Images of her and Beau on Austin's boat passed through her mind. She opened her eyes again, scanned the walls. It must be the manor, as Mrs. Miller suggested. It somehow resurrected old memories and feelings she had long relegated to a back corner of her heart.

She'd never been able completely forget the good times she and Beau had shared. She had tried. So she had made room for them. Like the trip she and Beau had taken to San Francisco where he bought her a beautiful rose quartz bracelet. Her fingertips traced her wrist, she could still feel the coolness. She inhaled, thinking she caught a whiff of the sandalwood and lemon verbena of his cologne. She shared her life with a ghost.

That Austin blamed her for Beau's leaving was absurd. Her suspicion was that Austin had lost his temper with his son and took things too far. He had to be the one who—

"I need you, Peyton." Her mother grabbed her by the shoulders and looked her in the eyes. "I need you to show him that we have cash coming in and we can afford to make the loan payments. We *have* to make this work!"

It was the first time she had looked at her mother since she arrived, really studied her. Her crows' feet were more pronounced and the skin at the front of her neck had slackened—small signs that she was losing her race with time. Her passion for saving Alcott Manor had bled into her every expression.

Her intensity reminded Peyton that her mother was capable of handling a difficult conversation when she wanted to. When they'd waited for over an hour for Beau at the church, all Peyton could do was stare to the window, her knuckles white from gripping the straight back of the chair. Jayne Ella was the one who had pried her hands from the polished wood and said, "He's not coming. You have to move on."

With her ability to be forthright, Peyton didn't know why her mother insisted on keeping secrets.

Her mother's tone was reaching a fever pitch and she had developed a wild look in her eye. It wasn't just that Jayne Ella wanted to save the manor, she needed it. For herself. This was going to be her new role in life. Her second wind, maybe. Her second chance.

"I think Peyton is remembering something from when she was a little girl," Mrs. Miller announced from the back of the room. She put a plate with two sandwiches and chips and a bottle of cola on a side table.

Peyton crossed the room and took a bite of the ham and

cheese sandwich so she wouldn't have to talk. She looked up, and realized all eyes in the room had fixed on her.

Jayne Ella sidled up to her. "Why would you have brought that up with Mrs. Miller?" Jayne Ella frowned like she was afflicted.

"I didn't. She was in the room when something came back to me and I guess she assumed. What does it matter anyway? She's heard me mention this before."

Mrs. Miller stared at Peyton with narrowed eyes. "I maintain what I've always told you—that if you were really here, that memory will come pouring back one day. The manor will insist. Maybe when you least expect it. Maybe it's coming back now."

"There's nothing for her to remember," Jayne Ella snapped. "She was never alone in the manor as a child."

Mrs. Miller smiled, like she toyed with Jayne Ella. "Maybe her memories are just a bit jumbled. Do you remember what you were wearing?"

"No, she doesn't," Jayne Ella said sternly.

"A white dress," Peyton said. A flash of the room that night came back. Panic hit her deep and hard, like she'd been punched in the gut.

"If it happens in the manor, it's never forgotten." Mrs. Miller's gaze traveled along the walls as if someone else were listening to their conversation. "The manor captures everything. Almost like it's on film. Right, Jayne Ella?"

Peyton's mother fixed her stare on the glass ceiling, her mouth twisted and her jaw working.

"Or maybe seeing Beau again triggered something for her. One of those flyers was pasted to the front pillar when we arrived. It's old home day for Peyton."

Jayne Ella finally looked at Mrs. Miller again and she lowered her voice, "We don't bring that up."

An argument ensued and their voices took on a hollow sound, like Peyton sank underwater. Images shifted in the back of Peyton's mind like the colors of a distant kaleidoscope, taking shape but not in a way that made sense. Someone cried. A man yelled. Panic crept through her like a thief, stealing what little bit of peace she had left.

Mrs. Miller locked into a stare with Jayne Ella, who, after a few moments, looked away. Her mother's face flushed.

Mrs. Miller put her skeletal hand on Peyton's shoulder. "Why don't you try on a few of these dresses, let me take some pictures with one of the old Alcott family cameras?" Mrs. Miller pointed to the rows of mannequins.

She stood, twisted away. Unable to bear the feel of Mrs. Miller touching any part of her.

"We can make new tintypes, place them next to the old ones. I think visitors will just love seeing Alcott ancestors next to living Alcott family members. And wearing the same clothes as they did in the same family home? They'll eat that up."

Peyton stepped away, let the idea run around in her head. She had hoped Mrs. Miller would leave the manor while she worked there.

But her suggestion had merit.

"I've given a lot of thought to this," Mrs. Miller said. "I could type up the history on some cards. Jayne Ella, I can tell you which rooms the mannequins and their outfits go in, I'll organize the right pictures so they'll sync up with the rooms and the outfits. Peyton, you can organize the exhibits —diaries and ladies' ornamental fans and china and so forth. You can tell us what changes you want in the exhibits from there, but maybe this is a start.

"And if we get this done before the bank rolls in tomorrow, maybe it will be enough to stave off Austin Spencer and his henchmen. That ought to leave you plenty of time to do the work you get paid for, sweetheart. And get married, of course. We can improve the tour as time goes along. What's most important is that we have a good, solid start." Mrs. Miller's smile lacked warmth.

Unnervingly, she was right. Their assistance would give Peyton the time she needed to work on branding and tourism alliances for the manor. And she could finish her proposal for work.

The breeze of an invisible presence left goosebumps on Peyton's skin. She rubbed her arms.

"Where is that draft coming from?" Jayne Ella asked. She crossed her arms

"It's the memories." Mrs. Miller squinted her eyes at the ceiling. "The house is full of them. They move through here constantly."

Mrs. Miller swayed side to side like she soothed a baby in her arms. She had always done that. Even more so when Peyton was little.

When Mrs. Miller's daughter asked her why she rocked like that she said, "Oh, Ruby Lee. I started doing this on the day you were born, and you loved it so much I guess it became a habit."

The bottom steps of the grand staircase came in and out of view as Mrs. Miller moved across Peyton's field of vision. Fuzzy images stirred in the recesses of her brain.

"Okay. Let's do it," Peyton finally said when she knew she really had no way out.

"The manor never forgets," Mrs. Miller mumbled to herself and she left the room. She ran her hand along the marble wall as she passed, like she stroked a pet. "Living memories. Secrets that won't be kept."

The woman had a special connection to a darker side of Alcott Manor. Peyton found that unnerving.

She didn't want to remember what happened in the manor when she was little, because she was certain that if those memories resurfaced, whatever they were, they would break her.

5

———

Peyton looked over the wide selection of dresses that were hung on a rack at the front of the room. Each of them was hauntingly beautiful. Bright golden orange with black lace, blood red with a deep v-neck. They were too pretty to be on mannequins, too exquisite to be relegated to an exhibit.

Mrs. Miller was right. Tour guests would love a historical photo next to a newly made tintype, both with Alcott women, and identical Alcott Manor outfits and backgrounds. They only needed a few of those, maybe one or two per room, possibly less. Those displays would be the talk of the tour. They might even make the paper with them.

Jayne Ella had gone for her curling iron, hairspray, and hairpins. Mrs. Miller had taken the camera to the kitchen to give it a good dusting. Layla was tired from work and went home.

Peyton paused in front of a light blue bustled dress. Delicate layers of fabric cascaded in measured lengths down the skirt. It was her color and the size looked about right. She also liked the white gauzy fabric that stretched over the décolleté. This dress was the same one from the tintype she'd seen earlier, the one with Beau's lookalike.

The energy in the room seemed to twist and swirl. It wound around her, knocking her off-kilter. It dragged her into its force, capturing her mind, monopolizing her thoughts. So many memories of her time with Beau spun through her mind, like a movie. She tried to get control, to direct her own thinking. But the room fell away and she was left with the first time he had spoken to her.

"Marry me, Peyton Alcott." Beau had driven up beside her in the high school parking lot while she walked from her last class to her convertible red VW bug. His light blue eyes were so intense they were nearly electric, like his future was bursting to get out.

"Get real, Beau Spencer." She rolled her eyes at him. But there was something in his melodic baritone that reached right into her chest and plucked the strings of her heart. Like only he knew how.

"Then let me at least take you to dinner," he said.

She stopped walking and looked at him. Straight blond hair poking out of the back of his baseball cap, his tanned arm perched on the rolled down window, he looked the part of the all-American boy.

"Come on, you can't resist." His smile picked up wattage.

She studied him for a long moment, then walked on. "Oh, I can, actually."

Beau Spencer was trouble. Hadn't taken her more than a half a minute to see that. It wasn't his good looks or the fact that his parents lavished their money on him. Unlike most teenagers in that situation, he seemed to have a mind of his own.

No, it was his eyes. Gypsy eyes, Peyton called them. The

boy was made to roam. Last thing she wanted was to fall in love with someone who would leave her.

Beau kept up this daily routine for weeks—following her, flirting with her, occasionally asking he out. Until one day after school he approached her, a 35mm camera slung over his shoulder. He asked her to join him for a sunset picnic on the beach.

It wasn't the usual movie date invitation. Neither was it the yacht club/country club dinner date she had heard from him before. But the thing she noticed most was that something had calmed in those brilliant eyes of his.

"Please?" he asked.

She wondered if maybe he wanted her more than he needed to drift around the world. She fought the one side of her mouth that wanted to tip in a smirk. "Fine. Since you said please."

She walked toward the kitchen, slowly, following the trail of her memories that wouldn't let go.

The night before the wedding, they held their rehearsal dinner on the great lawn.

Tradition said it was the groom's family who typically hosted the rehearsal dinner. But at the last minute Austin said they accidentally double booked their calendar. Peyton suspected Austin canceled the event.

The ocean crashed on the sand in the distance and the perfumed scents of roses, oleander and magnolia clung to the air. Tiki torches were lit around the perimeter. Everyone enjoyed shrimp and cheese grits, hush puppies, and buttered corn on the cob, catered by the Fish Shack.

Except for Austin, who just drank scotch.

Beau pulled her into the half-restored kitchen. His light blue eyes were darker in the shadows of the manor. A chill crept over her shoulders and down her back, like secrets tapped her.

She looked toward the heart of the house, where the grand staircase poured into a wide reception area. She tried to leave, Beau held her arm.

"I have to get outside, let's talk later—"

"My dad changed the terms of my inheritance. We can't travel, we can't leave. He says I have to work at his bank for a while."

She backed toward the door. "He can't' do that. Your grandfather put that money aside for *you!*"

"My dad can adjust the terms if he thinks I'm going to spend the money unwisely. Traveling the world to shoot pictures looks unwise."

"But there are travel magazines. You can submit the photos to them. They'll pay."

"Seven years isn't that long, it will pass before we know it."

"Seven years?!"

The idea of staying in Charleston, close to Alcott Manor and the memories she couldn't completely recall all but suffocated her.

"I can't stay in this town for another seven years," she said.

"I can't walk away from this money. It's my money." His cheeks flushed angry red.

They argued, their words fueled by passion and youth. And maybe, she thought, by the strangeness of the manor. It was crazy-making. Tragic and twisted.

"I *have* to leave!" she finally shouted.

Beau stopped mid-sentence. "What are you talking about?"

She placed her fingertips over her mouth.

"What's going on, Pey?"

Her eyes cut to the grand staircase. "I did something. A long time ago. And I need to get as far away from here as possible."

Beau glanced at the stairway, then looked back to her.

She told him what she had never told another soul. About the night she sat on the grand staircase, alone, wet, and with blood covering the front of her dress. That was the night Mrs. Miller's daughter disappeared.

"You were only ten back then, right? You wouldn't have—"

She held up her hand to stop him. "I-I don't remember specifically what I did. But I think I—Ruby could be so awful. She was a menace. She had this physical way of confronting people. I'm not saying I intentionally hurt her. At least I don't think I did.

"But it's possible she came after me and I fought back, because Ruby hasn't been seen since that night." There was a lightening in her chest, like a tiny part of her secret had broken free from its cage.

She tried hard to remember the specifics of what Ruby did to her. But critical pieces were missing from those memories, too. That part of her brain was silent, dead.

She could only recall a handful of infuriating instances. For as long as she could remember, she had wanted Ruby out of her life forever. At any cost.

Beau's mouth hung slightly open. His stare wasn't the usual gaze that held her close. Instead, it kept her at a distance, like she was someone he didn't know.

Her throat went dry.

"I have to get out of this town. Away from this place." She gestured to the manor that seemed to lean in and listen to every word she said. "Everywhere I turn in this town I think of Ruby—someplace we went together, some experience we shared, and the life she might have had if she lived."

"You don't know that she's dead. She could have been kidnapped. I know you, you would not have—"

"I have never forgotten anything in my life. I can remember what my sister wore to my fifth birthday party. I remember every book we read in kindergarten. I remember the color of the socks you wore on our third date. My mind captures everything. That night in the manor, I can't remember anything other than that one snippet. But I do remember how I felt. I know something horrible happened to Ruby that night and I think I'm the one who did it." She turned away, unable to look at him.

There was a loud crash. She spun around.

Beau had thrown his beer bottle against the wall. Pieces of brown glass lay on the hardwood floor.

"Why didn't you tell me?"

Her breaths were shallow and panicky. "I know this isn't something you ever expected to hear from me."

"No, you're right, it's not. I thought we told one another everything."

"I tried—"

He stared at her, shaking his head. After a long moment, he said, "I need time to think." He walked toward the door.

"Wait—what do you mean time to think?" She walked toward him. "We're getting married tomorrow. I'm still the same person I always was—"

"Maybe when you trust me, we can talk." He walked out the door.

That was the last time she saw him.

She remembered his bad habit of drinking too much when he was angry. For years she had worried that he had gotten into a car accident. Peyton squeezed her eyes shut for a long moment, not wanting to relive any more of that night.

She walked to the ballroom. An email alert buzzed and the message popped up on her phone screen. It was the caterer confirming the final menu for the wedding.

Her upcoming wedding with Ira felt strangely entwined with the tragedies in the manor, tangled with her unresolved past with Beau and frightful childhood memories that refused to come forward.

The manor's walls pressed more tightly around her. A mixture of Alcott stories with too much life to them still and the memory of Beau that reached for her.

She turned her attention to the gowns, undressed one of the mannequins, accidentally removing one of its arms in the process. She slipped out of her tailored black suit and wiggled into the blue dress, careful not to rip any of the antique stitching. She looked at her image in the foggy, dress-length, antique mirror. The dress was a tad short. She would have to pose for the picture sitting down. Or Mrs. Miller would need to move the camera closer so her bare feet and ankles wouldn't show.

Her line of sight fell on the edge of the torn flyer that stuck out from her purse. She bit her bottom lip. She had deleted the photos from her phone once she moved to Boston. She had to because she used to sneak peeks at them throughout the day and when missing him became unbearable. Back then she compared herself to a drug addict, her fix looking at photos of Beau, re-reading his love letters and thinking of what their life together would have been like. She resisted, trying not to think about the flyer and the tintype she had within her reach.

His presence from the photo was palpable, like he stood in the same room with her. "Pey," she heard his voice, using the same low, sweet tone as he did when he nuzzled her neck and said, "Promise me something..."

She dug her nails into her palms. The temptation held the strength of an underwater current. When the tidal force finally pulled her under, she snatched her phone. She enlarged the photo she had taken of the tintype and looked closely.

The image was grainy, she squinted to examine the details. The likeness was undeniable. His hair was styled differently, his attire was different. His expression was dissimilar. When she knew him, his smile was welcoming and gracious enough to sweep you into his world from the first hello.

In this 1850s tintype his lips were a straight line, his emotions hard to read. But the defined angles of his face were exactly the same and his eyes were pale and striking as she had always known them to be. It was as if the house had absorbed him right into its story.

She pictured him trapped somehow. Living in the dimension she could feel but not quite see.

She propped her phone against a small box on the table to keep his image in her view. Then she dug through one container after another until she found several other wedding photos that had to have been taken on that same day. If he were really here, there would be more tintypes of him.

In one tintype a woman wore the exact dress that Peyton had on, the one she had taken from the mannequin. She held the tintype close to her eyes, searching each face in the gathering to find Beau. When she didn't find him she opened another box and flipped through the tintypes more quickly. Metal upon metal clacked against one another.

Her frustration intensified with each passing image that

wasn't him. She caught sight of her reflection in the long mirror. Her eyes narrow and focused, her jaw set and hardened. She looked obsessed.

Her diamond engagement ring reflected the overhead light and sparkled. Her heart clenched. She leaned away from the box, sat on her heels.

The therapist had warned her. "Going over and over what didn't work out is a form of self-punishment," she said. "Woulda, coulda, shoulda have become your self-flogging tools of choice. Best to eliminate those from your vocabulary before you sabotage your future with Ira. This is a good man who loves you. Live in the present. Live in today."

She squeezed her eyes shut, tried to follow that direction.

She opened her eyes again, the memories were still there. Stronger than echoes, less real than actual people, and tangible all the same. She glanced at the grand stairway, turned to face the opposite direction. Shifted her focus to the project at hand.

Most Alcott weddings had taken place in the ballroom. She could replicate that setting as an exhibit. Maybe she would have a display entitled Alcott weddings. Or A Wedding at Alcott Manor with a sampling of the various wedding photos, guest books and bridal bouquet ribbons.

Peyton tugged one of the end tables closer to the window to match its placement in the photo. Mrs. Miller returned and together they set up the camera on its stand and waited for Jayne Ella to make her way into the ballroom.

"Is this the picture we're recreating?" Mrs. Miller pointed to the tintype that Peyton propped up on the table.

"No, I—"

"Do we have that wedding dress on a mannequin somewhere? It would be pretty to shoot that. Oh my. Look at him."

Mrs. Miller hovered over the tintype, lifted her glasses such that she looked through the bottom half of them. "Well, glory be. What do you make of that?" She tapped the image that resembled Beau, then squinted slightly like she expected to see him move.

Peyton stared, mesmerized. She twirled her engagement ring around her finger.

Mrs. Miller quickly straightened, like she had just remembered something important. "Do you ever think about my Ruby? Do you remember the night she disappeared? Earlier, when you remembered something, I thought maybe..."

Breathe.

She was silent for a long moment, the quiet stretching between them like a rubber band, getting thinner until she knew something would snap. Peyton didn't want to share just how often she thought about Mrs. Miller's daughter. She didn't want to tell her how Ruby's abrupt disappearance had haunted her for the last two decades. Not to mention the fact that she thought she had something to do with it.

The same old argument began in the back of her mind. That Beau might have been right—she might not have been involved. Ruby could have been kidnapped, Peyton might have fallen. It just didn't feel that way to her. And the blood on her dress flashed brightly like she had just seen it the night before.

"I don't remember anything about that night. I'm sorry."

Mrs. Miller pursed her lips, searched Peyton's face like she knew she was lying. "You're sure?"

Peyton pretended to work.

Mrs. Miller turned and fluffed a pillow from the couch.

"Did I ever tell you that I was the last person to see Beau alive?"

Peyton spun around. Her stomach tight. "No, ma'am."

"Mmm-hmm. I was still here after the family wedding social, making sure the caterers cleaned up well. Your mother had asked that he shoot the manor's progress. You know, the house had been in such an awful state and restoration was really starting to take off. At least we thought so back then. Your mother wanted him to take those before and after photos."

Peyton had heard from family members and police about Beau's last day, but never Mrs. Miller. Not like this. She wondered why the woman had never spoken up.

"I went with him to watch. He was such a good photographer. I asked him about his plans for travel, he told me about working with his father's bank. I never saw that as a fit for him to work with his dad. Austin always was terribly controlling.

Beau had that wild side, his independent streak. He needed that travel. Of course, your mother told me that you never really wanted to travel the world like that. She said you were just following Beau, following his dream." Mrs. Miller grinned like she had just told Peyton that she had spinach between her front two teeth. "Young love, I guess."

Peyton clenched her teeth. She *had* been following Beau and his dreams, but she didn't like hearing it aloud. She would have liked to think that, given some time, she would have found a path to her own dreams.

"I know I must be touching on painful memories, dear."

Peyton considered saying something polite like "that's okay." Then she thought that might open a door too wide where Mrs. Miller was concerned. "No, he didn't want to work in his father's bank. He would have preferred roaming faraway places, taking pictures with that camera of his. I found my passion. My career is doing well."

"I always thought the two of you made such a striking couple. Of course, as pretty and smart as you are, I guess it didn't take you long to find another."

Peyton studied her engagement ring. "Ira's a great guy."

"Ira..." Mrs. Miller took Peyton's hand and held it a little too tight. She eyed the diamond closely. Peyton had the sense that Mrs. Miller was thinking of her own daughter, and what this engagement ring would have looked like on Ruby Lee's hand, had she not disappeared. Guilt grabbed her gut with a mouthful of teeth.

"You're very lucky, you know, to have found someone else. Do you love him?" Her tone lilted with fake sweetness.

"Yes. Very much." Peyton tugged her hand from Mrs. Miller's grip, but she held on.

"My Ruby would be your age now. Probably married. She would have had a child or two, I suspect. She always wanted a little girl." Mrs. Miller tilted her head. "You know, the manor could help you remember that night if you would let it. Maybe you would remember something useful. If not something about Ruby, maybe something else about that night. Maybe your mother was with you?"

"There's nothing for me to remember," Peyton said sharply.

A groan sounded from deep within the manor's walls, like it disagreed with her, like it responded to the old woman's command, like unsettled memories stirred. The house became full with a swirling of stories, Alcott history. Voices that Peyton could almost hear, movement she could almost see. They seemed to reach for her with the same possessiveness she'd felt when she first entered the house, demanding that she know them, begging her to be a part of them.

A memory flashed in bits and pieces and in full color, as if the manor handed it to her: A much younger Mrs. Miller standing in the middle of the very same ballroom where they stood today. Peyton and Ruby, ten years of age, spinning around with their arms stretched wide.

Peyton wore the red antique hoop dress and Ruby Lee wore the gold one. There were party noises outside—chattering, music and laughter.

"Now don't tell anyone that I let you do this," Mrs. Miller said. "I'm going to get all the equipment and we'll get started. This will be so much fun!" She tweaked Ruby Lee's cheek and the little girl beamed with a special satisfaction. The kind where she knew her mother would do anything for her.

Peyton finally pulled her hand from Mrs. Miller's grip and held it to her stomach. She turned away, partial images flickered in her mind.

This was the first time she had remembered anything from the last time she had seen Ruby.

When Peyton faced her again, she said, "The night that Ruby Lee disappeared. We were here?"

"Yes," Mrs. Miller said. She drew the word out long and slow, coaxing Peyton. Her eyes narrowed, searching. "What else do you remember from that night, dear?"

Peyton held her breath.

"Oh my goodness, look at you in that dress!" Jayne Ella breezed in the room with two plastic grocery bags of supplies. A black cord dangled to the side of one bag. "You're gorgeous! You look like a spring flower."

The spell was broken. The manor released its hold on Peyton and its memories quieted. She exhaled hard.

"I'm going to sensitize the glass plates for the picture. I've set up a make-shift dark room in the pantry." Mrs. Miller stepped away.

When she was gone from the room, Jayne Ella held up the curling iron like she asked a question. Peyton nodded. Her mother plugged it in and organized a selection of brushes and hairpins.

"What was that about?" her mother asked. "Seems like I walked in on something."

A strange energy crackled in the air. Peyton shivered.

"She was asking me questions about Ruby," Peyton said.

Jayne Ella nodded once, like Peyton had just told her the temperature or had said that the library was closed on Wednesdays. She didn't like to talk about Mrs. Miller's missing daughter.

"Did you sleep last night? You've got the beginnings of some dark circles there," her mother asked.

Peyton situated herself in a chair and in front of her mother. She pressed her fingertips beneath her eyes like she could feel the dark areas. "Not much. Trying to get every-thing done before the wedding."

Peyton chose not to tell her that she hadn't slept well for a long time. Not since she knew she would have to spend several days in the manor near Mrs. Miller.

"So, what do you think of the renovation?" Jayne Ella waved to the rest of the room. "Turned out well, didn't she?"

A chill shot down Peyton's back at referring to the manor in the feminine. It was a female energy that inhabited the house.

Peyton's glass fell to the floor and shattered.

"Peyton! Be careful!" Jayne Ella took a paper napkin and soaked up the liquid.

"I—I never touched my glass." She looked around.

"The house did it," Mrs. Miller said when she walked in the room.

Jayne Ella looked at Mrs. Miller like she had lost her mind.

"Could be Bertha Mae, I guess. Makes sense that she would make herself known now," Mrs. Miller said. "The manor was hers first. Maybe she's not happy about this new era, Jayne Ella. Maybe she doesn't want to give it up." Mrs. Miller raised one eyebrow at Peyton's mother.

Peyton didn't know if Bertha Mae's spirit inhabited the manor. But she did wonder if Ruby's spirit did. She wondered if Ruby wanted to hurt her.

Her hair was finished and the dress was buttoned, Peyton organized the furniture according to how it was set up in the wedding photo. She tried to focus on the exact position of the side table and the couch. But her attention drifted to Beau in the photo.

Like flipping through a photo album, she saw one of the more memorable times they shared: Beau on one knee at the late night picnic he organized for them. The warm breezes, the cool sand around the plaid blanket, the fragrant scent of magnolias on the breeze.

She pressed her hands to her cheeks. They were warm. She needed fresh air.

"Are we ready?" Mrs. Miller asked.

"How many pictures are we planning?" Jayne Ella asked.

"I think just one to start. Make sure it turns out the way we want." Mrs. Miller stood poised behind the camera, a small smile on her face.

Peyton didn't like the idea of Mrs. Miller controlling things. But she didn't let on. "I'll sit on the end cushion of the couch. Check it but I think the camera is already pointing in the right direction. Mom, once I'm in position,

Mrs. Miller is going to remove this cap and leave it off for five seconds. I won't be able to talk or move during that time. After she replaces the cap, I'm going to develop the plate."

Mrs. Miller put the sensitized plate into the holder.

Peyton sat on the couch at the front of the living room, just as the other women had in the photo. Her posture was straight, her dress was fluffed, like she sat at an Alcott Manor gathering in 1860. "Okay...now." She gave Mrs. Miller the cue.

She removed the lens cap.

"We're doing a dry run on the ceremony set up tomorrow. This wedding is going to be fantastic!" Jayne Ella said.

Peyton tried not to grimace. Fantastic was the word her mother used when she was most interested in impressing someone. And when she was most insincere.

"I'm also having the photographer take a look at the manor and the great lawn ahead of time. So we can plan some of her shots."

Mrs. Miller finally replaced the cap.

Peyton said, "I'm going to develop this now, then I have to get to work on that proposal."

Mrs. Miller handed her the glass plate. "Good night, dear. We'll shoot more tomorrow. I left an apron in the darkroom."

"I've got to dash to the salon and get some more hairpins for tomorrow. How late are you going to be tonight?" Jayne Ella asked.

"I'm going to walk the main areas of the house to get some good ideas for the tour plan. Then I'll get a draft of the marketing and PR plan in place. I'll be home after that."

"You'll have the manor's plan ready by tomorrow when Austin and his henchmen come by?"

"It will be bullet points but I'll have the basic framework done. Do you think they'll give us a week to finalize everything?"

"Probably, we'll see. I've left a refrigerator full of healthy meals and snacks. There are also some less healthy snacks on the counter. You have a microwave and the coffee maker is on. I'll see you in a few hours," her mother said.

In the small pantry, her makeshift darkroom, Peyton put on a pair of large rubber gloves. She poured the thick chemical solution over the plate and tilted it back and forth until the glass was covered.

Peyton moved the glass plate to the next tray, confused by some of the darkened images that emerged. "Thanks, I'll see you later tonight."

The click of Jayne Ella's high heeled shoes faded. The kitchen door shut, the locks turned. Peyton immediately wished she weren't in the old family manse alone.

It was probably the fact that she was standing in a dark closet and surrounded by too many fumes. She had plenty of work to keep her company and well distracted. She'd pour herself a huge cup of coffee as soon as she got out.

All of her ideas were organized in her head, she just needed to document them on paper. It would only take a few hours.

She would show the bank that the revenue potential was real and imminent. That's all they needed to see in order to keep the loan in place. She hoped, anyway. If they saw that an accomplished professional was in charge, that should help.

She just hoped Austin Spencer would stay out of the process.

She dried the plate, turned out the red light and took the

print into the ballroom. "Dang it." She knew she shouldn't have let Mrs. Miller sensitize the plate. It wasn't right.

She walked toward the window that captured the last of the day's light. The lush green, magnolia-dotted lawn was laid out beyond the antebellum windows in storybook perfection. She had a particularly fond memory of playing in that grassy area with her sister when they were little.

She tilted the glass plate toward the remaining sunlight to get a clearer look. The camera and the chemicals had worked just as Mrs. Miller had suggested. There she was, a direct Alcott descendent wearing a vintage Alcott family dress, sitting on a family-original couch.

But she wasn't alone in the photo.

She was surrounded by four other people, one of whom was Bertha Mae Alcott.

She glared at Peyton, like she could see her.

But the one Peyton didn't see in the tintype, the one she would have wanted to, was her former fiancé Beau Spencer.

6

The exhibits marked a celebration of the old and new.

Peyton liked how this particular exhibition signaled how the manor was moving forward.

But the glass photographic plate that Mrs. Miller used had ghosted images of the 1860s bride and groom on the couch next to Peyton. Bertha Mae and Benjamin Alcott, Sr., stood behind her. She knew double imaging was entirely possible with digital and paper photographs. But glass plate photography?

A long creak sounded from the other room like the house shifted around her, settling its attention on her.

"Hello?"

No one answered.

She sat in a nearby chair. The grand staircase was in the distance.

A chill brushed along her neck.

The manor's energy closed in around her, she thought she felt a touch on her skin. It was cramped and claustrophobic in the vacuous room.

A scene spun to life, like a hologram, three dimensional and transparent—couples dancing, music playing, people laughing.

She quickly shut her eyes, a flicker of images spooled.

A man driving. His arm behind a red-haired woman in the passenger seat. His watch had a dark blue face and diamonds that sparkled in the low light.

She opened her eyes with a gasp. The room was quiet and empty.

Who was the man in the car?

The woman—that unmistakable shade of red hair. That was Jayne Ella.

That man wasn't her husband.

Peyton's phone rang, she walked to the ballroom. She lifted it from her purse and saw the missed call and a text message from Ira:

See you in the morning. Can't wait to begin our new life together.

She looked at the glass plate in her hand. Her relatives surrounded her, stared at her hard enough to break the glass. She popped the top on the Xanax bottle and tossed one tablet into her mouth, crunched it slightly, and swallowed the bitter pill without water.

She had never taken one before. Within a few minutes a serene calm swam through her veins and her worries about the manor, her past and Beau fell to the wayside. She wasn't sure what side effects there might be, if any. For the moment, she didn't care.

She grabbed her laptop and phone and headed toward the dining room. She tapped a message to Ira, letting him know how much she was looking forward to seeing him tomorrow morning. She tried to ignore the thread of guilt that curled through her chest. She shouldn't have been thinking about Beau so much.

She rationalized that it was inevitable. She was home again, where they had spent so many years together, and she was at the manor where he was last seen. Also she was getting married in a few days. Like a wave, the guilt tried to gather strength, but the Xanax quashed it. The pill was a temporary fix, she knew. Since she was stuck in the manor for the time being, she would take it.

She glanced around the room. The scenes that had played for her just moments ago were gone. The room was quiet. She smiled with relief. That had been her anxiety playing tricks on her. Everything was fine now. Xanax was a wonder drug. They should add it to the drinking water.

She spent over an hour in the rooms on the first floor. She sketched drawings of the tour path and made extensive lists of the family artifacts that would be on display. The anxiety about the manor, her past, Beau—was gone. It was glorious to be in control again.

She didn't have to take an inventory of objects or research their history and meanings. She already had that information. It was just a matter of organizing it and getting it on to paper. The tour and promotions plan would be wrapped up in a matter of hours.

Another groan sounded from somewhere, maybe upstairs.

The house. It studied her.

Crowded her.

She took a sip of coffee. The dark liquid seemed to sour in her mouth. She could barely swallow. The Xanax had its limits.

She made her way to the dining room, carefully avoiding the grand staircase.

She passed through an alcove with four golden arches, a small bust of Bertha Mae carved into the middle of every one. She stared down at Peyton, her strength almost palpable and certainly visible. Peyton wondered if the scenes she saw earlier were the manor's memories or Bertha Mae's. Or if there was a difference.

She would look up where Bertha Mae had died—if it had been in the house, maybe she and the house had become one.

Peyton imagined her ancestor counseling her, encouraging her to be strong. She remembered reading Bertha Mae's diary and how she had overcome unimaginable hardships with such grace and strength.

Peyton made a few notes for how she wanted the Bertha Mae exhibit to appear. They had several of her tiaras and fans, plenty of dresses and photos. And, of course, the diary. Bertha Mae was the original matron of Alcott Manor, and she was the example she wished that Jayne Ella would have followed—brave, humble, a model of beauty and courage.

She took stock of the dining room, its coffered ceilings, oversized fireplace mantel, stained glass windows and gold leaf accents. Her mother had been right. Once the house was open to the public for tours and events, all of Charleston society would want to align with the manor. And her mother. She shook her head. Oh, how the standards had changed from Bertha Mae to her mother. She couldn't imagine Bertha Mae being so self-serving or concerned about society's approval.

She framed her fingers around the beautiful designs in the stained glass windows, visualizing how shots of them would be featured on the website and in tourism pamphlets. A female figure passed across her handmade viewfinder.

She stumbled backward, held on to the table for support.

She heard laughter.

No. No, she couldn't have.

Peyton set her laptop on the dining room table such that the ocean was within her view. She studied the raised wall border print of peaches and cherries and delicate floral blossoms. The original wall design that Anna Alcott, Bertha Mae's favorite daughter-in-law, had crafted to match her wedding china in the 1880s.

She made a note to set up glass cases beneath the border to put the Alcott wedding china on display. She wanted to set the table with them. But they were irreplaceable pieces, and tour guests were coming through.

This was also the ideal spot for a few of Anna Alcott's wedding dress photos. She remembered just how many weddings had been held at the manor in its heyday. Several generations of Alcotts had been married in the manor and on the great lawn. She would make certain that the more beautiful wedding photos were featured on the wedding section of the website. And, of course, in the wedding display she had planned for the ballroom.

She had mapped out her business prospectus and marketing plan. Now she had to get it banker-ready. Financial projections were pretty easy to calculate. The family stood to do well over time, but there were no short-term gains.

When she put the final decimal point into the budget, darkness had long fallen over the ocean and taken it from her view.

Next she opened the proposal file for Sweet Chocolate

and started documenting her strategy in bullet point fashion. From the moment they called and asked her to submit a proposal, she'd had ideas on how to remedy their image problem. That was how it worked for her when a client was a fit, the ideas came immediately.

She worked tirelessly. Detailing every idea she had for Sweet Chocolate, listing the exact media vehicles she wanted, their costs. Most importantly they would combine a joint PR campaign and fundraiser with three major fashion designers to benefit breast cancer research. She had already spoken to the designers and they were all onboard. She was going to win this client and nail the partnership.

When it was finished she emailed the Sweet Chocolate plan to Amanda with a request that she approve the final budget as quickly as possible. Then she sent the Alcott Manor plans to her mother. She closed her laptop and left her hands resting on the cover. Like she could seal the fate with her pitch with Sweet Chocolate and the loan with the bank.

She checked the time: 3:30 a.m. She stood and stretched, a seam popped. It was then that she realized she was still wearing the light blue 1860s dress she had worn for the photo. She found the tiny hole in the side seam and made a mental note to hand stitch it back together in the morning.

She was exhausted. Jittery. Her stomach hurt. Coffee and Xanax were probably a bad combination.

She laid down on the blue print settee at the side of the room, exhaling hard. Bertha Mae would have slipped cyanide in her tea if she had seen Peyton lying across such a formal piece of furniture. With so much work to focus on over the last few hours, she hadn't noticed how constricting the dress was. Thanks to years of Jayne Ella's insistence that she and her sister Layla have good posture.

Of course now that she was curled into the small couch, she could barely breathe. She unbuttoned the top six buttons and drew in a deep inhale, stared at the gold vines that stretched along the green silk wall coverings. She was so wired and tired she thought she saw the vines sway.

Rosebuds appeared to open and bloom every foot or so on a repeat pattern. She relaxed her focus but kept her gaze on the swaying vines, surprised at how powerfully her exhaustion was taking her under. She wouldn't take Xanax again. She wouldn't spend long nights at the manor alone, either. She sat up, decided to leave.

The vines leaned away from their anchor on the wall coverings and let loose into the room. Her stomach pains worsened. "Have to get out," she said and stood. But the vines spread into the room with each back and forth, blowing in an invisible wind that she couldn't feel. The pain in her stomach was unbearable and she wrapped her arms around her stomach. She didn't have time to be down with a virus. Maybe stress—the wedding, the manor, the memories, work. They were all too much, using her up. Maybe, literally, making her sick.

She doubled over to the floor and closed her eyes. After a long while the room was quiet and her stomach felt better. She assured herself that when she opened them again the vines would be gone. She would see nothing but the furnished room, then she would hightail it out of there and home to her mother's house. Instead she saw a little girl standing in front of her, staring at her.

"Where did you come from?" the little girl asked. She had long dark wavy hair, pulled away from her face and tied into a ponytail with a red ribbon. Her muted gold dress was full below the sash and stopped just shy of tea length, the neckline was straight and extended laterally into off-the-shoulder sleeves. It looked turn of the century and wasn't the sort of standard dress a ten-year-old girl would wear. Peyton almost asked why she was dressed in costume. "If you were supposed to come for dinner, you just missed it." She leaned closer and whispered, "Your buttons are unfastened. That's not decent." Her breath reeked of garlic. Her sallow complexion and dark under eye circles detracted from her beauty.

Peyton sat tall and buttoned quickly. Conversation and laughter echoed from nearby. She looked up in time to see suited men and bustle-dressed women walking away from the dining room in a group.

She would never, ever take Xanax again.

"Evelyn, the men are going outside to smoke, let's play pinochle," one woman said from the hall.

"Excellent idea, Cora."

"Rachel?"

"I have to go," the little girl said to Peyton. "Hasseltine is calling me."

A tall African-American woman entered the dining room from the side door, giving Peyton only the briefest glance.

"Rachel," she scolded and grabbed the little girl by the hand. "You're too sick to be down here." They left. Peyton was alone once again in the empty room.

Of all the things Peyton expected to see when she opened her eyes, a gathering of people in Victorian costume wasn't one of them.

Gas flames hissed in the chandelier that hung over the dining table. A fire crackled and popped in the fireplace. Candlelight flickered from three silver candelabras, placed at thirds on the long dining table.

Peyton knew the candles hadn't been lit a few moments

ago. Certainly there weren't the remnants of dinner, like what had been left on the table in front of her. And she didn't remember if the light fixture had been restored to gas, but she really didn't think it had been.

She walked to the table and rapped her knuckles lightly on the wood. The cool, hard surface was solid. Which meant she probably wasn't dreaming. Dancing vines, women dressed in costume, a little girl—definitely hallucinating. The room even smelled of chicken and potatoes.

A subtle brushing of fabric against fabric startled her. She realized she wasn't alone in the room. Candlelight, gaslight and firelight left the far-reaching corners of the oversized room unlit altogether, it was impossible to see the source of the noise.

Embers from a cigar glowed hot in the swath of darkness, then faded again. Whoever stood in the shadows faced away from her and toward the window.

"Who's there?" her voice was breathless.

There was no response for a moment, the only sound the whisper of the gas that fueled the chandelier. Then, someone slowly emerged from the shadows on the other side of the room.

He was tall, well over six feet, with broad shoulders that slimmed into a narrow, vested waist. He sucked on a cigar and looked at his gold-chained watch, like he had too much time to pass.

He seemed oblivious to her. He clicked his watch cover shut, returned it to the vest pocket and blew sweet tobacco-scented puffs of smoke that floated like layered clouds above his head.

Adrenaline zinged through her chest and she pressed her hand to her heart. She fought the feeling that for as much as she had tried to hold herself together these last few days, that something had finally cracked. She had lost touch with reality, fallen into an Alcott Manor rabbit hole.

He stepped out of the shadows and into the lighted area of the room. His blond hair was slicked neatly into a short Victorian style, his skin was tanned and smooth and his light blue eyes fixed steadily on her.

Pinpoint dots blinked at the edges of her vision. Her head spun. "Is it you?" she whispered. She was struck with that feeling that she had missed the punchline on some horrible joke.

She squinted to focus on his face. There were differences between the man who stood in front of her and the man she was engaged to nine years ago. There were new worry lines across his forehead, the light was gone from his eyes, and his trademark smile was missing.

They walked toward each other.

Her heart kicked hard like it might burst right through her skin.

"Peyton?" he asked tentatively.

The sound of his voice reached inside her chest and plucked heartstrings she thought had died with his absence.

"Beau?" she asked.

When he reached her he ran his fingertips along the side of her face, as if to prove to himself that she was real.

She touched the top of his hand, realized she was shaking.

"Peyton—" He took her into his arms and held her close, kissing her cheek. She closed her eyes; the familiarity of his kisses was dizzying. She held on to him, memories pulling at her like a powerful ocean current, willful, strong and determined.

"How did you find me?" Tears filled his eyes.

In all of the time they'd shared, she had never seen him

cry. Her mouth opened but she didn't know how to answer. She studied him in the flickering glow of fire and candle-light, running her fingers over the features of his face, his neck, his chest. "Where have you been?"

He shook his head, like the answer wouldn't come, like he didn't know. He kissed her long and slow, lifting her in his embrace.

Unanswered questions silenced with the feel of his arms around her. Her mind filled with the nearly-forgotten memories of what it felt like to be loved by him.

When he finally set her down, he stepped away from her, their hands joined together.

"You're okay." She laughed, still unbelieving. "Where have you been?"

"Here." He gestured to the walls. "I haven't left the manor since the night of our rehearsal dinner."

7

They sat next to one another at the shadowed end of the dining table. He held her hands, kissing them now and then. The polished gentlemanly image she had first seen faded and was replaced by utter fright. Worry lines marked his forehead and fear illuminated his eyes. "How long has it been?"

Panic fluttered in her chest. She focused on the fact that Beau was alive. His bones hadn't been picked clean and scattered on some mossy forest floor, the result of a terrible accident or horrific murder.

Peyton licked her dry lips. "Nine years. What do you mean...you've been *here*?"

"Nine years," he whispered. His eyes widened like the breath had been knocked from his lungs. He cleared his throat. "Here. Stuck here, in its past. Actually, it's not the past. I mean, it is, but—time doesn't move here. Not linearly. We go from event to event. There are hard boundaries you can't escape."

Beau told her how he had searched for a way home, for

a way back to her and hadn't been able to find one. "Please tell me you can get us home."

Peyton closed her eyes. When she opened them again, she said, "Are you sure you're okay, because none of this is making sense. I mean the clothing, and you. I mean, are you—? You're really here. I think. And—" She looked at the gas-fueled chandelier and shook her head. Maybe this was a dream.

"You don't remember how you got here, do you?" he said.

"I fell asleep on the settee, sort of. I had a stomach ache. When it passed, I opened my eyes, and you and those other people were here."

"No, Peyton. We're not with you. You're here. With us." Beau stood, crossed the length of the dining room, rubbed his hands over his face. Then he returned to his seat and held her hands again. "You're not home anymore. You're not anywhere."

"Beau—I'm not— Where have you—"

He pulled her tight against him. A flood of memories swept through her: the way she held his waist when they rode home from school on the back of his motorcycle, their long Saturdays on the ocean in his father's boat, his proposal to her on the beach at sunset.

He was real, so real.

"I would never have left you. You have to know that," he said. "The house took me, I haven't been able to get to you."

Tears slid down her cheeks. She remembered the lesson she learned about the time the dry cleaner packed her wedding dress into a box suitable for long-term storage: That loving someone too much could wreck your life.

She couldn't help the way her heart and soul connected with Beau.

As it did once again. A familiar note, a familiar groove, a familiar love.

She looked at the table that should have been littered with her files and papers and her laptop but wasn't. Instead there were plates filled with remnants of food and she could still hear guests down the hall, people she didn't know.

"I don't understand what's going on here," she whispered.

"All I know to say is that we're in these memories and they...they seem to belong to the house."

She looked at the plates littered with half-eaten chicken and clumps of mashed potatoes and her stomach turned.

Ladies' laughter echoed from the front of the house and Peyton turned toward them. "Who are those people?"

He shrugged. "Your ancestors."

"My—what?"

He walked the length of the room again. Then he walked toward her, at a slow pace, licked his lips distractedly like the news he was about to share was not good. "I've searched. There's no way out. Unless you remember how you got here."

He handed her a rose from the centerpiece and she sniffed its fragrance.

Dreams didn't have scents, did they? She tried to swallow, her throat tight with terror. "I feel sick," she said.

She walked toward the front door, in the direction of voices. People chatting and laughing.

"Peyton—no!" Beau called after her. She stopped short of the foyer. Six women gathered just outside of the parlor, a photographer in front of them. The women faced an antique camera that was perched on a tripod. One that looked much like the camera Mrs. Miller had used to take Peyton's picture earlier in the evening.

The photographer placed the cap on the lens and when he noticed Peyton, stood upright and glared at her. "You!" he yelled.

She turned around and ran into Beau.

"Act as if you're my guest," he whispered.

A hissing noise sounded from overhead and she looked at the gold chandelier that hung from above, where gas flames flickered instead of the steady glow of light bulbs.

A group of older men stood in the formal living room across the way and stared at Peyton as though she were an uninvited guest. Horror shot through her at the realization that she wasn't simply in her ancestral home late at night. This wasn't a dream, this was something else entirely.

She ran her damp palms along the front of her dress. The house must have sucked her right into its history.

"You have gotten into my picture!" The photographer yelled with a French accent. He shoved a glass plate at them and tapped on its surface.

"It's okay," Beau said to the photographer. He raised his hands and tried to calm the man who clearly considered this to be a ruined work of art. "My fault. I was giving my friend a tour and I didn't realize you were taking a picture."

"Beau?" A woman appeared at the edge of the formal parlor, her wide smile blinding and magnetic. All eyes turned to her. Her dark hair was twisted high on her head with several long curls trailing just past her neck.

Peyton had seen this woman's image numerous times over the years—painted, photographed and even carved into marble and wood. This was Bertha Mae Alcott. Living. Breathing. Upright and beaming.

Panic exploded in Peyton's chest.

The photographer fussed and argued, his accent making it hard to understand him.

Bertha Mae stroked the outside of the photographer's arm and he visibly calmed. The lilting sound of her voice made her words sound like a lullaby. She spoke to him in French. The only word Peyton could make out now and then was the name Beau.

When she spotted Peyton, Bertha Mae stopped mid-sentence, the high wattage slipped from her smile.

"Beau," Bertha Mae said breathlessly, her accent full of Southern grace. "Who did you bring into my home tonight?" Bertha Mae pushed her way past the photographer and threaded her arm around Beau's. She patted his chest with her other hand.

Beau opened his mouth. No words came out.

"Beau?" she asked.

Peyton's head swam and a pain hit her stomach.

"Who are you, dear?" Bertha Mae leaned toward her.

Peyton thought she was going to be sick. She spun around and tugged on one of the iron double doors that led from the foyer to the front porch. When it opened just enough she slipped through.

She ran around the porch toward the beachside of the house. Waves crashed in the distance and she drew deep salty-air breaths into her lungs. She couldn't have just seen Bertha Mae Alcott.

Her sister Layla had said that the manor gave her strange dreams. That's probably all this was. A strange dream. A stress dream. A Xanax-induced dream. Beau, Bertha Mae, the dress, the history... She had been thinking about them too much, she had seen too many photos of them and they were heavy on her mind.

She would go back into the house and everything would be as it had been before she fell asleep—fully restored, decorated, quiet, empty of guests. Maybe Beau would still be there. Her stomach cramped hard again and it doubled her over in pain.

She dropped to her knees, her arms wrapped around her midsection. She squeezed her eyes shut. The dizziness hit again, only worse this time. With her eyes closed, the world spun beneath her.

She pressed a palm against the hard wood of the porch floor, trying to feel steady again. When the pain and the dizziness subsided, she rested on her heels. She opened her eyes expecting to see the ocean. Instead, she found herself on the floor of the Alcott Manor dining room.

She pulled herself upright. The dining table was empty except for her laptop and file folders and the empty coffee cup.

She glanced around the room. There were no plates or remnants of a partially eaten meal, there was no Bertha Mae.

And there was no Beau.

Beau Spencer stood at the side of Alcott Manor's wraparound porch.

The ocean crashed onto the sand in the darkness.

"Peyton!"

He walked around the back of the house, searched the area. He crossed the grassy lawn, knowing better than to go too far. Especially at night.

"Peyton!" he called.

He'd been trapped in the manor for years. He had searched every inch of the place and he hadn't found a way out. Had she found a way? Did he miss his chance?

The wind knocked him backward several steps. This was the night that a storm would hit, he remembered. He called for her again. There was no answer. He searched behind every tree and bush.

When there was no sign of her, he slow-walked his way to the side of the porch where the wind wasn't as strong. He replayed the evening in his mind. The rain pelted against the roof. Peyton's image was so vivid—the midnight black of her hair, the sparkle in the light of her eyes. She was even more beautiful than he had remembered.

He looked around, tried to think—did anyone come onto the porch on this evening? He usually spent this night in the dark corner of the dining room to avoid the party guests and the storm. He didn't have to sleep on the floor or outside on this particular night. That was always a welcome change.

He looked at the back lawn one more time, hoping to see her running toward him in that pale blue dress. Sheets of rain beat against the porch. He turned to go inside. He couldn't.

He leaned on the wall, slid down it until he sat on the floor. He drew his legs up, ran a hand over his wet face. Thunder crashed and lightning lit up the sky. In the time he had been stuck in this house, he had often prayed to die. Now with the chance to see Peyton again, he wanted to live. He wanted to be with her for the rest of his life. He'd known, from the first time he'd seen her, in just the same way they showed in movies, that she was the one for him.

He glanced at the second pillar from the far corner. After they had been dating for a while, they walked along the beach and ended up here at Alcott Manor. The house was run down then, or partially so. They were always in the midst of a restoration.

He had carved their initials in that pillar. It made her laugh and she called him crazy. "Someone will see," she said. He told her he knew he wanted her in his life forever and he didn't care who knew.

The wind blew the rain against his face. With a storm like this she would have come back by now if she could have.

He squeezed his eyes shut, wished for something to

numb the pain. On a normal night—not that anything was normal in the manor—he would drink the same whiskey that the Alcott men and their friends drank. He would wake up the next morning with a sick hangover and a naked woman sprawled at his side. Maybe a redhead, sometimes a blond. Never a brunette. Never anyone who looked remotely like Peyton. He couldn't be close to anyone who reminded him of what he had lost.

And no matter how much he drank, he couldn't forget the life he'd almost had, and he couldn't forget Peyton.

Hadn't he seen her tonight? Now he didn't know. He wasn't drunk. But she wasn't here. He looked at his hands that had just held hers, touched her face. He curled his empty hands into fists.

He scanned the empty porch, then lowered his head. Began to pray again to die.

The scent caught his attention.

He lifted his lapel to his nose.

Her lilac perfume, heady and spicy, was there.

9

Peyton sipped hot coffee and stared over the waves where the sun would soon reveal its fiery face. The breeze off of the water was cool and she pulled the light blue blanket around her shoulders. She dug her bare toes into the sand and squeezed.

The night before had been filled with too much work and too many mysteries, so she'd never made it home to her mother's house. She'd pulled her suitcase from the rental car, found her toothbrush and a change of clothes. Her Boston marathon t-shirt and black yoga pants were a welcome change from the formality of the pale blue party dress she had worn throughout the night. The simple ability to sit on the beach and draw her knees close made her feel more like herself again. Being outside of the manor, if only by a few hundred feet, helped, too. The coffee didn't hurt.

Seagulls called and her text alarm buzzed from where her phone lay in the cool sand. She looked at the screen:

Morning, honey.

It was Ira. Another message alert buzzed.

Be there shortly. You okay?

She could feel the comfort he had intended with his words, as if he had spoken them to her face to face, running his thumb along the side of her neck. His gentle touch could send goosebumps down one side of her body and up the other. She often mused that was because he was a doctor, he knew where all of the nerve endings were and he played them like a song. "Nope. I just know you," he would say.

He cared about her happiness—was the wine to her liking, was the temperature just where she wanted it?

She had started dating Ira two months after she moved to Boston and began her new job at the agency. She met him on a blind date that Amanda had set up. "He's a doctor!" Amanda had said like he was the largest prize on the carnival game shelf. She told Peyton that she should go for him and quickly.

Peyton actually enjoyed herself on that first date. They had a lot in common, talked with one another nonstop and when he held her hand in the cab on the way home, she thought the gesture was sweet. She liked him.

He left for France the morning after their date and by the time he returned at the end of the week, she had received two flower deliveries from him. "He's courting you!" Amanda had all but shrieked. "These cards, they're love letters!" she had said. "He said he can't stop thinking about you!"

Truth was she hadn't been able to stop thinking about him either. He called her the day he got back and that night she slept in his arms. His kisses continued to be as gentle as they had been on the night of their first date. That was important to her because she could tell a lot about a man by how he kissed.

She had refused second dates with men whose kisses were tight little pecks. That meant they were stingy, selfish and uptight. Same for men whose tongues were wild with exploration. Or stiff with restraint. She wouldn't suffer that lack of self-awareness.

But Ira's kisses were spectacular and she could have kissed him nonstop for days on end. The fact that his kisses were the same now as they were on that first date told her that he held nothing back from her. What you saw was what you got with Ira. No pretense. No secrets. That made her feel a little guilty because she had held a few things back from him.

She wondered if that hesitancy showed in the way she kissed him.

They developed a weekend hobby of finding the best wines in the city and an early morning habit of jogging through the Boston Commons. They both liked old movies and hated hot yoga. Somewhere along the way she realized she wasn't thinking about Beau every moment of every day. Her heart had made room for Ira.

She had fallen in love with Ira Byrne. He was funny and smart. Brilliant, really. He was one of the most sought-after pediatric surgeons in all of the Northeast. He was charming and sophisticated and it didn't hurt that he was from old money. He had surprised her on more than one occasion with an impromptu trip overseas. The first trip had been to Spain, then London. And finally, Paris, with a sojourn to the south of France. In the Mediterranean in Cassis, he proposed to her with champagne and a five-carat solitaire. She enthusiastically accepted.

When she thought of Beau just after Ira proposed, she thought that was because Ira had been the second man to propose to her. Beau had been the first. She was just someone who thought about those types of things. Even when she didn't mean to. She attributed it to her extraordinary memory. It was always coughing up details from the past that had a connection to the present. No matter how remote.

It was Ira who had given her a passion for work. One she hadn't realized how much she wanted. She had always planned on traveling the world with Beau because that was what he wanted. He had taught her the art of photography. Together they were going to travel, shooting and writing about faraway places.

But it was Ira who showed her how much good she could do with her knack for reinventing public image. "Think of all the people and the businesses who need a second chance," he had said. "You have a real gift for this. Nearly everyone deserves a second chance." That simple sentence set her on fire. Her work wasn't about money or prestige, it was about helping people. And using her natural talents.

A large wave crashed on the sand. She should have been on the phone with Ira right then, talking about how much they missed one another, discussing wedding plans. She should have been peppering him with questions about where he was taking her for their honeymoon.

But images of Beau flashed through her mind. He had returned to her life like a spray of fireworks, unexpected and beautiful and now she could barely think of anything else.

Ira had asked her once how she would handle it if Beau ever returned. Would she want him back? "It's not a possibility," she told him. "He's gone."

"But, assuming he did come back," Ira asked. "Just walked out of the jungle one day and said he wanted you back. How would you react to that?" She knew what he was doing. Limiting his risk.

Years ago Ira had proposed to Amelia Gilroy, his childhood sweetheart. Six days before their wedding she ran off with his best man. "Anything can happen," he said. "And usually does. So I have to ask."

"You don't have to ask me, because if Beau were alive he would have been at that wedding." She still felt bad about that comment. It was like she implied that Beau was better than Amelia because he would have shown up at their wedding if he could have. Or that maybe that she was better than him, somehow, because it was possible that her fiancé disappeared for reasons beyond his control. Unlike Amelia.

She apologized and told him that the point was he could trust her.

That was the night she knew that he was going to ask her to marry him. She didn't know specifically when he was going to ask, but she knew it was in the works. She knew in the same way she knew when a client was about to agree to the terms of their contract. She just knew.

So, even though she didn't think that risk could effectively be insulated in affairs of the heart—the heart loves who it loves, her mother used to tell her—she ultimately told him what he wanted to hear. That even if Beau walked in the door on their wedding day, she wouldn't leave with him.

Another large wave built in height, big enough to swallow her whole. It crashed loud and hard, the spray misted her face. She closed her eyes. She saw Beau: Blond hair, light blue eyes, full lips. Three piece suit. Smoking a cigar.

Her eyes flew open. He had walked right out of the shadows of the dining room, like he had been sitting there all this time just waiting on her.

Now he was away from her again.

Her fingers traced over her cheek, where Beau's lips had

pressed against her skin. She drank a long sip of her coffee. Her phone rang and she peeked at the screen. Ira. She hadn't yet answered his texts. She bit into the glazed dough-nut, her third that morning and one of a dozen that her mother had left on the counter the day before.

"Is everything okay?" Ira asked when she answered.

"Yeah, fine. Sorry. Just busy."

"You're sure? Your mom's not driving you crazy?"

"A little. But no, I'm good."

"I didn't hear from you last night."

"I worked most of the night and I guess I lost track of time."

"Listen, my mother wants to know if we're going to use the house in France for our honeymoon. I told her that I'd already made plans but if you'd rather…"

Peyton couldn't focus on wedding details right then. She stared at the manor.

"Peyton?" Ira asked. "I think I've just lost you."

"Sorry, Ira. I guess my mind is just occupied with…" She exhaled. "…stuff."

"Anything I should be worried about? Brides-to-be are supposed to be happy and thinking about all of these nuptial details, right?"

"The bank is giving us reason to be concerned about the loan, so I'm trying to help my family work that out."

"Are you having a hard time being home again?"

Anxiety tingled in Peyton's palms. She hadn't told him about the blank spot in her childhood memories. She wouldn't. She had told him that she and Beau had their rehearsal dinner there. "No, I um, I was just remembering how much photography I used to do when I lived here. I'm thinking that maybe I'd like to get back into it."

"Ah." Ira seemed to relax. "Well, if it's something you want to do again, you should do it. Do you have a camera?"

"They're all in Boston." Peyton looked out at the water and thought of the person she used to be when she lived in Charleston. She always carried a camera with her. She used to spend hours shooting photographs and creating exhibits for several local galleries.

"Then you should get back to that."

"Yeah. Yeah, I will."

"Good. Listen, I'm due in surgery in ten, I have to run. I love you. I couldn't be more happy that you'll be my bride soon."

They said their goodbyes.

She glanced at the house and frowned. Earlier that morning she had searched the manor for signs of Beau and Bertha Mae and the guests she had seen the night before, but found none.

Another text alert. Her mother this time:

Morning! Mrs. Miller is texting me. She says she's at the manor and that you're not there. Is everything okay? I checked and it doesn't look like you came home last night.

Peyton replied:

worked all night on a walk be in shortly

After Peyton pulled herself off the dining room floor that morning, she had walked cautiously to the front parlor. She found only the unpopulated room she had seen when she first walked in the manor the day before. No photographer. No tripod. No guests.

She could have written it off as a dream if it hadn't been for one thing.

Chills spread down her arms.

She drank the last of her coffee.

She had gone into the ballroom earlier that morning and found two black and white tintypes sitting on one of the tables. The first was Bertha Mae and several of her friends standing in the parlor.

Peyton held the tintype closer and focused on the woman in the background.

It was a blurry image. But there she was. In the corner of the picture, wearing the light blue dress she had worn yesterday.

She lifted the second tintype she'd found that morning —the Alcott family wedding. The man who resembled Beau had been standing to the side of the couch yesterday, looking like a wedding guest.

Today, he was gone.

10

Blair Spencer, Austin's wife and Beau's mother, had never stepped foot inside the manor. In years past, she had been quoted in several newspaper articles as saying that the manor was a danger to the community and should be razed.

Today Blair toured the home, examining every detail. At the moment, she stood silent in the middle of the front parlor, seemingly memorizing the finer features of the room.

Jayne Ella waited patiently, stood in the foyer of her ancestors' newly renovated home, feeling, finally, like the rightful matriarch of Alcott Manor. She had long dreamed of the day when she could claim Alcott Manor as the most elegant home in the county. And, she had often hoped to do that in the presence of Blair Spencer. Among a few others.

"I must say I am...stunned at how beautifully the home has been restored. It's beyond anything I expected," Blair said.

"Our family isn't afraid of a little hard work."

Blair Spencer's wide-eyed gaze covered the room. Her

blond hair was cut blunt at the shoulders and pulled off her face in a black velvet headband. She had worn that style since she and Jayne Ella were in elementary school together. Jayne Ella always hated the way the style made Blair appear blue-blooded. Like she had inherent rights to wealth that Jayne Ella didn't get.

But she had a family mansion on her side now. And it was even on the National Register. She let the quiet take over the room because Blair had to be the one to offer. She had finally figured out that that's how her social group worked. Invitations were extended and only rarely.

"You know, Jayne Ella, I don't know if you're aware, but The Charleston Women's League takes pride in the number of volunteer activities that we support during the year, and historical preservation is one of our favorite types of projects. I'm sure you have a grand opening coming up, and we could help with that. You might want to think about Saturday teas on the holidays, those could be a big hit. We could help with that. In fact, you might want to consider opening a year-round tea room with your gift shop. Those always do well."

Jayne Ella kept her smile professional. She didn't want to seem too eager. But Blair's support was a big key to making a success of the manor. "Thank you, Blair. We would love to have your support, and I love the idea of the tea room."

"I don't know if you've ever thought of joining our little group, but belonging could really help you to promote the manor. All of our members are extremely well connected."

Jayne Ella chose not to bring up the fact that she had tried many times to join the Charleston Women's League, but her requests had never been approved. The membership consisted only of married women who were extremely well moneyed, either through family or through marriage.

Jayne Ella's husband left her years ago for another woman. And though she had done well for herself, her savings didn't compare to the millions the members flashed about. Closest she ever got to the Women's League membership was doing their hair.

"I know our two families have had some trouble—"

"That's all in the past," Jayne Ella said.

"Austin was just upset that Beau—" Blair's voice choked and she gestured toward the walls of the manor. "That Beau was last seen here."

Jayne Ella placed her hand on Blair's arm. "We love Beau and we continue to have hope."

Blair's eyes became watery and she placed her hand on Jayne Ella's. "Thank you."

For the first time their relationship was markedly different. No longer was Jayne Ella the skinny and awkward little red-haired girl who didn't have any friends, the one Blair didn't want to have anything to do with. Neither was she just the hairstylist who did the hair of The Charleston Women's League.

She was their equal. Thanks to a fully restored Alcott Manor standing behind her.

She had the one thing no one else in the society group had—a historical property.

Most importantly, Blair's interest in being affiliated with Alcott Manor would shutdown her husband's interest to call the loan. Jayne Ella knew who wore the pants in that family.

Before Blair drove away in her dark blue Mercedes, she lowered her window and waved as if the two women had been friends for years.

Jayne Ella smiled and returned the wave, she watched Blair's car clear of the iron gate at the front of the property.

Jayne Ella turned around and startled at the sight of

Mrs. Miller standing in the open doorway. She held a mug of coffee.

"Making new friends, I see." Mrs. Miller's eyes held hers. "Blair Spencer certainly has a lot of influence in town, doesn't she?"

Jayne Ella tucked a lock of hair behind her ear. "She's interested in helping us with a few of our fundraising efforts. Called me right out of the blue!" Jayne Ella smiled like she could disarm Mrs. Miller.

Mrs. Miller's good eye seemed to focus more intently on her.

"It's unusual for her to play the charitable sort."

Jayne Ella didn't answer. She gestured for Mrs. Miller to go ahead of her into the manor. "Shall we go inside?"

Mrs. Miller didn't move.

"Isn't Blair's daddy the Chairman over at First Charleston Bank? I read about her father and the bank merger in the paper not too long ago. That merger made quite a news piece because it combines Charleston's two oldest banking families—her husband's and her father's.

"There she is right in the middle with all that money and influence. Newspaper said that Blair holds all of Charleston in the palm of her hand. Like a marble. One nod from her in any direction can make or break a business. Or maybe someone's world."

Jayne Ella nodded to the fact that she blocked the doorway. "May I?"

Mrs. Miller maintained her eye contact. She slowly stepped to the side.

Jayne Ella nodded a thank you. She took the key from the lock and shut and locked the heavy door behind her. A loud ka-thunk echoed through the main hallway.

"There was also an op-ed piece that said with her daddy

controlling one bank's loan strings and her husband doing the same with the other, businesses in Charleston didn't stand a chance if Blair Spencer didn't like you."

Jayne Ella pressed the hair that fell to the bottom of her neck.

"Is Blair finally letting you into their exclusive group?" Mrs. Miller took a long sip from her coffee mug. "Now that Alcott Manor has turned into something respectable?"

"She brought it up." Jayne Ella walked quickly to the kitchen, leaving Mrs. Miller standing in the foyer.

Jayne Ella lifted her tackle box of hairpins, brushes and styling products onto the largest table in the center of the room.

Mrs. Miller's slow, shuffling footsteps echoed along the hallway.

She gripped the top lid and squeezed. With any luck Mrs. Miller would have a heart attack and keel over before she reached her.

When Mrs. Miller finally arrived she said, "Why do you think they haven't invited you to join their exclusive group before now?"

"I've been busy with my salon, and the manor."

"No. You try too hard. Always did. They know you're a wanna-be. Not hard to tell with that bottle-red hair of yours, the bright red lipstick and your too-tight clothes. I would hazard a guess that most of those women think you're white trash." Mrs. Miller pointed a crooked finger at her. "That's why they've never invited you. And you shouldn't join their group. They'll chew you up first chance they get."

"I'm a successful businesswoman." Jayne Ella straightened her shoulders and tipped her chin upward.

"I don't think that's why Blair came calling, honey."

"Listen. I've been very good to you over the years. I've let you keep your job—"

"Oh, you *let* me keep my job. Yes, that's one way to look at it." Mrs. Miller lowered herself into the straight back chair at the side of the room. "Tell me, what do you think your new friend Blair would say if she knew you used to sleep with her husband?"

Jayne Ella looked around the corner to make sure Peyton wasn't around. "You and Austin have an agreement. Now as far as I know he's making his monthly payment to you on time, and you do still have your job here at the manor—"

"Did Austin ever mention to you that I have video as well as pictures? Or that I made copies?"

Jayne Ella swallowed against a tight throat. "Yes. He did."

Mrs. Miller smiled like she reflected on sweet memories. She dug into her right front patch pocket, placed three photos on the table. "These three are my favorite, I think. Here, take a look."

Panic shot from her heart to her head and back again. "Why are you carrying these around?"

"Because I just like to remind you of the cards I hold."

"I've never forgotten that. Not for a moment."

"Look at them." Mrs. Miller pointed to the photos.

Jayne Ella's first thought was that she looked so much younger then. It wasn't just the years that had not yet passed, it was something else in her face that gave that impression. She had been happier then.

In the first photo Austin held her face in his broad hands, his smile full of love and laughter. She held on to the sides of his arms—those strong arms that she thought were going to hold her forever. Her eyes were focused on his mouth and, most likely, whatever he was saying to her.

In the next image, he had lifted her against the wall. It

had been the back wall of the sunroom in the manor. His khaki pants hung low around his thighs. His bank had hosted their Christmas party on the great lawn that night with live music and festive food. The manor was enjoying yet another restoration attempt. Half of the first floor was completely restored.

Mrs. Miller was supposed to be babysitting Peyton along with Ruby Lee. She was also supposed to be handing out the guests' party gifts—local seashells that had been painted gold and turned into a Christmas ornament. She remembered Austin checking the area to make sure that no one was around. Somehow they missed Mrs. Miller and her camera.

"You realize that if Blair Spencer saw these, she would use every last breath in her body to destroy Alcott Manor. And her father would, too." She slipped the three photos into her tackle box of hairstyling supplies. "You would lose this job that you hold so dear. Not to mention that your leverage with Austin would be gone."

Mrs. Miller shook her head. "Austin would continue to pay. Blair might even pay. Because even if Blair knows about y'all's affair, she won't want that information public. Last thing either one of them wants is for photos like that to get out into the public eye."

Jayne Ella leaned in, her hands gripping the table hard. "Blair would pay to keep the photos quiet. But she would simultaneously destroy me and the manor. Think, Mrs. Miller. All she would have to do is tell Austin to move ahead with calling the loan. Which he would happily do. Which means you would lose your job. Did you ever hear the phrase 'win the battle but lose the war'? I'm already playing with fire by partnering with her. I don't know even why she reached out," Jayne Ella said.

Mrs. Miller's expression was calm, like she already knew the answer to the puzzle.

"Why did you bring these pictures here today? What do you want?"

"I'm concerned about that letter that Austin sent to you. He shouldn't be messing with the loan on this place. I thought I might need to remind him of these." Mrs. Miller nodded toward the photos with a slight smile.

"You called Blair, didn't you?"

Mrs. Miller shrugged. "I might have mentioned how beautifully the manor turned out."

Jayne Ella pressed her fingertips to her forehead.

"I also might have suggested that her society group could benefit from an association with such a prominent historical property. Someone needed to get her on our side. Plus, it's a warning shot to Austin. He's up to something. He wouldn't have sent that letter if he didn't know what his next move was going to be." Mrs. Miller ran her tongue over the front of her teeth.

How quickly their relationship had shifted between being enemies and being allies. As much as she hated the fact that Mrs. Miller had the photos of her and Austin, she did like that they had held Austin in line all these years.

On more than one occasion Austin had tried to buy her and the rest of the Alcott family members out of the loan.

"Concerns me, too. I can't imagine what he's thinking." Pain shot through her mouth where she had gnawed the inside of her cheek.

11

Peyton watched the wedding event company place 350 white folding chairs in rows on the great lawn for her wedding. Day after tomorrow was the rehearsal dinner, day after that she was marrying Ira Byrne.

Ira was supposed to arrive soon and he would want to know all about the final wedding plans. Her stomach tightened. She hadn't finished the plans.

She looked at the tintype where her image had been a few hours earlier. Now it was missing from the photo, too.

Jayne Ella paced along the outside of the chair formation like an army sergeant. Peyton figured her mother would do just about anything to make sure that this wedding went without a hitch. Ira's mother was the same way.

Peyton's first almost wedding was enormous. The formal sanctuary at the First Baptist Church was filled to the rafters with guests, standing room only. That didn't work out so well, and now she was superstitious. Last thing she wanted was a big wedding. But her mother and Ira's kept adding guests to the list.

Her mother hadn't said it aloud, but Peyton knew that Jayne Ella looked at this wedding as just one more rung to climb in her quest to achieve a certain level of social standing. She would get all of her mother's attention on this event, because it was useful to her.

Love by way of usefulness, that was Jayne Ella's style.

"I wanted some shots of the empty seating for the website and the brochure. The florist and the photographer should be here any minute to stage this for me, then your wedding flowers will be put out fresh day after tomorrow. Why are you just sitting there staring at that tintype? You're supposed to be helping me, this is your wedding."

"I thought we only had about a hundred guests?" she asked.

"We needed a bigger crowd for the photos so I expanded the list to include some family friends. We want to attract larger weddings and receptions, you know. Ira's mother added a few more, too."

"How many?" Peyton asked.

"A couple of hundred, I think? Maybe more."

"What?!" Peyton said.

Jayne Ella ignored her and began a conversation with one of the event coordinators who gestured to the tent.

After a few moments Jayne Ella called, "Come on, honey! Join me, this will be fun!"

Peyton stared at the side porch of Alcott Manor, remembering the night before. Then, a flash of Mrs. Miller running her hand along the hallway.

She startled at the slogan she had come up with for the manor—Where History Lives.

History *was* alive within those walls.

She looked at the tintype in her hand. Beau's location

had to have something to do with these tintypes. And the house. The manor had a second dimension to it, as if it existed in two different eras.

She stopped abruptly. Maybe it was the result of the authentic Alcott family clothing she put on while being in the manor? Had Beau done that? And how was it that she could see him in the tintypes?

She glanced at her mother, who waved for her to come to the tent. Then she looked at the back porch. Mrs. Miller stood there like she waited for her. Something she and Mrs. Miller did yesterday catapulted her into the home's memories.

"It's not the past," Beau had said.

What did that mean? Where was he, exactly? Where did she go last night in that house? How did she make it back and he didn't?

She walked toward Mrs. Miller, wondering what they had done yesterday that sent her into that other dimension within the manor. Was it the dress, the jewelry, making the tintype?

She looked at the house. It looked back at her through its tall shuttered windows that missed nothing. As if the house dropped the idea inside of her head, she thought: All of those things combined and only while in the manor.

Her imagination spun like old film flying off the movie reel. She got there somehow. And she got back. If she did it again, would she be able to bring Beau with her?

Her phone rang. It was her mother calling from the other side of the great lawn.

"Where are you going?" she asked.

"Work," Peyton said. "I need to get started on the rest of the pictures."

Ira arrived at the far end of the wide wraparound porch. He leaned on the railing, then waved when he saw her. His smile was so vibrant it could have powered ten cities.

Guilt seized her heart.

She walked toward him, remembering everything they had planned for their life together. She wondered if she was seeing Beau now so she could make peace with her past. Begin her new life with Ira with a clean slate.

They met about halfway between the ocean and the house.

He hugged and kissed her.

"This is quite a place you have here. You didn't tell me that it was all this." He gestured toward the great lawn and the manor and the expansive view of the ocean.

Peyton remembered the rusted chain link fence that used to line the property when the manor was in ruins. "It hasn't always been this beautiful."

"No sign of it now." He threaded her arm through his and walked them toward the rows of white chairs that faced the ocean. He exaggerated his steps as if they were taking a practice walk down the aisle. He gazed at her like she was the only woman in the world. He took one deliberate step toward the altar, then another.

She desperately wanted to stop the procession and tell him what had happened the night before, but she couldn't find the words.

"So this is where we're getting married." He pulled her close and kissed her. "My family is going to love this. It's the perfect place to blend your history with our future."

〜

WITH IRA on a tour of the property with Jayne Ella, Peyton went to the ballroom to prepare for the next set of photos that Mrs. Miller would take. Her heart thrummed with nerves.

Her past and her future were colliding.

When she first began dating Ira, she found a therapist. She asked if it was normal that she thought of Beau so often.

"It's not entirely out of the realm of normal," the therapist said. "Especially if Beau was the man you thought you were going to spend the rest of your life with. But we need to work on letting go."

Now she had seen Beau again, and her heart wouldn't settle. She ran her hand along the different dresses that hung on the mannequins.

She cautioned herself.

Strongly.

What if she wasn't able to come back?

She selected a dress and jewelry and thought about how she was going to do her hair for the photo. "So not smart," she muttered under her breath.

Ira was nearby, on the property. They loved each other and they were about to get married. So why was she risking her life and potentially ruining her future with Ira?

Because it was Beau. Because he had been missing for almost a decade. Because she might be the only one who could bring him home.

She fastened the necklace and slipped into the dress. What if it didn't work?. What if last night repeated itself— where she saw Beau but only she made it home again?

Could she still be with Ira knowing that Beau was alive?

She remembered Beau's daddy pulling her aside on the night of the wedding social between their two families.

"You're not right for my boy." He sipped his scotch. Then shook the ice in the bottom of the glass. "Now I'm sorry about telling you this at the eleventh hour. But he could have a very bright future with our family bank. Traveling around with you and that camera. That's a dead end for him. If you search your heart, I think you'll find that you're not really cut out to be a banker's wife. Set him free, sweetheart. You'll both be happier for it, I promise."

Heat rushed through her, gathered in her gut. Electricity sparked in her palms. She gritted her teeth so she wouldn't speak the words she wanted to say. She had been raised to be polite, respectful and to bite her tongue.

She never had the chance to tell Beau what his father had said. She wondered if Beau would have changed his mind about staying in Charleston if she had told him.

She placed the two tintypes on the side table, the glass plates rattling against the marble top. Her image had been there that morning, in the corner of the shot with Bertha Mae. Now it was gone. She had left the manor's memory world and then her image faded.

She grabbed the other tintype. Beau was gone. Had he moved to another tintype?

She rifled through the box of tintypes, searching for one that would hold Beau's image. Halfway through the second box she found it. A wedding reception on the back lawn. Beau stood under a white tent, sipping a glass of champagne and engaged in a conversation with a beautiful young girl.

Unexpected jealousy burned in her heart.

She pulled two dresses from the racks—one red, one orange and golden yellow with black lace trim. They each came with petticoats that the museum must have had made so they would hang right while on display. She chose the golden yellow gown and made her way toward the downstairs bathroom to change.

Once she was buttoned into the dress or mostly so, she pinned and curled her hair the way her mother had the day before. Her mind pinged between Beau and the love they once had, and the new life she had made with Ira. It was like watching a tennis match with no real winner.

When she made her way back to the ballroom, she saw the bottom step of the grand staircase. She stopped. A cold chill shivered down her arms. Blurred images flashed too quickly: She sat there, as a young girl, crying.

"Peyton." Someone called to her while she sat on the bottom step of the grand staircase. "Peyton, honey. You sit right there and don't move." She had never heard another person in that snippet of her memory before. And that voice, she knew whose it was.

"Good morning, Peyton."

Peyton startled.

"Did you get a lot accomplished last night?" Mrs. Miller walked one slow step in her direction, then another.

"Yes ma'am." Peyton backed up. How did Mrs. Miller manage to look so threatening with her fluffy white hair and sack-like dress.

The eyes. Glassy and dull and yet not missing much.

"Jayne Ella said you didn't come home last night." Mrs. Miller took another step.

"I was working and I lost track of time."

"So, you slept in the manor?"

"No. I just worked."

Mrs. Miller stopped. "Did you notice anything unusual while you were here?"

"What do you mean?"

"Oh, you know. This old house keeps secrets." She ran a hand along the wall. "I thought perhaps it might have shared one or two with you. Twice I was here working late and I dozed off. Just for a moment. I dreamt of my Ruby. Heard her calling to me just as clear as day. Mama!" Mrs. Miller called wistfully.

Mrs. Miller picked up the tintype of the wedding reception, the one with Beau standing under the white tent. She tapped the glass. "Isn't that something...looks just like him." She tilted her head and stared at the image through the lower part of her glasses.

"Did I ever tell you what Beau and I did on that last night of his? The night when he disappeared?"

A sick feeling dragged through the center of Peyton. Like she was drowning. "No, ma'am. You didn't."

Mrs. Miller sucked on her teeth and her mouth made a wet whistle.

"Let's get started on the new photos and I'll tell you all about it."

Peyton insisted on sensitizing the plates herself; she wasn't going to take the chance that Mrs. Miller could mess something up. She hadn't shown Mrs. Miller the double exposed plate from the day before. If indeed that's what it even was. There wouldn't have been any way to explain it.

Peyton showed her the wedding reception photo that she wanted to emulate. They set the stage as they had before, with lighting and furniture arrangement. Peyton's palms were damp and tingly.

She let Mrs. Miller take her photo, several this time since they knew what they were doing now. Peyton developed the photographic plates as quickly as Mrs. Miller took the pictures. After each photo or two, Peyton changed dresses and they took pictures in a new setting to match an old tintype.

"He was worried," Mrs. Miller finally said about Beau. "You and he had an argument that night. He wanted to prove to you that he loved you. He wanted to show you that he was joining your family—not just that you were joining his. He said he thought he'd made you feel like he and his family were calling all the shots. He wanted to do something to make up for that. Some sort of gesture."

Peyton stared at her.

"So, I made a suggestion." Mrs. Miller said. "I had some of the original Alcott family clothing in my car, a few pieces from the museum that needed to go to the tailor for repairs. I also had Bertha Mae's camera we've been using. I thought it might be nice if he dressed in antique manor clothing and I made a tintype that he could give to you."

"You took his picture with this same camera?" Peyton asked.

"Mm-hmm."

"In the manor, while he was dressed up in Alcott family attire?"

"Bless his heart he was so worn down from that terrible argument that the two of you had. He was a bit drunk, too. I just had to find some way to help him."

The camera, the clothing, the manor.

Peyton caved and mentioned the ghosted images of long-dead family members she had seen in the tintypes the day before. "Any idea how that happens?"

Mrs. Miller sat at the wooden table in the center of the room, sipping tea. "I don't know how it happens or why. Only that it can. Then we just have to wait," she said.

"Wait for what?" Peyton slowly squeezed a fist full of taffeta.

"You don't think I know, but I do."

"Don't know what?" Peyton asked.

"I know that you went into the manor's captured memories."

Panic darted around Peyton's chest.

"I know because I'm the one who sent you there."

12

Peyton stared at Mrs. Miller's crooked smile.

"Several hours after I took your picture, I came back to the manor. I spread most of the tintypes around the room and I watched them. It took a while. But then I saw you. You were there."

Peyton swallowed hard.

Mrs. Miller lifted her teacup with two hands and took a long sip.

"You were the one who left the tintypes on the table. You wanted me to find them," Peyton said.

Mrs. Miller stared at her, her lined face expressionless. "You weren't easy to find at first. But I've watched these photos for so many years, I nearly have them memorized. When I finally found you in one of them, I knew you would want to see it, too. And, of course, I wanted you to see how Beau had moved. I thought that would help me explain things."

"Explain what things?" Peyton shook her head in disbelief.

Mrs. Miller nodded. Her feet were placed wide and flat

on the floor in true old lady fashion. "That you're the only one. So far."

"The only one to what?"

"The only one to come back."

Dizziness spun through Peyton's body. She sat.

"Out of how many?"

"Dozens of people have died in the manor over the years. Only three people have disappeared: my husband Horace, my daughter Ruby and Beau, of course." Mrs. Miller tilted her head back, seemingly enjoying a strange power.

"He's really—"

"Here. Yes." Mrs. Miller's features settled into her usual smile that set Peyton on edge.

"You came back. That means when you go again, you can bring them all home. Like you, Ruby Lee deserves to have a career, get married, raise her family."

"Wait—you think Ruby Lee is in the manor?" Peyton's words spilled out quickly, her tone high pitched.

"Oh, I know she is. I've seen her."

Peyton let out a sharp exhale. "You've seen her?"

"Yes, that red hair is unmistakable. Are you alright, dear? You look pale."

"I thought—I mean, we all thought something terrible...happened."

"Yes, but I know where she is now. She's in this house." Mrs. Miller sipped her tea, oddly calm. At peace.

Had Beau been right all along? Had the blood on her childhood dress been from something that had nothing to do with Ruby's disappearance? Why didn't she remember?

"Your mouth is hanging open," Mrs. Miller said. "You'll make sense of it soon enough. What's most important right now is that you bring my family back to me."

"I don't know...what I did to get back here. I wouldn't

know how to bring anyone with me. I didn't even see Horace or Ruby." She couldn't believe she referred to Ruby as someone among the living. She'd spent her entire life believing she was dead, thinking she had been involved in that death in some way.

Mrs. Miller put her cup and saucer on the table, the delicate pieces of china clinked against one another in the stillness. She folded her hands into her lap, and her eyes crinkled when she smiled. "I don't get to see them that often, but when I do, they're usually in different tintypes. Different scenes. Usually Ruby is at the holiday gatherings. At the same time, Horace will be in another tintype altogether, playing poker or at the beach. Only once in all these years did I see Beau and Horace in a tintype together. I've never seen Ruby with either of them. I don't know why they're usually separate. Only that they are, and that they travel through the same tintypes, the same memories at different times.

"One day Beau will be at a wedding party, as you saw. Then, a year later, I'll see Horace there. It's like the manor spins through a cycle of these memories, and our loved ones go along with them."

"Why?" Peyton managed.

"Why does this happen, you mean?" Mrs. Miller asked.

She nodded.

"Because the manor has life to it. I think the manor is like a person—a living being. It started out with good intentions and a bright future. Just like the rest of us. Then life happened. And those life events were bad enough that the manor didn't get over them. The manor hasn't gotten over a lot of things, I think."

Peyton felt a wave of energy from the house, like it really was a person who had endured too much. Like it was someone who who had a secret to hide. She could relate.

"You've heard the saying—if these walls could talk?" Mrs. Miller stood slowly, shuffled to the far wall and ran her hand along its surface. Like she stroked a loved one's face.

Peyton leaned against the far table, nauseous and wanting to get outside.

"It's the manor, you see," Mrs. Miller finally said. "The manor, the authentic clothing, the jewelry. There's something about it all being reassembled here, they all sync together once again. Then there's Bertha Mae's camera. The tintype is made and it isn't long before the manor takes ahold of them. Takes them prisoner."

"The manor never lets go of anything," Peyton whispered. It was palpable. She felt it in the rooms, the furniture and the tintypes. As if the house were ruminating. The history lived on.

Mrs. Miller walked to the ballroom. Peyton followed her. Their heeled footsteps echoed in the stately marble hallways.

"My theory is that the manor has a secret. Something dark in its past that it hasn't been able to let go of. Something we don't know about. These tintypes where I see my family and Beau, those specific memories must be when something terrible happened. I think these must be the scenes the house keeps mentally touching. Thinking about. Otherwise none of this would be possible."

They stood in silence.

Secrets.

Peyton hated secrets. There were the secrets her memory kept from her, the secrets she kept to herself, Jayne Ella's lying about only God knew what. Now the manor had more secrets. All of them probably too horrible to see.

She looked at the tintype of the wedding reception with Beau. Then several pictures of Bertha Mae that Mrs. Miller had placed in a grouping. She looked closely at Bertha Mae and saw something she'd never seen before. Her smile was pleasant, but the eyes held the subtlety of something else. Some sort of emotion she had seen somewhere before but she couldn't place.

She didn't remember anything tragic happening at that point in Bertha Mae's life or even in the manor's history. She had read all the history books and diaries that mentioned the manor, but there was nothing disturbing in that particular era. In fact, it was one of the happiest times in Alcott family history.

She flipped through the tintypes, looking for a clue. But every tintype was filled with happy scenes—celebrations, parties, holidays. The air conditioner cut on, rumbling like thunder.

That was the nature of a secret.

No matter what someone painted on the outside, the secret created an anchor—often in the heart, perhaps even in one's soul. It left a part of you stuck in the past.

That's why Peyton insisted that her clients confess everything. Only then could they effectively move forward, create a new image. Otherwise, secrets literally ate a person up inside.

Ate them up.

"That's what the house is doing," she said. "Eating everyone up."

"That's what the desperate do," Mrs. Miller agreed.

The manor had seen murder, suicide, disappearances and tragic unfair endings in its existence, but none from that era. At least not that she knew about.

"You'll need to uncover the manor's secret. You have to

solve whatever mystery is hidden within these walls. Then, once the house has peace, I think this hidden dimension will fade and my family will be set free." Mrs. Miller's moist eyes glimmered with excitement.

The truth hit Peyton. The fear in her gut so intense she could barely move. She was on her way into whatever secret the house kept hidden. Knowing her ancestors' home, it was something macabre. She would have to unearth it, solve it, in order to get everyone home again. She nodded to the camera and the boxes of tintypes. "Since those items are involved, the mystery must be something that was captured with her camera."

Peyton hoped no one took pictures of Benjamin Alcott's hanging or the hauntings that began immediately after his death. Hopefully no one took pictures of Anna Alcott when she lay bleeding to death from a gunshot wound. That was the beginning of the Alcott family tragedies that lasted for over a century. Last thing she wanted was to be trapped inside the house when it was haunted, reliving the same dark days over and over.

"I would think so. Yes." She shrugged.

Peyton realized the woman didn't care which memories she traveled through, she didn't care whether Peyton lived or died. All she wanted was her daughter and husband back. Didn't matter to her how many people she had to throw at that problem to get it fixed.

"Why did I make it back home, when Beau didn't? He was right there with me."

"You'll have to figure that out. And that's only fitting, too. Since it's your doing that made it possible for him to go into the memories in the first place."

Peyton spun toward Mrs. Miller. "What?"

"Oh, honey. If you hadn't argued with him the way you

did that night, he wouldn't have been so devastated. Never would have gotten so drunk. I never would have been able to get him dressed in authentic Alcott attire, and I don't think I ever would have been able to take his photo with Bertha Mae's camera.

"I didn't—"

"I had tried and tried to get him to dress up and let me make a tintype of him. He wouldn't do it. Until that night. You not only opened the door for me to send him into the memories of the manor, you paved the way."

"You did this on purpose. You sent him back—"

Mrs. Miller settled into an upholstered chair, a slow smile of satisfaction spread across her face. "Yes, I did. But someone had to teach you a lesson. You needed to know what it felt like to have the greatest love you've ever known yanked away from you."

The horror of what Mrs. Miller had done stirred her fury. "You're a horrible old woman."

Mrs. Miller threw back her head and cackled. Her wide open mouth revealed grayish back teeth covered in silver fillings. "Me? You're the one who sent my Ruby away."

"I did not—"

"Yes, you did!" Mrs. Miller leaned forward and screeched.

Peyton jumped.

Mrs. Miller drew in a deep inhale and smoothed her short white hair. "Don't you remember?" Her voice was softer. "You insisted that the two of you play with those cameras. You begged for me to make a tintype of you and Ruby, but at the last minute *you* backed out."

Memories from that day at the manor with Ruby and Mrs. Miller became more clear. The house was in the midst of one of its earlier restorations, one that was doomed to fall apart yet again. Several rooms had been restored to the point of new flooring and paint and repaired windows. "I didn't back out. Ruby wanted the photo all to herself."

The images were fuzzy and few. She heard laughter, distant conversation, plates clinking together. Party noises. "Someone was having a party on the back lawn," she said.

"That's it, Peyton. Remember," Mrs. Miller coaxed.

She could hear the chatter and the laughter. Her mother complained about the heat and the air conditioners they had installed weren't pumping enough cool into the lower level of the house.

Caterers with white shirts, white aprons and black ties bussed platters and dishes and other supplies from their vans and into the kitchen area. "It wasn't our family that had the event. Because it was catered, our family always did a potluck."

"You're right." Mrs. Miller's gaze held steady as if she shared the same memories. "The party was put on by Beau's daddy and his bank. A big Christmas bash on the great lawn. Jayne Ella gave her permission for it and she even collected a fee."

"They decorated the magnolia trees out back with white lights."

"That's right, darlin'. It's all coming back now, isn't it? Keep goin'."

Peyton had forgotten this entirely. She wouldn't have remembered it if Mrs. Miller hadn't encouraged her to do so. And maybe not at all if she hadn't been in the manor.

"The manor never forgets." Mrs. Miller's gaze scanned the walls, like she connected with the manor's soul.

As if a switch had been flipped, memories spooled through her mind like old film through a projector. She saw Ruby's long, red hair, the sparkle from the necklace she always wore, her flower print top and matching pants. A white ribbon tied around her ponytail.

They played hide-and-seek at the side of the house. They spied on the party guests. "Ruby and I played outside." The chill Peyton felt in the manor crept along her back, like fingers danced along her skin, pushing her to remember.

Every cell in her brain pulled away from the memory, but the manor was too strong. The dead places in her brain, the spot that kept the memories secret, came to life.

"Eeny, meanie, miney, moe, take the ring or I'll take your toe." Ruby sang the words slowly, her eyes flat and mean. Black dirt beneath Ruby Lee's gnawed fingernails, her ungodly strong grip on Peyton's bare foot, a small knife pressed against her big toe.

"Stop it, Ruby!" Peyton screamed.

Ruby had knocked her down beneath the largest magnolia tree, pulled off her red Mary Jane and held her foot in a vice grip. The more Peyton tried to wriggle away, the harder Ruby Lee gripped the knife against Peyton's skin, blood trickled down her foot. Hot tears burned her eyes. The party music was too loud, no one heard her cry for help.

"Okay! I'll take the ring! Please, please, stop!" Peyton sobbed.

Mrs. Miller had brought various pieces of Bertha Mae's jewelry from the museum and placed them on display in the manor for the guests to see. Ruby Lee wanted the ring with the red stone, the ruby ring.

"I want it tonight," Ruby said through clenched teeth.

"I'll take the ring. Tonight. After everyone is gone."

"Take the ring. Or I'll take a toe." Ruby sliced the knife horizontally, leaving a bloody gash across Peyton's big toe.

Peyton vowed she would get Ruby out of her life one way or another.

Peyton could see Mrs. Miller, so much younger then, setting up a display in the music room for visitors to see—two box-like cameras and several tintypes of Peyton's Alcott ancestors. Mrs. Miller talked about the tintypes, what they were and the fact that she knew how to make them.

"You can make them!?" Peyton asked once she and Ruby were inside again and the guests left the room. "Make one of us." She jumped up and down in little hops, the cut on her toe burned. Blood glued her sock to her foot.

Ruby might forget about the ring if they were busy making tintypes.

Ruby tugged on a diamond necklace her father had given her, seemed to consider the idea. She often twisted the diamond charm between her finger and thumb, tried to get people to notice the fact that it was an actual diamond.

"We could put on those dresses!" Peyton pointed to the mannequins that wore Alcott family attire.

After much pleading, Mrs. Miller had finally given in and said they could wear the vintage dresses if they promised to be careful and not run around in them. First, she told them she had to drive into town for supplies. Peyton insisted they go with her, said her mother would never allow them to be in the manor by themselves.

While Mrs. Miller ran inside the photo shop to ask old Mr. Ferguson if he had the supplies, Ruby had a few things to say to Peyton. "You won't at all be pretty in that red fluffy dress that you love so much. You're pudgy and you shouldn't be in pictures."

Ruby snatched a pinch of soft skin under Peyton's arm and twisted and squeezed. Peyton acquiesced.

Ruby did this when she wanted her way. Twice Peyton

fought back and hit Ruby hard enough to leave a mark and a bruise on her face. But she got in trouble with her parents and Mrs. Miller for that. Ruby also had a way of convincing people that certain things weren't her fault.

When Mrs. Miller returned with the supplies she needed, Peyton told Mrs. Miller that she changed her mind and didn't want to be in the photo, that she would play photo assistant, instead. She rubbed her arm where Ruby had left a mark.

Mrs. Miller made the tintype of Ruby proudly wearing the red dress.

Peyton's private movie stopped and the screen went blank.

Mrs. Miller's lips flattened. "If you hadn't suggested the tintype, I wouldn't have lost my girl."

Peyton opened her mouth to tell her what a horrible little girl Ruby was. But she stopped. Mrs. Miller held too many cards, she held her life in her hands.

"I obviously didn't know that was going to happen." Peyton pressed her fingers to her temples where the pressure built.

Mrs. Miller paced around her like judge and jury. "You're going to bring her back to me."

Peyton licked her dry lips, expected Mrs. Miller to grab a section of skin under her arm and pinch. Just like her daughter used to. "I told you I don't know how I got back. It just happened."

"Then you'll do exactly what you did before. Except this time you'll bring Ruby back with you. And my husband, too."

Mrs. Miller flipped through the tintypes on the table. "It wasn't until I lost my husband that I knew where my sweet Ruby was. I thought she had been kidnapped on the way home that night. That's what the police told us. No body. No signs of foul play. They had said somebody probably picked her up. Just because they could. She was such a pretty girl.

"I beat myself up for years thinking that I never should have let her walk out of the manor by herself that night. Her daddy said that he was getting in the car and he was on his way to get her. He just asked that she start walking so he wouldn't have to be seen by any party guests leaving the manor. He said he wasn't dressed and he didn't want to pull down the long drive and have somebody see him in sweats while they were in their party finest. I kissed her goodbye in the manor's kitchen, and then I never saw her again.

"One day he disappeared, and I had no idea where he had gone. I thought maybe he just left. We never were the same after Ruby went away. Then one day I was working in the museum, dusting off the tintypes we had on display, and I saw him. Staring right back at me from one of the tintypes, like he'd been there all along. Like he was trying to get me to see him. That was the first time I knew where Ruby had gone."

"You found her?"

"Her hair is still red, just a little darker now that she's grown up." Mrs. Miller clicked her thumbnails against one another.

It was a quiet anger that defined Mrs. Miller, Peyton thought. It hadn't been there when she was younger and Ruby was alive.

"You made a tintype of him with the camera before he disappeared?"

"Mmm-hmmm. Your mother was trying to put together an advertising campaign to try to turn the community's perception of the manor to something more positive. She wanted everyone to remember its historical significance and forget about the hauntings and the disappearances that had made the news.

"It was a clever campaign, I'll give her that. Everybody loved my Horace, you know. So, she had him put on an Alcott tuxedo that we had in storage at the museum. Then she had me make a tintype with Bertha Mae's camera. The picture ran in the paper and she wrote a lengthy op-ed to go with it. I kept the tintype on display in the museum with the article beside it. It worked well, you know. The community thought Horace had lent his support to the manor, which he had, really. They backed off. Gave the Alcotts yet another chance."

"But then he ended up in the past." Peyton studied Horace's image in the tintype.

"It's not the past. They're memories. They move from tintype to tintype. Memory to memory." She took the tintype from Peyton, held it close to one of her eyes like she couldn't quite make him out, and ran her thumb over the image of her husband. "He's still very handsome."

Peyton looked at the photo in Mrs. Miller's hands. An aged Horace Miller sat at a card table with three other tuxedoed men, each of them holding a hand of cards and a cigar.

"That's why you won't leave the manor, no matter how Jayne Ella treats you. This is why you stay connected to our family and to our history. It's not the manor, it's the tintypes. You don't want to be away from them."

Mrs. Miller ran her hands over the tops of the tintypes. They clattered together. "I don't get to see them often. These photos are the only communication I get. I won't leave them. Not until you unlock the manor's secret and bring my family back to me."

Peyton finally put all the pieces together. "You knew

ahead of time that Beau would miss our wedding. You knew what that would do to me."

"Yes, I did. I had to take my one opportunity while I had it. I needed someone to bring my Ruby back to me. I thought Beau could be the one."

Peyton grabbed Mrs. Miller's teacup and smashed it against the wall.

Mrs. Miller jumped.

"You had no right to do that."

Mrs. Miller rose slowly, her stare hard and dark. "It's your fault I lost my little girl. I missed out on everything with her. And it's your mother's fault that I lost my husband. So don't tell me who has a right to do what. Your family owes me!" She banged her fist on the table.

"You suggested this whole past present photo gimmick, just so you could send me back."

Mrs. Miller nodded.

"What makes you think I could bring this Alcott secret to light?"

"You'll find a way. You'll want to rescue Beau. No one else would have the motivation that you do."

"And if I can't?"

"Then I think I'll take a picture of Ira to give you double the motivation."

"You wouldn't."

"I would. And if he doesn't work, I'll move to Layla. Then on to those cute girls of hers."

Peyton pushed her hands into her hair and squeezed her head.

"I've waited a long time for you to come home. You're the best person for the job. Also, I think you shouldn't be able to move ahead with your wedding until Ruby is able to have one for herself."

Mrs. Miller smoothed the front of her dress. She had been like this since Peyton and Ruby were little. "Anything Peyton can have, Ruby should have better." Peyton and Ruby walked into the museum one day after school and found Mrs. Miller singing that to herself. She sang the words to the old show tune "Anything You Can Do I Can Do Better."

"Mama!" Ruby Lee had said. "That's so funny!" She tugged the small diamond charm, pulled it from left to right.

But it hadn't been funny to Peyton. She remembered limping back to the manor that day when Mrs. Miller made the tintype. Ruby Lee put on the red dress and swished around in it. "It really does look much better on me, don't you think?" Ruby said.

"How did you get back?" Mrs. Miller whispered, as if Peyton would give her the real story this time.

"I told you, I don't know," Peyton said. "It just happened."

13

Ira's and Jayne Ella's voices carried from the upstairs like they were on their way down the grand staircase. Peyton thought of the vital meeting with the bankers that was scheduled for later in the day, the one that would determine the fate of the manor. And her family's wellbeing.

She printed six copies of her plan for the manor and reviewed the finer details of her strategy with her mother. Peyton's nerves felt like live wires in her gut.

Her mother needed to be prepared to handle the meeting alone. The night before, it had taken several hours for her to be propelled into the manor's memories. She assumed it would be the same timing today, but she didn't know for sure.

Ira toured the first level of the manor, then she took him outside to the back porch. They stood hand-in-hand and looked over their wedding site, the calm ocean sparkling in postcard-perfect fashion. He held her close.

His spiced cologne brought up memories of how they would laze for hours on Sundays—early morning bagels from their favorite shop with sides of eggs and bacon, hot coffee from his French press. The world had been only theirs then.

She felt badly that he didn't know it was a good-bye hug, that he didn't know she would be gone for a while, and that he didn't know who she was going to see. There was no way to explain any of that.

"You look quite good in this historical attire," he said. His kisses trailed along her neck.

She captured his hands in her own and pushed away.

"Not here," she said with her most pleasant smile.

A movement caught her attention. Mrs. Miller stood between the kitchen and the main hallway. Her stare was dark and flat. Her presence reminded Peyton that she had a job to do. Loved ones to protect.

She walked Ira out of Mrs. Miller's view.

"Does she always look at people like that?" he asked.

"Usually," Peyton said.

Ira shook his head. "I reserved a nice beach house for us so we could have some alone time before the chaos descends," he said.

"Ira." She ran her hands over his chest, not quite believing what she was about to say. "I know this is going to sound incredibly strange. Especially since we and—well, Jayne Ella have gone to all this trouble. But I can be terribly shy sometimes and—"

"I've never known you to be shy." He kissed her lips gently.

"Okay, maybe shy isn't the right word—"

"Did I tell you that Senator Michaels is coming to the wedding?"

"From Massachusetts?"

"Yeah. Our families go back a long way. It will be great

press for our family. And the manor. I'm sorry, sweetheart. I interrupted you. What were you going to say?"

Her stomach cramped and she pressed a hand against the pain. The signs were starting sooner this time. The additional tintypes that Mrs. Miller made must have sped things up.

"Are you okay?"

"Yeah. I'm fine. Something I ate, I think." She knew there was a chance that she wouldn't make it back in time for the wedding.

"Why don't I drive you to the beach house now and you can lie down?"

"No, I've got a ton of work to do between now and the wedding. I'm not sure how much time we're going to have together and—"

"Seriously?" He held her closer, his hands rubbing up and down her back.

"Yeah, I know. It's bad timing. But I can't very well leave the manor or my work unfinished." She flashed him her sweetest smile, the flirtatious one. Her skin buzzed with an electric current, it was another sign that she would be gone soon.

"You're too sensible for an almost-bride."

"Well, it's a lot of work and...I'm wondering if maybe we need to rethink the ceremony."

The force gathered in her stomach, formed a ball, twisting and spinning with increasing speed. Same as before. Soon she would be catapulted into the dark side of Alcott Manor that only a handful of people knew about—a shadowy reality of captive memories.

He kissed her and she could barely feel his lips on hers.

"I rented the beach house for us. It was going to be our

last few days together—before family arrives." He stroked her hair, kissed her on her forehead, her nose, her mouth.

He had an insistent way when it came to her and she had always enjoyed his attentiveness. Today it felt more like he wasn't listening to her. She placed her hands on the outside of his shoulders. "I won't be around much while I'm wrapping up all this work. Listen—"

"But I've already taken the time off from the practice."

"You can just stay at the house on your own. Get some R&R."

"Well, I don't know what I'll do without you."

"You can spend time here. With us." Mrs. Miller shuffled onto the porch, her smile wide, something black shifting behind it. "We'll keep you company."

"No!" Peyton said. "I'll be working. Remember?" With her eyes she silently begged Mrs. Miller not to send Ira into the manor's memories. It was like asking a snake not to bite, or a scorpion not to sting.

"Well, when you're at the bank and whatnot. He might need company." Mrs. Miller clicked her tongue.

Peyton imagined Mrs. Miller telling Ira about the tintype exhibit. How wonderful it would be if Ira dressed up in authentic Alcott wear as well. For a picture, with a special turn of the century camera.

"He's already made plans. He's going to relax and catch up on things."

Mrs. Miller turned to Ira and patted him on the arm several times. "Don't pay her any attention, you're welcome here any time, you hear me? Any time." She wagged a knowing finger at Ira as she went into the house, one slow step after another.

"Thank you, madam," he said professionally. "I may take you up on that offer."

"See that you do," Mrs. Miller sang.

"You don't need to be here," Peyton whispered to Ira and straightened his collar. "Don't let her make you feel that way. You don't take enough vacation. Enjoy this break—sleep in, take a run, read a few of those medical mysteries you love so much. Hopefully I'll be back soon. But I do think we need to talk about the timing of the ceremony—"

"What do you mean be back? Are you going somewhere?"

"I mean—I go into my own world when I have a lot of work. You know me." She smiled but it felt plastic, a betrayal of the honesty that had been central to their relationship.

"Do I need to be concerned about anything? Are we... okay? I get the feeling that you're trying to say good-bye." His laugh was nervous.

She stroked the side of his face and he leaned into her hand. She remembered how her therapist told her how pleased she was that Peyton had chosen someone who was so in love with her. "Not everyone does that. Sometimes, if we don't truly recover from the loss, we will partner with those who are unavailable in some way, emotionally or otherwise. It can become a repetitive pattern."

"I'm fine. We're fine. Everything is fine."

Fine was the farthest from the truth.

"It's just this place, too much history, you know? Sometimes I think it's going to devour me. Like a sickness that takes over. I need to close out my business at the manor and be done with it, and I think that's going to take longer than I anticipated. Plus, I'm just really uncomfortable here. It's hard."

He studied her carefully, his eyes narrowed. She wondered if there was something in her expression that revealed how less than honest she was being.

"What's hard?" Worry lines deepened on Ira's forehead. He ran a finger over her brow, smoothing what must have been her own lines of concern. "Wasn't this the last place you saw your former fiancé before he disappeared? I would guess the two of you spent a good bit of time here over the years."

She shrugged, suddenly feeling ten again. A little girl in a grown-up dress.

"I'm just saying it would be natural if you were remembering those times and if that left you feeling stressed. Maybe that's why your stomach is bothering you?"

Her stomach doubled over on itself and she groaned.

"You're not okay." Ira took her hand in his. He stared at her with the worried concern of a doctor.

"I'm okay. Best thing for me to do is get my work done. And, I'm really sorry but I think we need to postpone the ceremony."

His lips parted, pain and shock spread across his face.

"Just for a little while. Then, maybe we can elope." Something inside of her relaxed an inch.

"I knew coming back here wasn't a good idea. You have a lot of history in this town. Unresolved... romantic history, and girls, women, I mean, don't fully—" He exhaled hard. "What I'm trying to say is that, that stuff leaves a mark. We shouldn't have come back to the scene of the crime, so to speak." He tripped over his words, like they were loosely tangled rope around his feet.

"Your mother just told me about seeing Beau's photo and how that might have brought something up for you. She talked quite a bit about Beau and that day when he—the day you were supposed to—marry."

Hearing Beau's name on Ira's lips was wrong, somehow, like he had wandered into a forbidden area. Hearing him talk about that horrible day started her head shaking. "She shouldn't have done that."

"I thought we would be okay here. I thought the publicity would be good for the manor, a favor to your family. But obviously this wasn't the best location for us to mark the beginning of our life together. I should have seen that sooner."

"Ira—"

"Are you thinking of him and is that why you want to postpone?"

She started to say no, but the relationship book she had read, *The Clean Slate Theory*, popped into her mind. "Share, share, share. Communicate. Especially the difficult stuff. You're partners on a journey. You need to work through problems together and that requires honesty."

She wanted to be honest with him about what was going on with the manor and Mrs. Miller, so he would understand why she had to postpone the wedding. But that would take too much time, and right now she didn't have time to spare.

At the very least, she decided she should be honest and tell him that she had been preoccupied with thinking about Beau. That wasn't as resolved as she had thought. Besides, he had guessed anyway and if she denied it he would know if she was lying. They should work through this together.

She didn't want them to be the married couple that fell apart because of secrets, because they didn't or couldn't talk to one another. She certainly didn't want to be like her mother who kept everything hidden inside. If her parents had talked more, opened up to one another, maybe they wouldn't have split up.

She didn't think she wanted to confess solely to make herself feel better, as the book cautioned against. She genuinely wanted to talk with him about what was going on, what she was feeling.

But Ira was the one she should marry. She knew that. Her mother knew that, too, and often reminded her of all his attributes.

He wasn't one to walk away from.

Amanda, her boss, had told her as much, too. So, Peyton found herself standing there with her mouth open and saying nothing. The truth was harder to say aloud than she imagined.

"Do you still have feelings for Beau?" he asked softly.

She closed her eyes in a long blink and nodded. "The house is bringing up a lot of memories and it turns out my past is not as resolved as I thought."

He nodded, stunned. "Okay. Well. That's not what I expected to hear. But, okay."

"I'm sorry. I just wanted us to have honesty in this discussion for our—"

"Honesty's not really working in my favor today, is it?" He chuckled, but not in a way that said he thought anything was actually funny.

Ira had a bad habit of interrupting her when he felt angry or nervous. Stupidly she had forgotten that. She didn't think there was enough time at the moment to calm him, give him a sense of security and talk this out.

He stared at the ocean for a long while, shaking his head now and then, like he was in utter disbelief. There it was, Peyton thought as she watched Ira struggle. A blindingly obvious vote in favor of keeping secrets.

"Maybe I shouldn't have said anything. I just—"

"I want to be with you. And if you're having second thoughts then I guess I need to know. I mean, of course I need to know."

Ira turned toward the ocean again and bit his thumbnail. She had never seen him bite his nails before. Then she realized, he must be afraid that his past was repeating. Maybe, as her therapist suggested could happen for some, he wasn't entirely over his past. Had he chosen someone who wasn't completely available to him?

Ira turned toward her again, and there was an icy anger to his eyes. She panicked. Her mind flooded with all the many discussions they had had about second chances. How everyone deserved a second chance—people, businesses, relationships.

She almost asked for a do-over, a second chance of sorts. A kind of forget-I-mentioned-it, I-didn't-mean-it, don't-know-what-I-was-saying type of thing.

The house seemed to shift, change, like it enlarged itself around her. She felt small in its grasp. She thought of Beau. Then she realized. Yes, she wanted a second chance. But who did she really want the second chance with? Beau? Ira?

She shouldn't think that way. Besides, the idea was ludicrous. She and Beau had been apart for a long time. Even if he did come back, they didn't know one another anymore. He had been hell-bent on traveling the world back then. If he made it back, he would want that more than ever. Now that she had found a career she loved, she wouldn't leave that to follow him.

"I can't compete with the dead. They are saintly and perfect and there's no way for me to win that comparison."

"What? No, that's not what this is about. I'm—"

"I'm not going to convince you to be with me." He took her hands in his. "Tell me what's really going on in that head of yours. Because I don't understand."

"I no longer think Beau is dead," she said quickly.

His grip loosened. "He's alive?"

"It's just a sense I have. A feeling, you know."

"You've seen him? Or someone has? There's proof?"

She shook her head. "No. There's no proof."

He studied her closely. "Peyton. The stomach ache, the extra work, delaying the ceremony, could these be last minute jitters? Is that what's going on here?"

"I don't think so. I don't know. I just need to hit the pause button on our plans for a minute. There are some things I have to do. For the manor. For my family. For you. And for us. I know this is a lot to ask, but I won't be ready for the ceremony in a few days, and I'm trying to be fair to you."

"I should have realized the effect this place would have on you. There's always been this corner of your heart that I can't reach." He tapped the left side of her chest like he knew the exact spot. He eyed her carefully. "I always suspected, now I know what that secret chamber holds."

She thought maybe now he did know about the soft place she kept Beau and their memories. She hadn't been willing to share them. That was wrong, she knew, to keep that from him. But she didn't think he would understand and those memories were too precious to share.

She felt herself deflating. Like skin and muscle and organs melted from her bones and dissolved into the house. The manor finally owning her, the way it eventually owned everyone who spent time here.

He kissed her knuckles. "You take your time. Do your work, sort things out. And, my mother will kill me for even thinking this, literally. But if you would rather elope, I'll do it. We'll call the Senator's and the Governor's offices and let them know, there's still time."

"The Governor, too?" Her voice pitched high like an angry wind before the storm.

"It's not a big deal. He and my dad went to law school

together. My point is, that none of that matters, because I love you. I've never loved anyone the way I love you." He took her face in his hands and kissed each cheek, then her lips. "I want you to be happy."

With that kiss she remembered again what their life had been like together in Boston, when Alcott Manor was so far in the distance, she had finally been able to build something new.

"It's not that I don't want to marry you—" Her feelings about Beau and Ira had become too complicated.

His worried expression mixed with his smile. "We can leave. You just say the word. We'll go wherever you want. Hawaii? Bora Bora? Shoot, Detroit, I don't care. I just want you."

She felt a tugging at her stomach area. "It's too late."

"It's not," he said. "We'll leave right now. I'm so sorry, I should have realized."

"It's okay," she said softly.

He held her close until she wriggled away, offering him a pleasing smile. The dizziness was strong and she was concerned that she might actually disappear right there in front of him. She made him promise he would give her the next few days to think and work without interruption. He finally agreed.

His lip plumped in a mock pout. She caressed his cheek. Hard as it was to give him this news, it was better this way. He would have been devastated if she hadn't made it back in time for their wedding day.

Some women thrived on the control they had over a man, their affection or the withholding of it determining the strength of his soul. But she hated that moment when his happiness seemed to ride on her answers or whether he had access to the tiny piece of her heart she needed to keep for herself. Too much pressure. Too confining. It was infrequent, but it was there. That would change if they married, she hoped.

Things would settle once he had her final commitment. And everything would calm after she had escaped the manor's control, after she brought Beau and Ruby back. Horace, too. When she reached the end of her life and looked back, that's the way she would see things: Before and After. Before Beau left, and after he returned. Before Beau left she had been happy. After he returned, she knew she would be happy, too. She just wasn't sure yet how it would all play out.

PEYTON CLOSED the double doors that led to the ballroom and tried not to think about what waited for her on this next journey. "They move from tintype to tintype, memory to memory," Mrs. Miller had said.

She pulled a chair to the corner of the room. Hopefully, wherever she landed in Alcott Manor history, there wasn't anything going on in the ballroom at the time. If there was, she needed to be out of sight, not dropping into the middle of some public soiree. She tapped her left hand against her thigh three times, then tapped her right hand. Took a deep breath.

Her stomach hurt, it wouldn't be long before she opened her eyes to a memory. An Alcott Manor memory. And within it somewhere was a mystery that she would have to solve if she wanted to get back home with Beau, Ruby and Horace.

She hoped Beau would be there when she landed. Scenes flashed beyond the windows of the glass ceiling.

Suns, moons, light, dark, clouds rolling from right to left like she was being dragged through all the lifetimes of the manor.

She offered no resistance. Hoping she would be with Beau soon, that she would be able to bring everyone back and quickly.

Questions floated up like bubbles of oil in a tall glass of water.

Would Jayne Ella be able to handle the meeting with the bankers? Would Beau's father let them keep the loan? Did Beau still love her? Or had time and captivity destroyed what they once had?

14

Three bankers exited a black Lincoln town car in the front drive. Jayne Ella waved from the wide wraparound porch of Alcott Manor. She wore a wide confident smile as a testament to her bravery, but inside, her stomach had so many knots she could barely walk.

Each man buttoned his suit jacket. One removed a toothpick from his mouth and tossed it onto the ground. They all looked up at the manor, no doubt eyeing their investment. Maybe wondering how much they could get for it if the manor ended up in their possession.

She knew they would have calculated the value of the land to the final cent. Every investor who had loaned the family money to restore the manor knew how much the land was worth. There wasn't another oceanfront parcel as large as this anywhere east of the Mississippi.

Jayne Ella scanned the end of the long, white-pebbled driveway, hoping to see Peyton pulling in behind them at top speed, a last-minute rescue. She didn't want to handle this meeting on her own.

She had always been able to steer Peyton's focus away from that night at the manor. Because she hardly remembered a thing, it had been easy to tell her she was imagining things. But now bits and pieces tried to break through.

It was as if the manor was tickling Peyton's memory, trying to get her to cough up its secrets.

Jayne Ella would make certain they stayed buried.

She smoothed the front of her red sleeveless dress, extended her right hand. "Hello, gentlemen."

"Jayne Ella." The three men took turns shaking her hand.

Austin Spencer was the last, the tallest and the most handsome. His blond hair was now mixed with gray, and his year-round tan set off the light blue in his eyes. He greeted her professionally, like they had only just met. He was one of the best liars she'd ever known.

"Are we expecting your daughter?" Austin asked.

"Peyton had an unexpected emergency that she had to attend to," she said.

"Wedding errand?" he asked.

"No. She's very sorry to have missed the opportunity to speak with you. But I have her notes, so—"

"Must have been some emergency." His gaze combed the walls of the manor.

"It was. Please. Come in." She closed the heavy front doors behind them.

Austin didn't look at Jayne Ella but instead studied the ornate foyer. He hadn't stepped foot in the manor in several years. Whatever he thought the home might look like, she knew he hadn't expected this.

"So, we have effectively acquired all of the bank's assets and loans and so forth," Austin said.

"Yes, I gathered that from your letter," Jayne Ella said. A

phone call would have been nice, she wanted to say. After all we shared.

She couldn't believe that the manor's loan had fallen into the hands of Austin Spencer, a businessman in the community who had been very outspoken against the restoration of Alcott Manor. He was quoted in the paper as saying that the manor was cursed, that there was something evil about it, that it was a danger to the community and needed to be destroyed.

"Austin—Mr. Spencer, I saw your quote in the paper recently. Again, I'm very sorry for your loss. We loved Beau. He was family to us. I hope that some day you won't associate his disappearance with our family home."

He nodded without showing any emotion, poked his head into the long living room.

"And I hope that won't negatively color your judgment, considering that we have a business relationship with you now."

He waited a beat before he answered. His light blue eyes fell flat and cold with judgment. "Our relationship with you and Alcott Manor is no different than with any other client. Objectivity is one of the hallmarks of our bank."

She would have hoped to be comforted by that answer, but his tone sounded as though he would lower the ax on their agreement.

She wished again that Peyton were with her. She was supposed to run the meeting, show them the revenue projections she had prepared—the prospectus as her daughter had called it. These were the spreadsheets with all the revenue numbers and expenses, the ones that were supposed to show the bankers how they were going to make their money back and then some.

They sat at the dining room table with paperwork

distributed, Jayne Ella folded her hands in front of her. "Peyton has done a great deal of work and today I'm going to show you how we have organized the manor's revenue model. Peyton has run three different profit scenarios—one that is ideal, one that is middle of the road and one that is a worst-case scenario. You can see how they all show a profit.

"She's also drawn up a very detailed marketing plan that highlights all the different ways she is going to promote the manor to the tourist channels. She's listed hotels, bed and breakfasts, convention centers, tour boat companies, vacation home sites, the chamber of commerce and—oh! Even wedding planners. We're going to host weddings at Alcott Manor." Jayne Ella beamed.

She didn't necessarily expect the bankers to match her enthusiasm for their plans, but she did expect them to be at least a little impressed. Or ask questions. All she got in return were three non-committal stares. She felt her temper rising.

"Would you like to see the manor? I can give you a tour and show you how impressive the house has become. Oh, and Mr. Spencer, your wife's charity league has even offered to support our events here at the manor. They want to help us with a tea room and a gift shop. Those profits aren't reflected in this paperwork, but we can work it in for you."

Austin's line of sight left the numbers in front of him and landed hard on her.

She had crossed a line, one she had promised she never would. His wife was off limits to her. That had been their agreement.

"Good to know," he said. "Is Peyton the person in your organization who has the most business experience?"

"No, we have a few relatives on our board with business experience. But she is by far the one who has the most marketing and promotion experience. She's up for a partnership with a prestigious firm in Boston."

The other men stayed glued to the numbers in front of them.

Jayne Ella looked at her phone screen, hoping to find a text from her daughter.

Howard, the tallest, thinnest and most frugal looking of the three bankers, with his long face, wire-rimmed glasses and uber-short, dark hair, asked if the Alcott family trust was really prepared to execute this plan. Could they really show revenue potential by executing an organized business plan?

"We are, Howard. I can assure you. Peyton is the best at what she does. She's in very high demand in that city."

"How is she going to execute this plan while she's in Boston?" Austin asked while looking at the prospectus in front of him.

Jayne Ella knew where Austin was taking this. "We'll execute locally. My plan is to sell my salon and focus on the manor exclusively. There's quite a bit of money to be made in the manor, we're sure of it. I think you know that, too."

Austin jerked his head toward her.

"Running this organization is quite different from running a hair salon, Ms. Alcott."

"I'm aware of that, Mr. Spencer. With all the support behind me, I won't have any trouble. And I hope you realize this is more than a houseful of pretty finishes and furnishings. By investing in us, your bank has played a role in preserving history. United States presidents and senators have stayed here. Lived here, even. You remember that Benjamin Alcott, Senior and Junior were both senators for our fine state. Not to mention that we've made all of our payments on time. We've never defaulted, even when times were difficult."

Austin inhaled slowly. He looked at the surrounding area skeptically, as most people who knew its history did. Jayne Ella silently scolded the house to behave. She didn't want any strange drafts or noises. At the moment, the manor's beauty belied its tragic past.

"This is a lovely home you have here," Austin said. "But the truth is that the Bank of Charleston invested heavily in several large commercial real estate projects that went belly up earlier this year. We're not sure we can keep this loan."

Adrenaline surged in her chest. She cleared her throat and sat tall. "We're very close to making some real money here. As you can see from our projections, we will be able to pay back the loan in full."

"Our research shows that you have borrowed heavily from family financial resources after you obtained the bank loans. Technically, that is a violation of the terms of our agreement. Frankly, it has given us cause for concern."

"You will need to show a ready amount of revenue, and your other loan amounts. Those amounts aren't reflected on your projections." Harold tapped the report. "You've overextended yourself. We can't afford to take the loss, you understand. We're just circling our wagons."

Frank, the banker with the deepest tan, cleared his throat. "Hedging our bets."

"It's not a personal decision as to which loan accounts we keep and which ones we call. It's a numbers game. We're just doing our due diligence," Austin said.

"I understand numbers, I've run a business for the last twenty years. But this is our family home. It's our past and our future, you can't just rip it away from us. We can make a go of it this time, I'm certain."

"I can give you thirty days. That's it," Austin said. "At that point we have to see actual revenue coming in. Otherwise we'll have to call the loan."

"Mr. Spencer," Jayne Ella said. "Might I have a word with you in the kitchen? Privately?"

Austin waited, then nodded once. He whispered something to the other two men who immediately stood, as if by command. They shook Jayne Ella's hand and left through the front door.

She and Austin stood alone in the kitchen. She closed the door behind them. "You and I both know that our family is not going to default on the loan. We've fought long and hard to get this house up and running again, we're obviously not going to do anything to screw things up at the eleventh hour. So, lay off of this loan nonsense or else."

"Jayne Ella." Austin's tone was patronizing as it often was when he thought he had the upper hand. "This isn't entirely my bank anymore. Your loan isn't within my control, so don't threaten me."

She shook her head. "You realize that Mrs. Miller wants the manor open and doing business. She could choose to tell Blair, show her the photos. Or the video. Not to mention that I still have something of yours that you want. In a way, I hold your future in my hands."

"Or maybe it's the other way around now." He raised an eyebrow at her and she remembered that look. It was not just the one that said he had a plan, it was the one that said he had nothing to lose.

"Frankly, I've had enough of being held at the wrong end of the leash. I decided it was time that things turned around."

Jayne Ella's teeth clenched and pain shot through her

jaw. "So, you're just going to take the manor away from me now? Because you're fed up? That's what you get to do?"

He pointed his finger at her. "That's exactly what I get to do. I'm taking the manor and everything that goes along with it—the land...and our past."

Jayne Ella smacked his accusing finger away. "If you break our agreement, Mrs. Miller will send those pictures to Blair. I don't think your wife will take that kind of humiliation lightly. She'll divorce you. She'll turn her father against you and then where will you be without your bank?"

Austin leaned against one of the side tables. "You see, that's where you're wrong. I negotiated quite a bit of stock for myself in this recent bank merger. So, I have a lot more control now. I'm not as beholden to my father-in-law as I used to be. I also negotiated a large sum of cash when I agreed to this new position, and I've decided to take a portion of those proceeds and invest them in myself. My future."

Jayne Ella's body sagged. The fire drained from her temper. "What are you talking about?"

"I had a meeting with Mrs. Miller early this morning and I've made her an offer that I think she's going to accept. Assuming she does, she'll be a very wealthy woman and my life will finally be my own again."

"What have you done?" Jayne Ella whispered.

"Mrs. Miller has some health issues. Because of the hardships she's endured, her life expectancy is probably less than yours or mine. So, now that I can, I've made her a lump sum offer to put this matter to bed once and for all. So to speak.

"We've more than paid the price for our indiscretions and I simply suggested to her that, at this stage of her life, she might be happier on a beach somewhere. Or, if she chooses to stay in town and with the museum, that she would enjoy the unique privileges that come with wealth."

"Why would you think she would be happy giving up this hold she's had over us for so long?"

"Because I think we all reach a certain age when the security of money calls to us more loudly than leveraging the grievances of our past. I think she might be there. She has the hip problem, she's not aging well, she's alone. I think I may have gotten her to see that wealth is the best revenge of all."

"What makes you think she'll give you all of the photos and videos that she has of us? Why wouldn't she take your money and send Blair copies of what she has?"

"She might. If that happens I have control of my bank now. I've made enough to retire on. Because of the merger, it won't affect me as much as it used to. Blair can divorce me. My father-in-law can refuse to speak to me again. Ultimately, it won't matter. Not like before."

"It would still matter to me. If Blair finds out about our affair, she and her group won't support the manor. They'll make sure that I'm ruined!"

"I can't help you with that," Austin whispered. "You should have let me take the gold from the manor a long time ago. It's mine anyway."

"It's ours, don't you mean? And I couldn't. You know that. There was no way to dig it up without getting caught. Not the way you buried it. And not with all the publicity surrounding it. I've had people in here day and night for years. Not to mention security cameras. And security guards and the local police patrolling the house and the grounds. Don't you think I would have taken it out if I could have?" Jayne Ella caught herself chewing her cheek.

"I wasn't the one who poured cement over the hole. And

I've told you that I would do everything for you," he said. "If you had just given everyone a few nights off."

"How would my family have responded to that? With all the theft and trouble we've had over the years? Suddenly I'm just going to cut the security detail, the security cameras? How will that go over?"

"You could have found a way. Maybe you still can."

"Did you see the piece that cable ran on the theft just last week? It's the twenty year anniversary of the great Charleston gold theft. Stolen from *your* bank, Austin. They included original footage of your interviews: 'Someone managed to break in and take the gold right out from under our noses. I don't know how, we have state of the art security systems.'" Jayne Ella lowered her voice to make it sound like Austin's.

"My family has paid your bank hundreds of thousands of dollars in loan payments, doesn't that mean anything?"

"I couldn't have predicted that my bank would have merged with my father-in-law's bank, the one that held the manor's loan. Now that we have, everyone is taking an honest look at its assets. Truthfully, the bank is in an awkward situation. It has to call a few loans to get them off the books, that's not my doing. However. If you were to give me unfettered access to the manor for one night, without a security detail, I might be able to persuade the bank to, say... shift its attention from your loan account to some others for a while. Give you an opportunity to turn a profit."

Jayne Ella crossed her arms, leaned against the table. He finally had her cornered.

"How am I supposed to get rid of all the security cameras? The company monitors the feed. They'll not only alert me when there's a problem, but texts and calls go out to two other family owners, as well. The owner group is serious about protecting its investment. The banker side of you should be happy about that."

"I've told you this before. Tell the company that you've found a new monitoring system, and you have to cut their service. When I'm done in here, call them back, tell them the new company didn't work out and reinstate the service."

Jayne Ella shook her head. "I wish you had never brought me into this."

"You're lucky I did bring you into this. Do you know how much gold has gone up over the last twenty years? It's—"

"Two hundred and fifty percent," Jayne Ella said. "I'm aware."

"That means we have—"

"Four point three million. I know. I did the math."

Austin raised his eyebrows like he was impressed. "It's time to take it out."

She stared at him for a long moment, remembering the night when the gold disappeared from his bank. They had been in his office after hours, which wasn't unusual back then. It had been a convenient place for them to be alone together. Twenty years ago there weren't any security guards for his community bank and no one stayed to work late. Except for him.

He had been so excited to impress her, to show her the gold that a customer had momentarily parked in his bank vault. Had she ever seen one thousand pounds in gold? He ran his finger down her neck when he asked her. As if he knew his words were an aphrodisiac.

One of the bank's elderly clients had recently passed. Not a particularly wealthy one, or so they thought. He only kept a few thousand in his accounts. But when his son cleaned out his father's house, he found one thousand pounds of gold stored in plastic containers in the basement.

"He lived through the depression, didn't trust banks," Austin said when he showed Jayne Ella the gold. "Neither did he trust cash or stocks. Started buying gold when he was young. Kept trading up and buying more over the years. Just kept sticking it in his basement. His son is leaving it here for about a week until he can arrange to have it converted into cash."

Jayne Ella ran her fingertips over the cold, thin bars. She'd never seen so much gold before. "Are the security cameras on?" she whispered. "I want to be with you, right here with the gold."

"I checked. The security tapes are rewinding." He looked at his watch, took a long swallow of his scotch. "We have twenty-two minutes."

"What if a couple of bars went missing?" Jayne Ella asked some time later with a giggle. She pretended to tuck one in her waistband. "Oh, they're heavier than I thought they'd be."

"Where would you hide the gold if, say, a few bars went home with you?" Austin buckled his belt, checked his watch and guided Jayne Ella from the vault.

"That's easy," she said. "Considering the fact that everyone is too terrified to go in the manor, the gold would be safe for years. Depending on how well you buried it, I guess."

They stopped in the hallway and stared at one another. Shortly thereafter, they had their plan.

Under normal circumstances the security tapes recorded nine hours of video at a time. Then someone had to rewind them and any activity was recorded for the next nine hours. But on this night, Austin rewound the security tapes every thirty minutes so that, if some techie checked, it would look like a glitch in the system. Just to be safe, he rewound the tapes again before they left.

They pulled a few bars from every stack but mostly they took the gold from the rear stacks so that from a front view, it didn't look like anything was missing. With the dollies they used, it only took two trips each to remove two hundred and fifty pounds of gold.

They put half in his trunk and half in hers. Then they drove to Alcott Manor and buried all five hundred pounds beneath the side of the grand staircase. Workmen had left their tools lying about, and Austin was handier with them than Jayne Ella would have guessed. Turned out he had spent several summers as a teenager helping out on a construction crew.

The hardwoods hadn't yet been lain near the outer wall behind the grand staircase, and the subflooring panels weren't difficult for him to lift. He worked the gold bars deep into the black dirt, keeping them in short, neat piles. After he covered them, he replaced the subflooring. "No one will be the wiser." He kissed her, the scotch was still strong on his breath. His blue eyes sparkled in the low morning light. She felt exhilarated and yet ashamed, she knew she would have done anything he asked.

It wasn't until the next day, when she was fully sober, that she came to grips with what they had done. They had gotten away with it.

"The twenty year anniversary of the theft is getting a lot of press," she said.

"They're doing that as an interest piece for ratings. The police aren't focusing on it as an active investigation, neither do they have any new information. The timing is right, just like we planned, remember? If we're careful, we can make this work." He dragged his index finger along the bare skin of her arm.

Jayne Ella could have gotten the gold out a long time ago and probably safely. But she liked keeping it in the manor. For one, the location gave her a measure of control. During one of the earlier renovations, she instructed the workers to pour a thin layer of cement over the subflooring to keep out the moisture. But it was really so Austin couldn't take the gold and run, as she often suspected he might. And, if ever she needed to keep him in line, all she had to do was remind him about the gold. Not that he ever forgot.

Two, it wasn't her personal home. Lots of people had come in and out of the manor over the years. If the authorities found the gold, it wouldn't be hard for her to plead ignorance. But now, if he managed to take the manor, he would have access to the gold without her.

"I'll give you some advice on how to convert the gold to cash without raising any suspicion. I have contacts I could share with you."

Austin leaned harder against a table and several glass canisters clinked against themselves. His eyes softened and she caught a glimpse of the man who used to love her, too.

"It's risky," she said softly. "If anyone sees what's down there, you would be implicated. If you remem—"

"Oh, I remember, Jayne. Not a day has gone by in the last twenty years that I've forgotten how I could be implicated." His fingertips rubbed his left wrist where he used to wear the platinum, diamond-studded watch his father-in-law gave him on his wedding day.

He was the only one to ever call her Jayne. The sound of her name on his lips made her remember the many nights they shared together in their hideaway at the beach.

"The watch was a thoughtful gift," she'd once told him.

"It was a threat," he'd said. "The back of the watch is engraved with *Welcome to the Family*. He capitalized the F in family. I have no doubt that if he discovered I cheated on Blair, I'd be wearing cement shoes at the bottom of the ocean by next week."

Apparently, Blair hadn't fallen far from the proverbial tree.

Two weeks after he buried the gold beneath the manor, he called Jayne in a panic. He needed to dig everything up, break through the cement she'd just laid down. "My watch is down there," he'd said. "It must have slipped off."

But three teenagers had broken into the manor that week and one fell to her death. Police were crawling through the manor like cockroaches.

He was never the same after that. It was the vulnerability of it all, she suspected. The fact that his watch sat with the gold, that she could have turned him in whenever she wanted.

Not anymore, though. Not now that he had the upper hand. If she made an anonymous call to the cops, if they found the gold and put Austin in jail, the bank would still move ahead with calling the loan.

Truth be known, she wanted her share of the gold.

He stood and looked out the window at the ocean in the distance for a long while. Without thinking, she slid her arms around his waist and held on. It was the first time she had touched him like this in recent years. She wanted a moment of feeling close to him. She was prepared for him to pull away.

She hadn't been prepared for him to turn and kiss her.

His kisses had always been passionate, never the stiff-lipped pecks she had seen him give his wife. For a few precious moments she felt as though they were a couple again, planning the next few hours they would steal with one another.

When they parted, his eyes stayed closed for a moment. He licked his lips like he savored her taste. "I've missed that," he whispered.

She wanted to say, "Me, too." But she held her tongue. She had learned the hard way that she couldn't trust Austin Spencer. Not when it counted. For years he'd told her that he was leaving Blair for her. But when she finally divorced her husband, Austin didn't go through with his end of the bargain. He'd stayed with Blair. For money and status, she knew. That was when she began to use the gold and his watch to her advantage.

"I've spent too much of my life reliving what happened here and worrying what would happen next," he finally said. "I'm wrapping up all my loose ends."

She reluctantly let him go, ran a finger below her bottom lip to remove any smudged lipstick.

"Give me unmonitored access to the manor—inside and out—for twelve hours," he said. "As long as you keep paying off the loan on time, I'll find a way to keep the bank off your back. Then, I'll pay off Mrs. Miller. If Blair does find out about our past, I'll do what I can there in terms of damage control. If Peyton is as good as you say she is, then maybe she can get enough tourists coming in even without Blair's clout."

"That wouldn't be easy."

"I agree with that. But at least your family wouldn't lose the manor."

"Dang it, Austin. Why can't you just let the gold sit there for a while longer? Digging it all up right now is going to put us more at risk."

"Do you know how many times you've give me that excuse? There's never a good time."

She ran her hands over her face, worry clawing at her from the inside. "Your plan is missing one consideration."

"Oh? What would that be?"

"Peyton."

Austin shrugged. "She hasn't remembered anything in the last twenty some odd years. She's not going to remember now."

"That's where you're wrong. She *has* started remembering that night."

15

Peyton arrived in the corner of the 1850s ballroom and her vision was blurry. She was hunched over in a chair that was exactly like the one she had seen in pictures over the years and placed in the same location she had begun.

Only a hundred years or so of difference.

Couples twirled about in pairs to the music of a chamber orchestra. She rubbed at her eyes, the people in the room resembled a fuzzy Renoir painting. Swirling, tilting heads, leaning this direction and that, to the lilting tune of a waltz. Somewhere beneath all the beauty was a secret deep enough that it was still destroying lives.

She stood. Woozy. Several people approached her through the crowd. She fumbled for something to say. She hadn't thought to assemble a cover story. What would she tell people in terms of a name and background? How would she find Beau?

Maybe these were Alcott relatives wondering who she was, wanting to see her invitation to the soiree. She cleared her throat, pressed her hands against the front of her dress to smooth the wrinkles.

"You came back to me," a man said from behind her. His voice was as smooth as liquid chocolate.

"Beau!" So excited that she had made it to the right location, the tintype where he was, she leaned toward him, nearly hugged him until he stopped her. He laced her hand around the crook of his arm. "Let's get some fresh air."

They began a formal stroll across the ballroom floor, in step with one another. He held tight to her hand, kept it pressed to his arm. Beau nodded to other couples who passed by in their Sunday finest.

"Mr. Spencer," one woman said with a polite smile.

"Ms. Harper," he replied.

When they reached the parlor, Beau pointed to a black gap in the floor. There wasn't light shining through, it wasn't a mark on the floor, it was nothing. Just a black strip.

"Step over," he said firmly.

The black gap appeared at the other end of the room as well. Again, they stepped over.

They strolled through the two front iron doors that were propped open by two large flower pots. The black gap appeared every so often and she pointed to it. "What is that?"

He placed a finger over his lips. "I'll tell you in a moment." They walked to the side of the wrap-around porch.

When he was certain that no one else was in sight, he kissed her, lifting her close to him such that her toes left the ground.

She held on tight, remembering with a rush of emotion what it was like to be in his arms, remembering the future they had promised one another. The way life was supposed to be felt oddly within her grasp once again.

He kissed her cheeks. "I could not have lost you one more time." When he released her, he kept her at enough of a distance to study her. His fingers grazed over her hair, her cheeks, her lips. "Always so beautiful," he breathed. He brought his mouth within just a whisper of an inch from hers and waited, like he savored the moment.

Finally, he leaned into her and kissed her softly. His full lips tasted of love, passion and champagne. His kisses had the same effect on her that they always had. They filled her with happiness, made her feel that dreams really did come true and they sent a flood of heat through her body that curled her toes.

There were two thoughts in her head, and they were hooked on repeat: He was alive, and he hadn't left her.

A familiar sound. The ocean breeze whipping over the lawn and through the pines, whistling as it picked up speed. With her eyes closed, Peyton almost believed she was home: Beau's kisses, the endless ocean nearby, she prepared herself to feel the wind on her skin. Instead, the gray boards beneath her feet shifted. Beau jerked back, grabbed her by the arm. "It's changing. We have to move."

"What's changing?" she asked.

"The scenes. The story. This." He searched the ground.

The decking slid beneath her feet like a flat escalator.

He held her hand and guided her to follow the natural movement of the flooring. "Watch out—" He pointed to the black space in the floor, about five inches that spread from left to right. He held her hand to make sure she stepped over the gap.

The flooring stopped at the great lawn where a large white tent had been erected. A fairly large crowd milled about. The same people from the ballroom, Peyton thought.

"I remember this one." He breathed a sigh that sounded like relief. "This is the wedding reception. We can get around in this one, too."

She told him how she had seen him in one tintype and then later, he had moved to another. "Is this how that happens?" she asked.

"It's like the house changes its mind, moves on to a different memory and the landscape changes. I move with it." There was a hardness to his eyes, a mix of fear and rage. "We can't stay here." He pointed to the gathering. "Follow my lead. Play along. Don't reveal where you're from or how we actually know one another. I'll take care of that."

They arrived at the reception, he lifted two champagne flutes from a waiter's silver tray and handed one to Peyton. He tapped his glass against hers and they both sipped the cold, bubbly wine.

He looked over his shoulder, nodded toward the manor. "These scenes, the manor's past, they play on repeat. This is the twelfth time I've been to this wedding."

"Twelve times?" She felt an irrational sense of guilt.

He nodded to something behind her. "We can step inside the kitchen in this scene, escape the crowd for a while. You'll follow my lead." He phrased his words as a question but his tone gave no such request. It was a statement, almost a command.

"And the black lines?" she whispered.

He pointed to a man in a black suit coat and tie standing behind a camera on a tripod. "Bertha Mae has several photographers that take photos of everything you see out here. The black lines delineate the edge of the photo, and they aren't actually lines at all. They are the gaps between the photos. If you step on them you'll fall into them, I've made that mistake before. If you fall into them, you'll leave this sequence of photos and end up in a different set of photos altogether. I don't know how you and I would find each other again if that happened."

Peyton ran her hand across her forehead, remembered the boxes of tintypes that were stacked in the ballroom in her time. She imagined herself falling from this tintype and landing in one that was several boxes away from where they were now. Their trip through the manor's memories, through the tintypes, could be like dancing through a shuffling of cards.

"Horace and Ruby Lee could be anywhere in the collection," her voice pitched high with worry.

"What?"

She told him how Mrs. Miller accidentally sent Ruby Lee into the manor's memories, how Jayne Ella accidentally sent Horace. And how Mrs. Miller deliberately sent Beau, and now her, as well.

"You may have been right all those years ago. I may not have had anything to do with Ruby's disappearance." She couldn't believe what she was saying, still couldn't figure out what she didn't remember from that night.

Beau ran a hand along his jaw, sighed deeply.

She expected him to be angry. He'd tried to tell her the last time they were together that she couldn't have done such a thing, that she couldn't have hurt anyone. If she had known that, or been open to that possibility, then maybe they wouldn't have argued. Maybe Mrs. Miller wouldn't have been able to send him into this realm. And maybe they wouldn't have been apart these last nine years.

"And the blood?"

She shrugged. "I don't know."

He nodded patiently as if to say they would figure that out another time. She realized that being in this hidden universe of the manor had changed him, humbled him.

"Mrs. Miller is insane with grief over the loss of her daughter. Unless I get Ruby Lee and Horace back to her, she's going to start sending other members of my family into this realm. My sister, my nieces, my mother." She left off the fact that Ira would probably be first on her hit list. Another wave of guilt washed through her, this time because she hadn't yet told him that she was engaged.

Beau started shaking his head before she even finished. "We can't let her do that. This place has nearly broken me. I can't imagine what it would do to a child." He told her how he had seen Horace several times over the years, but that they'd often gotten separated. The fear she had seen in his eyes the night before was back. She wanted to take him in her arms. She took his hand.

"What about Ruby Lee?" She looked at their hands, they had always fit together so well. His thumb stroked over hers. He used to call her his split-apart. He'd said that when God made him, he made her at the same time, as his perfect other half. That he never truly felt at home unless she was in his arms.

She told him with a grin that he was being possessive.

Truth be known, she felt the same way.

"I haven't seen her since we were kids. I'm not even sure I would recognize her after all this time," he said. "Have you seen her in the tintypes?"

"Mrs. Miller showed me a picture. It's hard to tell in black and white, but it looks like she still has her red hair. That should help narrow down the options for us."

"I have seen a few redheads here over the years."

"Mrs. Miller said she was usually in the holiday tintypes."

"Usually? As in she stays there?"

Peyton shrugged. "She wasn't specific. Maybe she's only out and about in the photographs during the holidays?"

"I didn't think you could stay in the scene when the tintypes shifted, but maybe she figured out something I haven't."

"We have to find her. Are there any holidays coming up?"

"Thanksgiving. We'll find her," he said. He kept her hand in his and clasped it even more firmly. Kissed the top of it and held it to his chest. It was as if his feelings for her traveled from his heart through his hand, down her arm and into her soul. It was a visit with what used to be, what they used to have, what she'd thought had long been lost.

She leaned into the sensation, enjoying the firmness of his chest. His personality used to be so much stronger than hers—his drive, his dreams, his need to travel. Even his love for her had been overpowering. She had never been a shrinking violet, but his strength defined their relationship in many ways. Even how they would live their lives after they were married.

It wasn't that she minded, necessarily. She loved his strength. But it could, at times, suck all the oxygen out of the room. His certainty, his determination, left very little room for her to have her own thoughts.

"We have some time before this scene changes again. It's a good idea to eat while you can. Sometimes there isn't food for a while. It all depends where we end up next."

She cursed under her breath. If there was hunger in this world, there could also be pain and suffering without the remedies they were accustomed to, like penicillin and painkillers.

They walked until they reached the kitchen door at the back of the house. The reception was still in full swing on the great lawn. Beau slipped into the kitchen through the screen door, motioned for Peyton to wait.

"Hasseltine," he called to a tall, full-figured African-American woman who stood at the sink. The same woman Peyton had seen the night before. Beau turned on his light-up-the-dark smile and she grinned in return.

"On the stove, Mister Beau." She gestured with a nod to the stove where a plate was piled high with chicken, mashed potatoes and other vegetables.

"Thank you, love." Beau kissed her on the cheek and she swatted at him with a towel, shaking her head.

Beau introduced Peyton and requested two forks and a knife. He motioned for Peyton to sit with him at a long wooden table.

When Hasseltine put the silverware on the table, she gave Peyton a nervous pat on her back.

Peyton leaned toward Beau. "We can interact with them?"

"Oh, yes. They're alive," he said. "Or at least the memory of them is. Living memories, I call them. And as long as we follow events in a certain order, they'll remember you. I came to see her earlier this morning and asked her to put this plate of food aside for me."

"Hello, Hasseltine."

The young girl that Peyton had met last night in the dining room walked into the room slowly, her black patent shoes thudding against the hardwoods as if there wasn't an ounce of energy left in her. The circles beneath her eyes were darker. The bow in her messy ponytail was crooked, obvious she'd tied it herself.

"Honey-child, you're supposed to be in bed," Hasseltine scolded.

"But I want to see everyone. I'm tired of being in bed. I'm bored. And I'm tired of not feeling well." The little girl sat on a nearby chair. Even with her sallow complexion and downturned mouth she was one of the most beautiful children Peyton had ever seen. Like a walking doll. It was hard not to stare.

"My name's Rachel."

Peyton's head tilted back with recognition. With her illness, the little girl didn't look like she did in the tintypes Peyton had seen. This was Bertha Mae's daughter, the one who drowned when she was young. "Hello, Rachel," Peyton said. "Are you feeling okay?"

"Your mama said you weren't allowed to attend today's gathering. This is no place for children." Hasseltine pressed her lips to the girl's forehead, then touched her fingers to her own lips. "You need to rest, somethin's not right."

Bertha Mae walked into the room, her dark hair piled high, ringlets cascading in ideal contrast against her white dress. She paused at the sight of Rachel, her lips tight as if met by a rank smell.

Peyton flinched.

"Mama, don't be mad at me, I just want to be with everyone. I don't want to miss out."

Bertha Mae turned to Peyton, assessed her red dress in an agonizingly long up and down. Her cheeks flushed.

Hasseltine lowered her arms from the little girl's shoulders. Waited. Her dread filled the room like black smoke. "This is Miss Peyton, Mr. Beau's friend."

"So thoughtful of you to help us celebrate today, Peyton."

"Thank you," Peyton said. The words barely found their way out of her throat. She rose out of the chair, folded her hands in front of her.

She had always thought of Bertha Mae as a benevolent woman—caring, compassionate, kind. She had been a heroine of Peyton's, someone she long wished Jayne Ella could have been. But the soft brown eyes Peyton had seen in the tintypes were darker today. Hard and accusing, like an insect's.

The house felt sick, its energy made Peyton cringe and nearly cower. She wanted to open the windows and doors to the manor, let the salty ocean breeze sweep through the house. Cleansing everything in its path, removing the sickness, like a purge.

Bertha Mae took a step toward her. Peyton backed away, knocking the chair behind her, and she stumbled.

A half smile cracked Bertha Mae's face, like she was pleased.

Hasseltine tucked her hands into her white apron and looked at the floor.

Bertha Mae turned toward her daughter. "You'll take your medicine and then you'll go back to your room."

"Noooooo," Rachel wailed. She dropped her head back, tears slid from her eyes.

Bertha Mae pulled her shoulders back, like she concentrated on becoming the better version of a caring mother. She stroked her daughter's hair, gently kissed her forehead. Her tongue darted over her lips as if she didn't like the taste.

Shockingly it reminded Peyton of Jayne Ella. The love and care she had given to her and her sister in later years had been measured, slightly distant and never enough.

"You need medicine because you're sick." She poured an oily liquid the color of tree bark into a spoon and poked at the girl's lips until she opened her mouth and swallowed.

"There, there." Bertha Mae's tone softened and she held her daughter's head to her hip. For a brief moment she appeared to be the person Peyton suspected she was—the truly giving, long-suffering matriarch of Alcott Manor. The woman Peyton had always wanted her mother to be.

Hasseltine stirred a pot of boiling potatoes, her lips folded into a tight seal.

Bertha Mae left the room.

Rachel held her stomach, appearing worse after her dose of medicine.

Hasseltine waved at her to go upstairs.

The little girl didn't move. "I want to go outside," she cried.

Hasseltine kept her head low and focused on the potatoes. Her eyes shifted toward the doorway where Bertha Mae had disappeared. Watching.

"I won't go near the water," Rachel said.

"That's never my concern with you," Hasseltine said.

"I just want to be outside."

Peyton kept still.

"Go on," Hasseltine said to Rachel and shooed her toward the stairs.

The girl stood and vomited onto the floor. The wet scent of heated sick filled the room.

Hasseltine grabbed a towel and rushed toward the girl. "Baby, baby, baby."

Rachel cried, wiped her mouth with her hands. "Every time! Why does she make me take that horrible stuff?" She threw up again, coughing brown liquid down the front of her red dress.

Peyton grabbed a towel from the long table next to her, wet it and wiped Rachel's arms and hands. She didn't know what Bertha Mae had given her, but it didn't agree with her. It must have been one of the many harebrained medicinal remedies doctors gave in this era.

Peyton wondered if Rachel's death was the mystery that needed solving. Maybe Rachel snuck out to swim, but the medicine made her sick while she was in the water. Or maybe her death wasn't an accident. Could someone have drowned her? If there were foul play involved with her death, that could be what kept the house's memories on repeat.

"Did she get sick?" Bertha Mae appeared in the doorway with a teapot wrapped in a white cloth.

"I'll take her upstairs, ma'am," Hassetine said. She grabbed another towel and ushered Rachel out of the room. The little girl's cries could be heard all the way up the stairs.

"I'll have to go check on dear Rachel." She said it like Jayne Ella. Wore her mothering responsibilities like a badge of honor and sacrifice, and yet she didn't seem to do mothering all that well.

"I'll make you some tea first." She mixed her smile with an exacting stare. Examining Peyton's dress. Looking for flaws. Peyton felt increasingly uncomfortable.

"Mothering may be the most important thing I've ever done. Everything I learned about mothering I had to come up with on my own. I had a difficult mother."

She watched Bertha Mae bite her bottom lip while she spooned two heaps of white sugar into the teapot. Peyton chose not to tell her that she didn't take sugar in her hot tea. She didn't even want tea now that she had seen Rachel get sick. And why wasn't she tending to her daughter? Maybe she was accustomed to letting Hasseltine take care of the cleaning and the bathing.

She gave Beau a wide-eyed look.

"Mrs. Alcott, I can finish the tea. I know you're busy," Beau said.

Bertha Mae waved him off.

Hasseltine returned, scurried across the kitchen and threw a towel over the mess on the floor. "She's in her room, ma'am. I've changed her clothes."

"Thank you, Hasseltine. I think I'll go check on our guests first. Finish Miss Peyton's tea, would you?" Bertha Mae pointed to the iron teapot on the table. "Just needs water."

Hasseltine nodded a long, slow yes.

When Bertha Mae was out of sight, Hasseltine ushered Peyton and Beau from the room and onto the porch. "Go on, now," she whispered. She seemed to know that no one wanted tea or food or even to be in the kitchen. Not after everything that had just taken place.

"I know some place where we can go." Beau looked at the sunny skies. Checked the gold watch that hung from his vest. "We'll get some snacks from the reception."

Halfway across the lawn, Peyton turned to find Bertha Mae Alcott approaching them with a young blond girl at her side, the same girl Peyton had seen in a tintype with Beau. Maybe at this very same reception, in this same location.

Bertha Mae stopped, spoke to a man setting up the camera and tripod. It was a different photographer than Peyton had seen the night before. Bertha Mae gave him instructions, pointed to the gathering under the tent. She waved at Beau with her picture-perfect smile.

Peyton was bothered that Bertha Mae showed no

outward sign of concern for her daughter, that there was no frantic rush in her step to get back inside to comfort her.

Peyton wanted to call the doctor herself, but she had seen how the remedy the doctor prescribed seemed to do more harm than good. Plus, she reminded herself, these were memories. They couldn't be changed, what's done was done. Rachel would drown soon, no one could prevent that from happening. Maybe this was how parenting was done in this era and if you had help in the house. Or was the manor's secret that Bertha Mae wasn't the good mother that history painted her to be?

"Mrs. Alcott," Beau said when she arrived. "Beautiful wedding, you've outdone yourself. And such a lovely day for a celebration."

"Thank you, Mr. Spencer," she said and eyed Peyton cautiously. "I hope you enjoyed your tea, Miss Peyton."

She nodded, smiled with her lips pressed firmly together, and crossed her arms in front of her.

"Then I'd like to introduce you to my niece, Martha, whom I've told you about. She arrived this week from Virginia." Mrs. Alcott ushered the young woman closer to Beau.

"Pleased to meet you, Martha. I hope your travel was pleasant," Beau said.

"The scenery was the most beautiful I've ever seen." Martha's blue eyes sparkled and her smile was slow and budding with interest. It was clear that Mrs. Alcott had handpicked Martha as a match for Beau, and she was quite pleased with her selection.

"Even more so than your trips abroad?" Beau asked.

"I don't think anything compares to the beauty of one's own country. Do you?" Martha swayed and lowered her chin such that her gaze fixed on Beau.

A twinge of jealousy tweaked Peyton's heart. If this exchange had happened in her current day, she knew that Martha would be wearing a low V-neck blouse with a tight skirt. Had they been seated together, Martha would have found the occasion to gently rest her hand on Beau's thigh. Maybe after laughing at one of his jokes.

Peyton realized women here weren't playing for boyfriends. They were playing for keeps, they were playing for life and livelihood, they were playing for marriage.

"I agree, Martha. No land is as beautiful as one's own country," Beau said.

Peyton smiled and nodded, carefully studied her surroundings. There had to be some reason why the manor held on to this memory, as well as the one where Rachel got sick in the kitchen. She searched for Horace and Ruby.

Bertha Mae's eyes narrowed on her. A chill shot down Peyton's back. She had seen this calculating expression before, with Jayne Ella. Possessive, competitive. Her mother didn't deal kindly with a threat. Perceived or otherwise.

"Beau, I wonder if you might do me a favor and bring me a glass of champagne? The heat is too much for me," the blond said and cooled herself with an elegant fan printed with yellow roses.

"I would be delighted, Martha," he said. Beau slipped his hand around Peyton's and pulled her toward him.

Bertha Mae eyed Beau's fingers on Peyton's waist. "Beau, do tell me how you met Miss Peyton."

"Yes, ma'am. Martha, Mrs. Alcott, allow me to introduce Miss Peyton Smith. My fiancée."

~

PEYTON SPENT the entire reception glued to Beau's side, listening to his conversations, watching the surroundings carefully. Though she didn't want to, she ate the wedding cookies and small sandwiches that Beau handed her. As he had said, there was no way to know when they would eat again.

Beau knew everyone at the gathering, and, curiously, they knew him. Peyton pieced together her recollection of family history and Beau's introductions to form a pretty solid understanding of who everyone was. Nothing odd happened at the reception at all. Other than the fact that Peyton thought Bertha Mae should have checked on poor Rachel. Instead, she flitted around the reception like a new bride, while her precious daughter lived what would be her last few months. Her callousness had to be tied to the mystery they needed to solve.

Beau played his part well. She watched him laugh effortlessly at jokes he must have heard all twelve times he had attended this event. She remembered that laugh, full of life and full of joy. That sound was one of the many things she missed after he disappeared. She wondered if that was what was happening here. Was the house also remembering precious details?

"Smith?" she whispered to Beau when he handed her another glass of champagne. She knew the answer as soon as she asked the question.

"Your Alcott name wouldn't have worked. I told her the truth about us because she's always trying to set me up with someone. She needs to understand why I'm spending time with you, so she'll leave me alone. Here, follow me. I think we can scoot out of here now." He glanced over his shoulder at the thinning crowd, took her hand and led her to the beach.

Joy unfolded in her heart at the feel of his hand around hers. They fit together as if no time had passed between them. She squeezed her eyes shut for a moment. She shouldn't be holding another man's hand. Not Beau's or anyone's. Ira was waiting for her at home, they were getting married.

She slipped her hand from his and shared her theory with him that these scenes must be leading up to something —the real secret they had to uncover. Possibly something to do with Rachel's death.

"We'll find it," he said. But his tone was only half-assuring and she wasn't sure if he believed what she said.

She bent down and unbuckled her shoes. When her balance wobbled he held her at the waist. It was a simple move, a kind gesture. There was no reason why fireworks should explode in her chest. But they did. She looked into those blue eyes she once thought she would wake up to every morning, and she thought she might fall in.

She looked away and dug her bare toes into the sun-warmed sand.

Beau put his hands in his pockets.

She held up her hand to block the glare of the setting sun, estimated the time to be about six o'clock. She figured she had been with him for about an hour before she was sucked home the last time. An hour must have passed by now. They walked in silence.

"There was no sign of Horace or Ruby Lee today," she finally said.

He pointed to the wedding guests. "I know from experience that they stay up there for the rest of the night. No new guests come in or out. Maybe tomorrow, or rather the next scene."

She looked at the area: various sections of Alcott Manor

land, bordered by the sea and separated by the black gaps. Like pieces of a strange skin held together by black adhesive. She studied the manor and the room she knew to be Rachel's, feeling badly that she was up there all alone and sick.

The ocean waves crashed hard and sent a salty spray over her skin in a fine mist.

He stared at the sand as they walked. She looked at him out of the corner of her eye, drank him in. His tall stature was clothed in an expensive but ill-fitting suit, and he was still sexy and beautiful. He took her hand again and she let him, once again feeling that they were home, together. She slid her hand against his, her heart soaring. The feel of his touch mended the broken places of her heart.

"When you left last night, where did you go?" he asked.

She wiped the water spray from her face. "I went back. Completely. All the way home."

He stopped, owl-eyed and mouth partly open. "Back to the reality we know?"

She nodded. "I don't know how I did it. But it happened. I was able to do it. I think once we have Horace and Ruby with us, we need to repeat the steps that I did last night."

"Except that nothing repeats right away in this world. We'd have to wait about a year to see that particular scene again."

She looked at the sun that was rapidly dropping from view and knew more than an hour had passed. Disappointment and worry crept up like a building wave. What if she couldn't figure out how to get them home? What if they were stuck here forever? Her confidence that she would quickly return home with Beau had shrunk dramatically in the last few minutes.

She went over the events of the night before, ending

with how she was caught in the making of the tintype. "I'd say that we need to have our picture taken in order to get back, but—"

"I've had mine made numerous times."

"And that obviously didn't work."

He shook his head. "Unfortunately not." He took his jacket off, along with the elegant cravat that was tied at his neck. He unfastened several buttons on his starched white shirt. He picked up a sand dollar, side-pitched it into the ocean such that it skipped seven times along the water. His body and movements were strong and fluid. She flashed back to watching him pitch at high school baseball games. She was often the one to hold the radar gun. His pitching speed came in at 86 mph. Which was another reason why he and his father didn't get along. Austin, being the over-bearing father he was, thought Beau ought to have tried to play professionally. He wanted his son to do high profile work, or high paying work, but not photography.

She looked at the ocean that wasn't really there, thinking of those days. They felt like another lifetime.

He stroked her cheek gently with the back of his hand. "We can do this. Don't worry. We're always a force together."

He'd read her mind, he always did. Knew when she worried, knew how to calm her. He knew everything about her. She had forgotten until just then how he never let her suffer alone.

"We always did manage to sort of part the Red Sea when we were together."

His smile dropped by half, as if he had just gotten bad news from some inner report she couldn't hear.

Were together, she figured. Past tense. It was only past tense to her. She would have to tell him about Ira. The corset dug into her ribs and she tugged at it. She wanted nothing more than to exchange it for an old sweatshirt and a pair of jeans.

The ocean smelled of seaweed and fish, the briny mixture that reminded her of home.

"I remember feeling what you're feeling right now. Lost. Trapped. Angry. Come on. Put your toes in the water." He helped her gather her wide skirt until the hem was up around her knees.

The cold saltwater washed over their feet in the cadence of a normal tide. She was having a hard time believing any of it.

"Feels good, doesn't it?" He squeezed her hand.

Except for him. She could believe it was him, she had no trouble with that. It was stereotypical to think it, but he had been her knight in shining armor. He had always shown up whenever she needed him most.

They stood there hand in hand, facing the horizon. Or at least the moving photographic version. "Have you been swimming?"

He shook his head. "Too afraid in this place. God only knows what would happen if I swam out there and stumbled on to one of those black lines. I assume there's one out there. Probably a lot of them. I figured I would drown or something. Not the way I want to die."

A sob came up and she stopped it in her chest. For years she'd thought Beau was dead, or worse. She cleared her throat. "You've fallen through them before?"

"In the beginning I did. I'd been here for a couple of weeks. I didn't know what was going on when the ground shifted and I fell right into one of those black spaces. I got separated from everyone I had become familiar with. I ended up in an entirely different set of memories.

"I think I've traveled through all of them now. There are

some I'd like to avoid, but all in all, I find that order helps when you're stuck in a place like this. It gives me familiarity. A way to predict. Which means something to me while I'm in a world I can't control."

"How did you figure out that these were photographs?"

"Mrs. Miller told me."

"She did." Peyton nearly gasped. "After she took your photo?"

He nodded. "She shot me with that antique camera, had me convinced that if I did those photos that you would appreciate them. She said, 'Beau, you're asking her to give up so much— Show her that you're joining her family as well.' Of course, if I hadn't been three sheets to the wind I wouldn't have done any of that."

She turned her head to the side. The angst and worry, built up over all those years, wondering what happened to him, it threatened to spill over. "She—Mrs. Miller has an oddly effective way of getting people to do things. She leads them down the primrose path and traps them before they realize what's happened."

They walked along the beach and away from the manor. The sun had nearly disappeared behind the manor. Its weight sinking to the other side of the water oaks and magnolias that were far shorter, thinner and younger than when she had seen them when she was at home.

"Do you mind if we look around the front of the house? I don't want to miss anything. Especially if Ruby or Horace might be there. Plus I just have to look around while I figure out a plan."

He stared at her with narrow-eyed intensity, standing so close that she could almost feel the warmth of his skin. There was a heat between them that pulsed, its strength taking on a life of its own. She looked away. Told Beau about the loan, his father's bank merger and how he was trying to take the house from them.

Beau shook his head. "I never thought he would do something like that. I wish I were there to try and stop him for you."

"Jayne Ella is probably cursing my name right about now since I missed the meeting with the bankers. Of course, when I do make it home, if I make it home, there will be all sorts of accusations about my selfishness, how I abandoned my family when they needed me most." She walked quickly and knew she sounded chatty.

To the side of the house she saw the lush green gardens and tall hedges that had been sheared into a labyrinth, something else she had only seen in photos. Squeals of children's laughter could be heard from inside the maze. She slipped her shoes on, the remaining sand on her feet rubbing against the inside of her shoes like sandpaper. They passed a young magnolia tree and Peyton remembered Ruby Lee tackling her in that spot, how she held a knife to her toe and sliced the skin. She wondered if Ruby were more subdued now, too. Or had she become worse?

The perfumed magnolia scent was so thick and strong, it was three-dimensional. Clinging to everything in sight, defining a visitor's experience at Alcott Manor. That was what Bertha Mae had written in her diary, that she had planted the magnolias to define a visitor's experience, even before they reached the house.

They rounded the corner of the manor and she half expected to see the familiar—the white pebble and shell drive that crunched under her step, Jayne Ella's light blue Cadillac, and maybe a few other visiting cars.

Instead, the curved driveway was light brown dirt.

Horses and carriages were parked where cars should have been. Several of the horses stared and snorted.

She gathered her skirts and walked all the way to the end of the long drive, passing one gentleman in a tuxedo who tipped his tall black hat.

"May I help you, miss?" he asked.

"No, thank you," she said and hurried her steps.

Just past the front entrance was a narrow dirt road and beyond it were acres of cotton plants. She didn't know where she was going, she just kept walking. Beau was several feet behind her but he might as well have been right by her side for as close as she felt to him. She turned left, grit and dust kicking up from the road and irritating her eyes. Her face slammed hard into something solid, and pain shot through her nose and cheekbone.

Peyton stepped back, feeling foolish that she hadn't seen whatever it was that she'd run into. There was nothing ahead of her except for miles of an empty dirt road with crops on either side. She stretched her hand out and her fingers met a smooth, thick surface, like the glass of a window pane. She searched for a way around it, looking like an idiot, she suspected. When she found the invisible barrier immovable and without edges, she turned around and found Beau standing with his hands in his pockets. As if he had been waiting for her to discover something he already knew.

"What is this?" She touched the invisible wall that kept her contained.

"This would be the last photo that Bertha Mae had someone take today." He pointed to the visual horizons that surrounded them on four sides. "Therefore, there's nothing beyond what you can see."

16

T hey reached the ocean side of the manor. Beau placed a finger over his lips and nodded toward the opposite end of the beach. "Follow me. I want to show you something."

They snuck past the wedding reception by sticking close to the dunes.

"They can't see us?" Peyton whispered.

"Right now, Senator Alcott is making a toast to his niece, the bride. No one is paying attention to anyone but him. Heard that speech several times, he's a captivating speaker." He pointed to the white tent where the man in a black tuxedo stood on a platform with a raised glass of champagne.

He held her hand and guided her over several black lines, making sure she didn't fall in. He couldn't bear to lose her again. He honestly didn't think he would survive that.

They headed toward the forest that, in this picture at least, was much closer than it was in their current day. He hadn't realized just how many trees had been removed over the years until he ended up here. There was a luminescent glow to the area, like spirits blinking and swirling around the trees.

"What's going on there?" She smiled like a fairy-tale princess.

He escorted her the rest of the way, knowing that ocean, forest, and sand was her favorite combination. In fact, it was in a place not unlike this where he had taken her on their first date. He had seen her expression when she found the hard edge of their world. He knew that exact feeling of devastation, felt it many times in this land of trapped Alcott reality—there was no way out.

She needed a break, a distraction, so that she wouldn't lose hope.

"Lightning bugs!" she said. "There must be thousands!"

"Nothing to scare them off, I guess. Not many visitors to this area at this time of day. No vehicles of any kind. I guess Bertha Mae caught it with her camera."

It was a magical scene, thousands of lightning bugs coursing through the forest, flashing their courtship messages. She walked through the fluorescent crowd, several landed on her hands.

"It's amazing that she captured this! Well, I guess her diary did say that she took pictures of everything."

Beau wrapped his arm around her and pointed to the back porch in the distance. A photographer stood behind the camera on its tripod. Bertha Mae stood behind him, her arm extended, pointing in the distance as if to direct his efforts.

Thunder rolled through the air. Dark clouds appeared to move in their direction. None of it happening in real time, and yet its danger couldn't be ignored. On the great lawn there was a commotion and guests began to file inside the manor.

"Why, would be my question," Peyton said. "What is it about her or this camera that causes that to happen?" She raised her hand and another lightning bug landed on the tip of her finger.

Beau put his hands in his pockets, studied her. "She reminds me of this professor I had in college, he was a former green beret. He took pictures of everything. I mean, everything. The outside of the communications building, the inside of the classrooms, the hallways. I saw him take pictures of students and teachers when they didn't even know he was watching them. He was obsessive about photo-graphically documenting every event. It was like he was creating his own world, one that didn't require an actual connection."

"Maybe he was trying to compensate for something he saw in the war. Maybe he had too many bad things happen in his life and he was desperate to create some sort of ideal world. Maybe one where certain horrors didn't exist."

"That's what I thought. Like maybe he needed to paint a better picture for himself. She started early this morning, making tintypes of the house and its interior. She shot the grounds in every which direction. She had someone else shoot the wedding and the reception, but she kept a close watch on them. She checked the tintypes they made as soon as they were ready. If she didn't like them, she made them do the tintypes over. I think she has an iron fist tucked inside of those white gloves of hers. If she had been born in our time, she would have been some sort of social media fiend.

"It's like a disorder, that she has to document her life like that. She's constantly painting a particular version of her life story." He picked up a shell and tossed it into an oncoming wave. "She's covering for something. Hiding something," Beau said.

Peyton nodded like his words resonated in her, as if they had struck a tuning fork. "The manor has always kept more than its share of secrets, and the Alcotts have constantly tried to cover them."

"She's photoshopped the Alcott Manor image to hide her secret." He took her hand, rubbed his thumb over the fingers of her left hand. He remembered kneeling in front of her in an oceanfront setting much like this one and slipping the yellow diamond on her ring finger. He expected to see that same ring on her hand fifty years into the future.

She pulled her hand away, pressed it to her midsection. "History paints Bertha Mae as an ideal mother, but that's not what I saw today. She has no love for that child. I wonder if we reveal how the little girl actually died, if all of this just falls away." She gestured to the forest around them. "Even if we don't find Horace and Ruby Lee, if the truth comes out, maybe that would be enough to get us home? Maybe it would be enough to get all of us home."

"It's worth a shot," he said.

"Then I'll find the camera that Mrs. Miller used to send us here and destroy it. That poor girl." Her chin trembled and she wiped the tears that slid down her face. "I'm sorry— I—I wasn't expecting to feel this way."

He held her close. "What's going on, Pey?"

Her face crumpled and the quiet sobs seemed to come from somewhere deep within.

She finally lifted her head from his shoulder, she looked at the ocean, drew in a breath.

"When I was young I used to idolize Jayne Ella. She was my heroine—she was so strong and fierce. She had her own business, she was so in charge. She was everything I wanted to be, and believe it or not, we were so close. I was like her doll. She would choose my outfits and do my hair every day. She tried to be that way with Layla, but those two never synced the way she and I did.

"Anyway, when I was about ten, that all changed. The closeness went away when I told her I was stuck in the manor the night when Ruby disappeared. She told me I was making it all up, especially the part about the blood. I've never been able to forgive her for that. She should have been there for me, she should have had my back. She should have known I wasn't lying."

"You're right. She should have." Beau thought about the night of their rehearsal dinner, the last night he had seen her. "I'm sorry that we argued when you told me what happened that night—"

She shook her head, ran her hand along his jaw. "No, you were right. About part of it, anyway. The blood obviously wasn't Ruby's. I didn't have anything to do with her disappearance. Not directly, anyway. And apparently she's not even dead!" Irrational laughter burst out of her mouth. He put his arm around her, to ground her, to let her know he cared.

"Mrs. Miller intervened about then. She introduced me to Bertha Mae by showing me all the tintypes in the museum. I read Bertha Mae's diary, fell in love with who I thought she was—this morally upstanding woman who honored her family, overcame the odds. I've even designed a series of exhibits at the manor to honor her—her tintypes, her diary, her clothes!" She tried to laugh again but the noise was quickly stifled into quiet crying.

"Jayne Ella was not an easy mother."

"I always wanted Jayne Ella to be more like Bertha Mae. Unfortunately, I think she is." She sniffed and studied the glow of the fireflies that surrounded them like fairy dust.

He pulled her closer still. "Both of them seem to have their own agenda."

"I actually thought that if I worked on the manor for her, that this might bring us closer. Even though it was hard to spend any time there, I thought it was important to mend my relationship with my mother. But, forget it."

Peyton mentioned the darkness she had seen in Bertha Mae's eyes. "Like some kind of evil," she said. She launched into all the different ways Bertha Mae could have hastened her daughter's death, like ignoring the fact that the medicine wasn't working, or encouraging Rachel to swim when she was too sick.

Beau had seen that in Bertha Mae, too. "At the funeral, she behaves more like a host, like she's the center of attention," he said. "Almost like she's energized by the event, somehow."

"She doesn't deserve children. We need to follow Rachel, ask her questions."

He pushed his hands through his hair. "We don't really have time for that."

Peyton's eyes owled.

He knew how the fear was getting ahold of her. He'd always had that ability to calm and center her. To bring her home, so to speak. She was stronger now, more independent. But he still had a fierce need to protect her and he definitely wanted to help her find a way home.

"What do you mean?" she asked.

He turned toward the manor, double checking his memory of the events he'd lived through too many times. "The next scene we shift into is Rachel's funeral."

"She's dead by tomorrow?"

He nodded.

"Beyond tomorrow, how long before we see Rachel again?"

He rested his hands on his hips and tried to remember. "If we stay in order, there are about three or four hundred tintypes, I think, before we go all the way through to the beginning—when the tintypes started. I would guess another hundred or so before Rachel appears after that. Not every memory lasts a full twenty-four hours, so, about a year."

"So, we have no shot of figuring out what Bertha Mae did to her, at least not for a long time?" She pressed her hand to her head, paced back and forth. "Our only shot is to find Ruby and Horace."

He tried not to look discouraged. The lead they had on Rachel's death was the first he'd had. "I think so."

"What about going into one of those black gaps together? We might end up coming out in a better place in the order?"

"I thought about that. But we could also get separated."

Disappointment and resignation shadowed her face and caused his chest to ache. She was trapped. Anchored, leashed to this world that offered very little explanation for its existence. He wanted to tell her that they would find a way out, but he didn't know if they would.

"At least we have each other." He offered her his hand and she accepted it. "We won't give up, we'll keep trying."

"We'll keep trying," she said softly.

He kissed her left hand. "You left your engagement ring at home, I guess."

"Yes, it's at home." She turned toward the wind. He watched her stop herself from chewing on the inside of her cheek. Sensing bad news, the worst news, he felt sick and dizzy.

"Beau—" A shadow crossed her face. He let go of her hand.

"I waited...for almost six years. I kept thinking that maybe—" Her voice caught in her throat.

Never did he think he would be hearing this from her.

"I kept thinking that you were going to come home somehow."

"I had no way to get to you," he said.

Thunder rolled through the sky, a long and angry warning.

"Your family. They made a grave for you in the cemetery on the east side of town. After you had been gone so long that you were considered legally dead. I guess they decided it was time to— Oh, gosh. I'm so sorry. I realize this must sound heartless."

He didn't respond. Just stood there, thinking that he would have preferred living what was left of his miserable life without hearing this news. "You're married?"

She shook her head, licked her lips.

He exhaled hard. Not married. The wind blew her hair. He wanted to grab her shoulders, tell her that she was his. Instead he kept still and quiet, curled his hands into fists.

"Everyone kept telling me I had to move on, that I was wasting my life. So, I finally accepted dates, let myself get set up on blind dates. I was trying to be healthy.

After a couple of dinners, I would inevitably find a reason not to see these guys any further. Friends and family criticized me for being stuck in the past. Everyone said I needed a therapist. I finally did see a therapist for grief counseling, because I couldn't get over you." She wiped the tears from her cheeks.

"When I finally told the counselor that you had disappeared several years previously, she said I *had* to find a way to move on. Either that or get on medication."

Pain shot through his jaw as his teeth ground together, because he knew that she hadn't chosen the medication.

"What's his name?" he asked.

She waited a moment before answering. "Ira."

He turned toward the darkening sky, feeling as if his soul were being ripped from his body. When he looked at her again, he asked, "Do you love him?"

"We're engaged."

He nodded, short and quick like he'd been shot.

"He's a good person. I think you would even like him."

He stepped closer to her. "Under the current circumstances, I rather doubt that." Then he realized that she hadn't answered his question. "Do you love him?" he asked again. His voice strained, it took effort to keep it calm.

She squeezed her eyes shut for a moment and winced.

He thought she might regain her composure. But when she didn't, he tried to find peace in that. If she was conflicted, that wasn't the worst thing she could feel. And he thought that meant she would tell him the truth. They had never kept anything from one another, at least not until they had been parted.

"Yes," she said.

He didn't move at first, but he kept his eyes on her. His chest pumped up and down too quickly. He looked to the ocean and faced the oncoming wind. His mind was filled with unfortunate images of what she and Ira must have shared, how deeply they must care about one another.

"I thought you were dead!" she said above the noise from the crashing waves.

He walked toward her, calm, though a piece of him was

broken. Nine years, he reminded himself. He had been gone for nine years. The hurt had a grip on his heart. Not anger. He wasn't mad at her, he understood. Life moved on. At least for her it had.

The heartbreak nearly swallowed him whole.

"I watched constantly for some sign that I could hang on to, something to give me hope that you were still alive—there was nothing." Her eyes filled with tears and when her expression softened with emotion, they streamed down her cheeks.

"It's okay," he reached for her, wiped the tears from her face. "I was gone. You had no way of knowing where I was. You thought I was dead. I hear you on that."

Nature whipped around them with building fury and yet something peaceful settled between them. Something solid. Her tears stopped.

"Would you have fallen in love with him if I hadn't left?" he asked.

A flash of lightning ripped through the sky, thunder crashed and startled her. The clouds opened and rain fell in fat, heavy sheets.

He jogged away from the beach with her in tow. He led them to a small red barn not far from the house, one that wouldn't be there in the current day. Just shy of the horse barn, he pointed to the thick, black border. A new photo.

She gathered her skirts, jumped over the line.

Once inside the barn they faced one another. Rain soaked their formal clothing and dripped onto the floor. The barn was filled with the clean scent of sun-dried hay. Bermuda hay, he guessed. Horses grazed in their stalls.

A barn swallow swooped twice like an acrobat and Peyton ducked to get out of its way. Beau found a pack of matches and a gas lamp. He lit the lamp, and the barn filled with an orangish glow.

He stared at her. What little bit of makeup she had worn earlier in the day was gone and her hair had mostly fallen from its pinned-up style. She was the most natural beauty he had ever known.

She hadn't answered his question and he thought twice about asking it again. If she said she had met the love of her life in this man, it might just kill him on the spot.

He stood close, leaving only room enough for the heat between them. "I just want to know the truth," he said.

The rain pattered on the roof, filling the silence.

"No," she said. "I would never have fallen in love with him if you had still been around."

He drew in a deep breath.

"And now?" he asked. "Are we over? Is it too late for us?"

She ran her fingers along the side of his face, and he closed his eyes. He could still feel the future they once promised one another. It was vivid, alive, even though so much time had passed. He had been so driven to leave Charleston with her, to leave his father, to figure out where he belonged in the world.

They were going to travel together for the first year, seeing as much of the world as possible. Then settle into a house on the beach, in a small town, maybe in North Carolina. Someplace with a porch where she could watch the waves and he could play his guitar. They planned to open a photography studio, one they could run out of the house or in a spare room over the garage.

"Is it?" he whispered. He opened his eyes.

Her lips were parted, like she searched for the words. To let him down easy? He wondered.

"Beau—" She shook her head.

"Just tell me the truth." He would have to have that. At least.

Her eyes filled with tears. "We've never been over. Not for me."

The years of desperation, the years of missing her, loving her and needing her converged into that one moment. She leaned toward him and he wrapped her in his arms, holding her close and feeling, for the first time in too many years, that his world had fallen into place.

He kissed her, the sweetest kiss he'd ever known. Her lips soft, her mouth lingering. He paused. He knew, for as much as he'd prayed to go home, what he had really wanted all these years, was to go home to her.

He kissed her again, sliding her close. Knowing he'd do anything she asked. She was the only heaven he'd ever known. His hands gliding gently through her hair, across her back. His entire world safe once again in his arms, but for a moment or a lifetime, he didn't know.

She turned to the side, stepped away. "I'm sorry. I—"

"It's okay." His heart ached with the same excruciating emptiness he'd only known in the last nine years. His breath left his lungs in a slow exhale, like life seeping from his body.

She walked further away from him, looked out the window, the rain driving hard against the glass. When she turned toward him again, her expression had changed. She held still and his breathing stopped.

She moved toward him fast and with determination, air filled his lungs in a rush. He caught her in his arms, stumbling backward. Her kisses passionate, her arms around him, holding on, holding tight. He lifted her against him, her mouth on his, adrenaline shooting through every nerve ending like a drug.

She'd never been the aggressor with him before, she'd never had to be. Jealousy competed for first place in his mind at how she had changed. Images raced with her and this other man. He pulled away, their breathing ragged. He yanked his vision in a better direction and reminded himself that she was in his arms now. She had said that their relationship wasn't over for her. Did she still love him? He didn't know.

She took his bottom lip between her teeth, tugged.

He lifted her, spun her until her back was flush against the wall, held there by his body. She pulled at his wet jacket until it was freed and on the floor.

There was nothing real beyond what they shared in this moment. Even the walls around them would fade in a few hours. In its stead would be some Alcott facade that hid unspeakable horrors. Those secrets kept everyone trapped, unable to move forward. Those secrets had stolen his life.

He peeled his wet shirt from his body. He buried his face in her neck, her rose-scented skin an echo from their past.

It had been years since he had known her like this.

She was his past, he had once been her future, and for as long as he could remember her love was wrapped tightly around his heart. He built a makeshift bed for them on the floor out of hay and blankets, he kept an eye on her. Her pale skin glowed in the yellow lamplight, her smile soft and tipped to one side, like he'd often seen in his memories. He wondered if she would act differently as time passed. Was this a temporary reunion or was she the girl he had wanted for all time?

"I missed you so much I thought I was going to die," she breathed. "I think I almost did."

Her eyes were bright and clear, locked onto him like she had finally found what she wanted. He'd forgotten what it was like to be next to someone he truly loved, to feel the endlessness of the connection, the sensation of coming home.

She curled against him, and held him. She asked how he survived for nine years in this world without a home, without family or friends.

"I'd replay moments I'd shared with you, over and over. Just to remind myself that life was worth living, that you and I had been real. I found a black diary in the library, and I filled its empty pages with every memory I had of our years together—where I took you on our dates, the catchphrases you used, your mannerisms, the outfits you wore. I forced myself to recall every detail about you.

She smiled and it was like warmth from the sun. For the first time, he felt life in this place.

"There's nothing better in my life than being with you," he said. "My life is yours, Peyton. It has been from the moment we met. I'm yours forever if you'll have me."

17

Mrs. Miller checked the time and she paced in front of the row of tintypes.

It seemed later than what the cream-colored watch face read. She checked her cell phone, noting her watch had been slow. She wound the knob on the side of the slender gold watch. She didn't think they made wind up watches anymore, but her husband had given her this one when they first married. She refused to give it up.

She adjusted the vase full of fresh flowers she'd brought to the ballroom for her daughter's arrival. She shouldn't have cut any of the flowers from the manor's garden out back. But pink and yellow roses were Ruby's favorite, and her homecoming deserved the best.

Peyton came back so quickly the first time, she really had expected to see her family by now. She pulled the small bottle from her pocket, tilted her head back and squeezed two drops into each eye.

"Age-related macular degeneration can be caused by psychological stress," the doctor had said. She nearly fell over when he told her that. First Peyton causes her to lose her daughter, then she causes her to nearly lose her eyesight before Ruby Lee returns. If she didn't come back soon, she would make sure Peyton lost everything.

She reached for her necklace with the large, gold owl charm, the one with the magnifying glass in the middle. Holding it over the tintype that had been made at an Alcott Thanksgiving, she stroked the image of her daughter's hair. Her baby girl was all grown up, and thankfully she had kept her red hair. It was darker now that she was older, a lovely auburn. She ached to run her fingers through those soft tresses, wondered if her daughter would let her put them in a braid.

She gripped the frame more tightly. She had searched fifty-nine tintypes that day, looking for Peyton. It took her almost two hours and looking at so many tiny details nearly ruined what little bit of eyesight she had left. But with the help of her owl magnifying pendant, she found her. She scratched at the glass that held Peyton's and Beau's images. They stood in the distance, hand-in-hand, facing one another at the forest's edge.

That was the day of Benjamin Alcott's niece's wedding. Peyton and Beau should have been searching for Ruby and Horace, not enjoying some reunion.

The way she and Beau had loved one another, Mrs. Miller didn't think Peyton would ever recover—which had been part of her goal. But now that she thought Peyton was enjoying the love of both Ira and Beau, it was an injustice she would put right.

She would make Peyton pay again—this time for not bringing Ruby home like she was supposed to and for thinking only of herself—while she and Ruby and Horace suffered.

She wondered which authentic Alcott family suit Ira

would want to wear. He would look dashing in Benjamin Alcott's black tuxedo, or he would also look nice in Senator Alcott's tan suit. Maybe Ira would be able to bring her Ruby back to her. At the very least, he would be an unwelcome visitor in Peyton's life.

She slipped her black handbag over her arm and headed toward the door. She needed to bring Bertha Mae's camera back to the manor today. She passed by the tintype of Rachel Alcott. That dress would be just the right size for Peyton's youngest niece, Emma Catherine. Perhaps she would photograph Ira and Emma Catherine together. Jayne Ella would be happy to help her set that up.

18

In the flickering light of the lantern, Beau's face drifted in and out of her focus. He looked like a dream. The shadows played tricks, making Peyton wonder if he might disappear.

He stroked her hair. He placed gentle kisses on her forehead that melted on her skin.

She traced his broad chest with her fingertip. She lingered over his muscles that must have been maintained through hard work and chores. Certainly not the obsessive gym workouts he used to do.

She told herself that everything would be okay. They could find Ruby and Horace, they could find the secret that made the manor hold on to the past, they would find a way home. But the wind rattled the square window on the opposite side of the barn, and reality seeped in.

Mrs. Miller clipped Beau's wings on the day she made those tintypes. His beautiful soul, the one Peyton thought belonged more to the world than it ever did to her, would want to explore more than ever when they got home.

She had effectively ruined her relationship with Ira,

which was unlike her. She remembered *The Clean Slate Theory* and what it said about revealing secrets only to clear your own conscience. But she didn't think she could keep her feelings for Beau from Ira. Her mother might be able to keep secrets for decades on end, as could Bertha Mae, but Peyton wasn't cut from that particular Alcott cloth.

Then she wondered, what if they made it back and Beau didn't want to travel? What if Ira still wanted to marry her, even once he knew that she had spent the night wrapped in Beau's arms? What would she do then? Her heart pumped adrenaline through her body like water through a firehose.

But Rachel was dead. There would be no way to figure out how she died. Not until the manor shuffled through all of these specific tintypes and worked its way back to the beginning. Only then could they follow clues that would help them solve the mystery.

Horace and Ruby were nowhere to be found. There was no way out. No way back. Perhaps not for a long, long while, if ever. By then Ira would have moved on. She couldn't blame him, she had had to do the same thing. But she would have been lying if she'd said it didn't smart.

Beau ran his finger along the side of her face, and his magical touch brought her focus back to him. He was the secret she had buried deep in her heart. The one she kept from everyone—her mother, her friends, even her therapist and certainly Ira. But here in this strange reality that was hidden within the walls of Alcott Manor, she had finally opened all the deepest corners of her heart.

As if Beau knew, he kissed her again. And again. He worked his way around to her collarbone, until she no longer cared what they would wake up to.

They kept on for hours, talking, laughing, kissing, making up for lost time. Dozing only occasionally. When she thought the darkest part of the night had passed, she rolled over to see if he was awake, to ask him about the next day.

His face was peaceful and yet radiant, happy, like everything was right in his world. She lightly traced a finger around the frame of his face and his eyes fluttered open. He realized she was gazing at him, and he smiled. They didn't talk or kiss or touch. They just looked at one another for a long while, their unspoken connection speaking volumes.

"You are the one who kept me alive," he finally said. "I prayed every day and night, I believed that we would be together again. That's the only thing that kept me going."

She rested her head on his chest, wrapped her arm around him and held on.

Don't leave me, Beau. Don't leave me.

Was it okay for her to think that? She had spent so much time trying to let go, trying to put him in the past. Trying to start fresh, begin anew. She had set up mental guardrails, to keep herself from thinking too much about the future they didn't get to have. Now those were blasted away. Memories of her life with Beau flitted around Peyton's mind like butterflies, beautiful, airy, fleeting.

She finally fell asleep and she dreamed of being in the Alcott Manor ballroom in the wide-skirted party dress, waltzing with Beau. The walls shifted and morphed, the room fell away and the temperature dropped to near freezing. Her legs were short and bare, her shoelaces were untied. She sat in the back seat of a car she didn't recognize. One with black seats. The seatbelt was too high and its thin edge cut against her neck.

Her mother turned around from the front seat. Her hair was longer then, sleeker. The way it looked when Peyton was young. The scenes flipped forward, frame by frame. Choppy, like an old silent film.

"You okay, sweetheart?" her mother asked.

She nodded her head. Slowly. Something was wrong.

"It's late. I know you're tired." Her mother flashed her wide smile, the one that came naturally when she'd had too much wine to drink. She reached over the seat and patted Peyton's knee. "Too pretty for your own good," she said.

When she returned her arm to the front seat her mother's fingers rubbed the back of the driver's neck.

"Mmmm," the driver groaned.

"Daddy?" Peyton asked.

The man laughed and stretched his arm around Jayne Ella possessively.

That wasn't her father's laugh.

"Daddy's at his poker game tonight, remember? Cose your eyes for a few more minutes." She leaned close to the man, ran her fingers through his hair. "After you drop me at the salon, I need you to take Peyton to the house, please. The sitter will let her in, she's taking care of Layla."

The man looked in the rearview mirror at Peyton. She recognized those blue eyes.

"You don't want to just take her with you?" he lowered his voice. "The sitter might see me."

Jayne Ella shook her head. "The sitter is glued to the tv, she won't see a thing. All you have to do is stop at the end of the driveway, Peyton can walk in by herself. Brenda called me about an hour ago. She came down with the flu and left without counting out the cash drawer or getting tomorrow's deposit ready. So I have to do that."

The man sighed. "I don't know—"

"Please? Peyton feels warm and I don't want her waiting around on me. It's late, she's so tired and I'm hoping she's not coming down with Layla's flu bug. Seems like everyone's getting sick this time of year. I'll make it up to you..."

He faced her mother, his greedy smile turned Peyton's stomach.

"She asleep?" he asked.

"Gettin' there," she whispered. "Few more minutes she'll be out. Car rides are better than sleeping pills for my girls."

Peyton closed her eyes almost all the way, pretending to be asleep. Her mother wouldn't notice the tiny slit of her open eyelids. Whatever secrets they were going to discuss, she wanted to hear them.

When her mother buried kisses on the man's neck, she changed her mind and closed her eyes all the way. This wasn't her father! Her mother wasn't supposed to kiss other people like that.

"Mmmm, baby," the man said.

Peyton plugged her fingers into her ears. The man's cooing sent her skin crawling.

The scene changed again. Now she stood next to the grand staircase, the man with the sparkly watch digging a wide hole in the floor. Stacks of something shiny, golden on the floor. Her mother spun around: "Peyton!"

The scene changed again. It was much colder this time, she sat on the bottom step of the grand staircase of Alcott Manor. Shivering, chilled, afraid. There was a banging noise in the background. Wood breaking, splintering. A man grunting with each whack.

The wood split and she jumped to her feet. One step, then another toward the front door, determined to get out. A mix of cold and fear had her moving at glacial speed and shaking so hard involuntary noises leaked through her mouth.

"I said sit down!" the man growled.

She backed up, knew this was where she would die. She would never again see her sister or play with her dolls. She would never get to have her own business or get married or travel to Egypt.

Tears fell onto her cheeks and sobs ratcheted up from deep in her chest. She crouched onto the steps again, holding her knees against her.

"Just a few more minutes, okay? Just sit here and be a good girl." He sounded like her art teacher when he fussed at her over jars of spilled paint. The words were kind, but his tone was scolding. The man stood in front of her, covered in sweat and dirt. She knew him. It was Beau's daddy. Mr. Spencer. She looked down at her white dress smeared with dirt and blood.

She woke with a gasp, the cool breeze blowing across her upper body, and Peyton shivered. Confusion riddled her brain when the sweet smell of hay filled her nostrils. Where was she?

"What's wrong, sweetheart?" Beau's voice was deep and smooth like warm whiskey and honey. She turned and melted into his arms, told him everything she had seen.

Her body shook like she was still ten and cold and frightened in the manor. Beau wrapped the scratchy plaid blanket around her shoulders. He had long known about her missing memories and how they frightened her. This wasn't the first time he had comforted her.

He slumped a little. He stared toward the rough brown wall of the barn. "I suspected that he had affairs, but I never suspected Jayne Ella. My mother would have ruined him if she had known. She would have ruined Jayne Ella, too."

"I think this must be why your dad didn't want me to marry you," she said. "He didn't want me to talk about their affair, or whatever they hid in the manor."

Beau jerked his head like someone smacked him. "How old did you say you were when this happened?"

"Ten, I think. I remember getting this little butterfly ring for my birthday that year and I know I was wearing it that night."

"That would have been..." He counted back the years. "When I was twelve, going on thirteen, and that was—I'm almost positive that was the year there was a theft at the bank." He told her about the gold his dad had agreed to hold in the bank safe for a client, how some of it disappeared, and no one knew when because the security cameras didn't catch anything.

"Gold..." Peyton thought about the shiny golden stacks from her dream.

"I didn't know about it until a few weeks before I ended up here. The police reopened the investigation, my dad had to go down to the police station. Ultimately, they said it was either an inside job or the client simply didn't store as much gold in the safe as he said he did. Small town, small bank, there wasn't any paperwork on the transaction. They gave everyone at the bank a lie detector test. No one failed. Not even my father. Which doesn't mean anything. I don't doubt that he could beat a polygraph if he wanted to."

"Why wouldn't Jayne Ella have cashed it in by now? Our family needed the money too much over the years."

"Maybe they've been keeping the gold hidden until they could safely trade it in. The gold has gotten a lot of publicity."

"Maybe he's taking the manor because he wants the gold now and she's not willing to give him his share. Or maybe it's impossible to get to it? That digging noise. It must be buried under the floorboards."

"Wouldn't that area go to the basement?"

"Not on that side of the main staircase. That first floor, what they called the summer quarters, isn't as wide or as long as the top two levels of the house. Some of the main level sits flush to the ground. But it would be underneath the hardwoods, and the cement foundation, too, probably. I remember she said he couldn't be trusted. The affair could have ended badly," she said.

"She was right about not trusting him," he said.

"I remember she told me once, that a long time ago, when she really needed him to come through for her, when she trusted him to do the right thing, he didn't."

"My dad has never been afraid to put himself first."

"Maybe he left her."

"I'm sure he did. Probably led her on until the fun was gone, or until he had a good hiding place for the gold. He might have even planned the whole thing in advance."

She lowered her guard where the manor was concerned, opened herself up to the night in question, and tried to remember. She could hear the thwack, the definitive sound of wood splitting. Her brain spun in circles. This was the same feeling she always had around the manor. That feeling of being captive, dragged, needing to escape.

Peyton felt like she stood on a slippery bank of layered secrets, hidden truths that shifted beneath her feet and kept her unstable. One wrong step and she thought the lot of them would take her down. Her grandmother was wrong in this case. If truths were revealed from that night, she didn't think they would set her free. Knowing them felt like they might destroy her.

She glanced in the direction of the manor. Another little girl who disappeared long ago popped into her mind—Rachel. Partial memories jolted loose, elbowed their way to the forefront to be seen. Ten-year-old Peyton sat on the lowest step of the grand staircase, wind and rain rattled ancient windows, whispering from around the corner, a hole in the floor—a sharp inhale.

She turned back. Beau studied her, ran his hand along her cheek.

"What if Rachel didn't drown? What if her body wasn't lost in the ocean like Bertha Mae's diary said it was? What if Bertha Mae killed her and buried her body in the manor?" Her voice sounded hollow, as if it weren't her own.

The idea of finding Rachel's dead body, seeing the little girl's small bones beneath the floorboards sent off all sorts of bells, buzzers and flashing lights inside her head. Like she had hit the bullseye. Something let go from the inside.

"That's entirely possible."

"Maybe if we find her body and can figure out what happened to her, that will bring an end to all of these memories."

"That's a plan." The warmth of his compassion told her that he celebrated this victory with her.

She tapped three times with her left hand, then three times with her right. The images unsettled her, her memories still weren't clear.

"We're probably losing the manor as we speak." She picked up a piece of hay and cracked it into two pieces. She pressed the end of her finger onto the sharp broken end, feeling the prick on her skin.

She thought of the manor being torn down—once Austin recovered the gold, she knew that's what he would do. The few times he had been on Alcott Manor property all he could do was ask about the land. How many acres do y'all have here again? How much of it is oceanfront?

He would tear it down and the bank would sell the land. A developer would snatch it up before it could even be advertised. The best properties sold on word of mouth. Maybe he would even buy it himself for pennies on the dollar. Then her family's land would be subdivided for McMansions or a resort. But that wasn't her most pressing concern.

"If your dad tears down the manor, what would happen to us?" she asked.

Beau made a noise like someone jabbed him in the heart. "Without the manor, I don't see how there would be a way for us to get home."

It was still dark and raining when Beau roused her and explained that the scenes would change soon. She yawned and stretched, not at all enjoying the way she felt. At some point in the little bit of sleep she managed to catch the night before, snippets of her old reality wormed its way in. Guilt knocked on the outer walls of her newfound peace and tugged at the renewed happiness in her heart. She was engaged to someone else and yet she loved Beau.

Their short time together was proving every bit as right as life always had been. But now her heart splintered. Ira—a kind and brilliant man who had been good to her. He loved her. And if she was going to be honest with herself, she knew that she still loved him, too.

Beau must have picked up on the delicateness of the moment because he began to make small talk—not something he had ever been too good with. He was too busy, quickly on to the next thing. But now his questions to her teemed with genuine interest. While he put on his shirt, his blue eyes focused on her with kind intent. He asked what she did with her time back home.

"I work a lot. Crisis PR mostly. Corporate image stuff. I'm up for a promotion, Senior Vice President for an agency in Boston." She felt silly for saying that.

"Boston...wow. That's a big change from what we had planned."

She bit the corner of her bottom lip. "Truth?"

He ran his hands through his blond hair, nodded hesitantly, like he wasn't sure that was what he wanted.

"I was excited about leaving Charleston with you, and I was looking forward to the writing and the photography. But the travel might have been more your dream than mine."

He put his hands on his hips. "You were such a good writer and photographer, I didn't realize—"

"I never told you. At the time I guess I didn't really know what I wanted. Other than to leave town and be with you."

He buttoned his vest and walked toward her.

"Apparently, I'm good with turnaround opportunities. It's a good fit for my talents." She had not told him that Ira had helped her see how her natural interests and talents fit with her career choice. But a shadow crossed his face, as if he knew. It felt like Ira was in the room with them.

"If we make it home—when we make it home—how will you handle things with Ira?" he asked.

His question hit her so squarely in the chest, she stopped to catch her breath. Guilt, her abiding demon, stood strong by her side, stealing the love they had found again. "I don't know," she finally managed.

"You don't know?"

"I mean, I don't even know if we're getting home. It's not a bridge I've come to. I haven't had a chance to even think —" Her answers sounded weak. The minute they left her mouth she wanted to yank them all back inside.

"You haven't thought about it," he said flatly. He knew she was lying.

"No—I—I didn't exactly plan any of this." She couldn't believe this was her own self talking. If he had said these things to her she would have been crushed. She wasn't prepared for this conversation.

"So, when we get home, if we get home, you're just going to go back to him? Get married like none of this happened?" He waved to the blankets on the floor where they had spent the night in each other's arms.

"My words are not coming out the way I mean for them to."

She hoped he would nod and agree and let the issue go. They had other things to resolve. But he didn't, so she said, "Okay, assuming we get home, I'll have to tell him how I feel and he's going to be heartbroken. He trusted me, and I blew it." She pressed her finger against the building pain behind her left eyebrow.

"You regret this?"

"No, I—dang it, stop putting words in my mouth!"

"You're saying this is a mistake?" He gestured to the two of them.

The features of his face appeared to sag from the years of hurt and loneliness, she suspected. She realized what he was feeling, she knew it all too well. Emptiness was heaviest in the heart. That sort of weight could take the rest of you down with it. She'd had too many days when she thought the grief might just drag the skin from her bones. She licked her dry lips.

She waited a beat. Not because she didn't know the answer but because she was afraid to say it. "No. Okay? We aren't a mistake. Not for me. But this is all incredibly insensitive to someone and— Right now I don't even know what tomorrow looks like. I have to try to work that out first. Then I can figure out the rest of my life." She glared at him, half furious that he was pressuring her about the two of them and half relieved that he still cared for her.

"You're right. I'm sorry. I've waited a long time for you. I've waited a long time for us. I can't expect the same of you, our situations have been different." His shoulders drooped.

She coughed up the barbed worry that had long been stuck in her heart. "It's been almost ten years since we've even seen one another. I've changed. I'm not the same person you left behind. I don't know what your experiences have been since we've been apart, but I can tell they've changed you, too."

He frowned at her.

She wanted to feel the overwhelming love she had for him the night before. But all she felt were questions. She felt panic, guilt, worry. "I know we're not offering one another any guarantees."

He jerked backward like she had smacked him on the face.

Silence screamed in the room.

Something fierce and painful passed through his eyes and she felt a stab deep inside her chest.

She looked away which just made the pain hurt worse.

He exhaled slowly, like his patience ran thin. "You think we don't know one another anymore. But I know you, Peyton. You haven't changed that much. You're doing the same thing you always have in situations like this. You're thinking about what this Ira person wants. You're thinking about me and what I want. But you're not at all thinking about what you want." He waited for her to respond. His mouth stayed open with frustration, his hand was in the air, palm up as if it asked a question.

"It's not as simple as that," she said.

His hand dropped slowly, his lips closed. He stared at her for a long moment. "Actually it is. Once you know what you want, once you know what's right, everything else becomes pretty darn simple."

~

PEYTON WATCHED Beau put the final touches on his outfit—buttoning his white shirt, brushing dust and hay from his jacket. Like he was going to work.

His absence in her life meant she had spent the last nine years with an ache that kept its full-fisted grip on her heart. When she'd met Ira, that pain lessened. But Ira said she kept a piece of her heart closed off to him. A private chamber, so to speak. Now she wondered if that hiding place hid a wound, or did it keep safe a love that would never die?

"Rachel's funeral is a busy day at the manor. There are lots of tintypes, so, be wary of all the black lines. The barn disappears because she doesn't have tintypes made on this side of the house." He glanced at his pocket watch, wound the knob on the top.

Beau's tone was all business and it made her feel alone. The connection they shared was broken. She tapped her left leg three times, then tapped her right leg three times—her yoga instructor's method for balance. She repeated the pattern on each side, hoping a centeredness would come over her. It didn't.

She thought of Rachel. The secret of how she might have really died, whatever it was, was big enough and hidden enough that it might keep her and Beau trapped in these tintypes forever. Once again, she was taking her secret to her grave with her. If they couldn't find her body, they would have to wait a year before they would find Rachel alive again, before they could follow any clues that might reveal how she died. By then Austin would have claimed the manor and torn it down. Peyton, Beau, Horace and Ruby would all cease to exist. The manor, its memories and everyone trapped inside of that torrent of recall would be gone forever.

Buried secrets. Peyton's life was full of them—her mother's affair with Austin, the gold that was probably beneath the floorboards, the childhood memories at the manor she couldn't completely recall. They lurked in dark corners and threatened to grab her by the ankles.

"We only have a few minutes left before things begin to change. Do you need help with anything?" He gestured to her dress. His expression wasn't the peaceful sort of happy she had seen the night before, but it was resolute.

She pushed the last hairpin into her hair that she had twisted into a loose bun. "How do I look?" She winced, expected a sarcastic remark. Not just because of the tenor of their conversation, but because she knew she must look a fright. There was no place to shower or bathe, no hairbrushes and no mirrors.

He stood in front of her in his black 1850s suit, his eyes full of her. The combination of his towering height, sun-bleached hair and blue eyes was just as arresting as the first day they'd met.

"Beautiful," he said.

J ayne Ella stood to the side of Alcott Manor's grand staircase, staring at the hiding place she had helped Austin create over twenty years ago. She bit off tiny pieces of skin from the side of her thumbnail. The area was already raw If she didn't stop, it would bleed. She kept chewing. Nipping at the skin, the sharp pain strangely satisfying.

Austin and his henchmen were gone.

Before Austin left the front porch, he whispered to her one last time, "You have a choice. You can give me access to what we hid together, or I can take the manor and help myself."

In front of his associates, she offered a polite laugh to the whispers they couldn't hear. But when they stepped away, she whispered in return, "Need I remind you that what you want is buried in a hard to access corner, beneath hardwoods and cement? That there is no way to dig—" She turned around to see if anyone could possibly hear what she was saying. "There's no easy way to dig that up. This place is crawling with volunteers night and day, and cutting through wood and cement makes a heck of a lot of noise." It actually wasn't an impossible situation, but she wanted him to think that it was.

"I'll come at night when everyone is gone." His finger found her hand and stroked it gently. "Take care of security and I'll do it for you."

She moved her hand out of his reach, propped it on her hip. She didn't like the effect his touch had on her and she didn't trust herself around him. "You won't get through that much flooring and cement in one night, the reconstruction done on this place is extraordinary. I'd also have to clear the repair with the security company and the county cop that patrols this place at night. Blasting through cement is not a quiet project. Not to mention that I don't know how we would explain the giant, very deep hole in the floor as a needed repair."

"It's more important that we get all of it up and out. No one is going to think anything about a hole in the floor. Repairs in this place aren't an unusual thing. Let me take care of it for you."

Jayne Ella knew what she had to do. She would dig up their gold and move it somewhere safe, someplace he didn't know about. If he wanted his share of the gold back, he'd leave the manor alone.

She imagined Austin making his own move. Buying all the right equipment today, somehow getting into the house and sawing through wood and cement this weekend. If she confronted him, she could also imagine him pulling a gun on her, shooting her before she could scream, then burying her underneath Alcott Manor until the end of time.

No, she would get to it first. She would also film the entire process with her camera, so that when his watch was uncovered, that proof of his original participation, proof that he was there when the gold was buried in the first place, would be evident. She wasn't entirely sure that his watch was buried with the gold. She didn't remember him losing it that night. But she would be prepared to capture proof just in case.

Taking a page from Mrs. Miller's book, she would make copies upon copies of the video, and she would tell him that she had left instructions in her will that the video was to be taken to the police in the event of her untimely death.

That would be enough to keep him away from the manor. She couldn't anticipate how her move would affect his temper. He'd said it many times, he didn't like being held under someone else's thumb. He might just grab her by the throat and strangle her on the spot. Or he might coil like a snake in the grass and wait until he figured another way to strike.

20

Whon the tintype shifted, Beau held Peyton's hand tight. The ground slipped beneath them, the hay-covered dirt floor morphing into grass. The horse barn that had given them shelter for the night disappeared completely, leaving only open sky in its place.

The towering hedges of the labyrinth she had seen yesterday stretched out before them still, and to the side of the house. It was fitting, she thought, that Bertha Mae would have constructed a complicated maze next to the manor—it was most likely her memories that had, in effect, become the complicated maze where Peyton and Beau were trapped.

A hairpin slipped out and a chunk of Peyton's bun fell. She fussed over the style.

"Hasseltine will help you," Beau said. "She'll probably help us find new clothes, too."

Mourners began to arrive by simple, black horse-drawn carriages. The muted clomp, clomp, clomp of horses' hooves sounded from the dirt drive. Bertha Mae stood next to a photographer on the front porch, the camera perched between them on a tripod.

Peyton assumed she and Beau would appear in a tintype at home and she wondered if Mrs. Miller would be watching them. Maybe she tapped on the glass. Peyton wondered if she would feel the tapping like thunder or an earthquake.

Peyton knew from studying family history that Rachel drowned. What she hadn't known was how much Rachel hated the ocean. She doubted that Bertha Mae would let her little girl swim, not with her health history. And she didn't think there had been much swimming in the 1850s anyway.

When she and Beau arrived in the kitchen, Beau made up some story about traveling, losing luggage and requested Hasseltine's help with clothes. She agreed and disappeared upstairs.

Peyton and Beau slipped around the corner and found Bertha Mae in a wide-skirted, black taffeta dress talking with several women. Her hair had been perfectly styled and her gardenia-scented perfume filled the room. She looked too well put together to be a grieving mother.

"We tied a rope to her waist." Bertha Mae chewed at her bottom lip. "The end of it was tied to the cabana. I never left her, of course. But a wave took her under and when I tugged on the rope, she was gone." Bertha Mae wiped falling tears with her white handkerchief.

The women cried together, shook their heads and took turns hugging Bertha Mae. They told her what a beautiful little girl Rachel had been, how lucky Bertha Mae was to have had her in her life if only for a little while. The more they lauded her with their sympathy, the more she seemed to plump and glow. Like she fed on their attention.

"I'll never get over losing her." She bit her lip so hard a drop of blood appeared at the lower corner.

Eventually the women shifted their stances like they became increasingly uncomfortable with the situation, like they were afraid Bertha Mae's loss might be contagious.

There wasn't a casket in the living room. Just two silver vases of lilies on either side of a long table in the middle of the room. In the center of the table were several tintypes of Rachel in healthier days, appearing beautiful, almost unreal, like a prized doll.

Bertha Mae moved from group to group, circulating, like a bride at a reception. Peyton thought of her own mother and how she seemed to draw energy from others' attention.

When Bertha Mae fanned her face and turned toward the hallway, excusing herself from the group, Peyton took Beau by the arm.

"Let's go," she whispered. She didn't want to be caught watching.

They scurried to the kitchen where Hasseltine had returned with their clothes. She pointed to the black hoop-skirted dress. "This is Mrs. Alcott's dress. She has several black ones, she won't miss this one."

Peyton and Beau slipped into one of the upstairs guest rooms to change clothes. When they were dressed, Beau shoved their old clothes into the back of an armoire. "The scenes will change soon enough, they'll never find these."

The idea of spending the rest of her life sleeping on barn floors and living off of leftovers made her want to scream. She was starving, in need of a bath and desperately wanted to find a way home. She smiled, in part to try to make Beau feel better. It wasn't his fault that they were stuck here.

Something in her expression must have revealed her true feelings because Beau sat next to her on the bed.

"I know," he said, rubbing his hand along her arm. "This is no way to live."

"Are you mind reading or are my thoughts that transparent?"

"You have this sort of half smile you do when you'd rather be anyplace but where you are. Then you look down and to the right. Like you're too polite to be honest. That, and I know you." He raised his eyebrow at her. Then he stood in front of the dresser mirror and adjusted his cravat.

She wanted to say that he didn't know her as much anymore, but it seemed that he did.

The manor was quiet except for the low din of conversation from downstairs.

"I guess it's an Alcott trait. Maybe none of us can lie too effectively." She thought of her mother's many expressions, her little tics that shined a light on the emotions she tried to hide. "Jayne Ella has this tell whenever she's lying or trying to hide something. Her mouth twists to the side and she chews on the inside of her cheek." She told him what she had seen downstairs. "I think we're on the right track with Rachel's death. I think Bertha Mae is lying when she says it was an accident."

Beau searched the walls like he waited for them to react.

She paced over the hardwood floors, the too-tight antique shoes pinching her toes. "There have to be clues. And where is Rachel? I doubt she ever even went swimming."

"Funeral home?" he asked.

"I think funerals were all held in private homes back then." She tried to remember something, anything from all the tintypes she had seen over the years that might help. "Bertha Mae is lot of Jayne Ella. Proud of her children in some ways, jealous in others. I think Bertha Mae hates being a mother, but she likes the attention she gets from having a sick child."

"And now she gets attention from being the mother who lost a child," he said.

Peyton pressed her palm to her forehead. "That must be why she doesn't have the body on display. There must be proof of how she died, a wound of some kind, maybe marks on her neck."

"We have to find her body," Beau said.

"She has to be in the house somewhere." She and Beau searched what rooms they could on the second level. She half expected to find Rachel lying on the bed with her hands folded over her chest.

When they exited the last room and hadn't yet found her, Peyton stood still in the long, narrow hallway. "There's no way to search the main level, not with everyone there."

They stood at the top of the grand staircase and looked down at the empty receiving area. Peyton's nightmares came back to her, the hand reaching up from the stairs, grabbing her and dragging her below ground. Then the sense that someone was screaming. She told Beau about the dream.

"The lowest level, is there an outside door yet?" she asked.

"Not yet. Only access is a door through the hallway."

Beau took a gas lamp from one of the bedrooms. Then they tiptoed down the back steps, past the kitchen, moving quickly toward the basement door. Several visitors who had come to pay their respects were gathered in the foyer, the crowd of people spilling out of the large living room.

Several of them turned when Beau and Peyton were about halfway to the door. Beau took Peyton's arm, threaded it around his and slowed his pace. He nodded in a gentlemanly manner and hid the lantern behind his back. Peyton smiled her most gracious smile. The group eyed them suspiciously in return.

They opened the basement door like that was the most normal thing to do—go to the basement during a funeral.

"Hurry," Peyton said. "Someone is going to come down here now that they've seen us."

The downstairs was dark and dank and the light from the lantern only allowed them to see a few feet ahead. The furniture was simpler than it was upstairs. The rooms were smaller. Peyton had seen the area once before in her normal world, when her sister stayed there, and it had been filled with light. But now she felt oddly unwelcome. The strange scent of raw meat wafted through the rooms.

The rooms were significantly cooler than the upstairs and a chill covered her neck and chest. She held tight to Beau's hand.

Beau held the lantern up to send more light into the space. It cast a dim glow onto empty couches and chairs; a blue and beige rug covered the floor. She checked behind and beneath the furniture. "Nothing in here," Peyton said.

"The grand staircase would be about there." Beau pointed in the lightless direction of the ceiling at the opposite end of the hallway.

She grasped tightly to his arm. One step, then another. If they found Rachel, they might be set free. If they ran into Bertha Mae, they probably wouldn't survive.

"She might have used an ax," Peyton whispered. "Might have cut her head clean off while she was sleeping. Or maybe a gun."

Beau's arm muscles tightened in her grip.

In the back room, a food storage area was packed with bags of grain. Glass jars of jams lined the shelves, slabs of raw meat wrapped in burlap hung from a rack. Blankets covered a table behind the meat. A tripod stood in the corner.

"Shine the light in there," she said.

When she took another step, Beau placed his hand on her arm. "I'll check," he said. He led the way, walked to the blankets and lifted the corner.

Brown hair tied back with a blue ribbon was the first thing Peyton saw. She gasped, lifted a hand to her mouth.

Beau pulled the blanket the rest of the way. Rachel Alcott laid still, her mouth slightly open and eyes closed like she slept. But there was an emptiness to her body that told her Rachel was long gone.

Peyton glanced at the tripod. "She must have made the tintype earlier in the day."

"That stench." Beau pressed the back of his hand to his mouth.

Peyton bent to the floor and held one of Rachel's small, cold hands. White horizontal lines crossed her fingernails. "She was poisoned. Arsenic."

Beau lowered himself to squat beside her. "How do you know?"

She leaned closer to the little girl's mouth, the scent became stronger. "Garlic," she said.

Beau leaned close and sniffed, scrunched his nose.

"The scent was really strong on her breath the first night I saw her. I thought it must have been something she ate. Then she got sick in the kitchen and that smell was really strong, and now, look at this." Peyton showed him Rachel's fingernails.

"In one of my college photography classes we talked about how the photo chemicals used to have arsenic in them. Most chemical formulations had arsenic in them, like paints and so forth. You could even buy arsenic at the chemist. The pharmacy. I think they used it as rat poison. We got into this big discussion about arsenic poisonings in history, how some of it was accidental, some were intentional. The Borgias were partial to arsenic." Peyton tucked the little girl's hand under the blanket. Left her hand on top for a moment.

Beau covered the girl's face.

"Out of curiosity, we started searching the internet for arsenic poisoning symptoms. The strong scent of garlic and white horizontal lines on the nails were two of them."

"So, Bertha Mae did it on purpose," Beau said.

"With that so-called medicine she gave her, I would bet."

The pressure in the room intensified, a contracting that made Peyton feel her organs were being squeezed.

Beau stepped back, grabbed his head.

A crackling noise sounded in the room. They both looked up to the source of the noise and saw the edges of the room turning black, like singed paper.

Beau grabbed Peyton by the arm and they backed away.

"What's happening?" he asked.

"I think we finally found the manor's best-kept secret, and now it's letting go of these memories," she said.

"With us in it?" He guided Peyton toward the stairs. "If this is its last secret, then it should finally allow us to go home, right?"

"It looks like solving Rachel's death was enough to dissolve this world." She watched as bits and pieces of the room tumbled inward and fell away, leaving nothing in its place. "But I'm not sure it was enough to get us home."

They dashed up the stairs, Beau taking them two at a time, pulling Peyton close behind him. They shut the door that led to the basement.

Guests had left the foyer area and the low chattering

noises of party-like conversation drifted from the living room.

Beau pointed to the doorknob that began to twist and melt. The upper corners of the doorway turned black and dissolved.

Peyton's heart seized. "We need to get outside, buy us some time to figure this out."

Hand in hand they ran down the long hallway to the kitchen, stopping short at the wide doorway.

Bertha Mae stood in the middle of the room. Hasseltine stood in the back with her hands folded in front of her. To the side of Bertha Mae was an older, mustached man in a black suit who held her camera and a tripod in his arms.

Peyton knew him at once, had known him since she was a child.

His hair had once been a thick shock of jet black, but now it thinned such that his white scalp shone through the sparse gray strands. His cheeks were sunken, like he hadn't eaten well in years. And his physique had shrunk from lumberjack strong to nearly skeletal.

But it was Horace, nonetheless. Mrs. Miller's husband.

His mouth opened and hung there like he had been struck. Finally, he said, "Peyton?"

Peyton hurried toward the kitchen like a scared rabbit, jumped over the black edge that ran across the end of the hallway. She motioned to Horace to follow them outside, but when she opened the screen door she ran smack into a hard, smooth surface. The outdoors weren't an option. They didn't exist anymore.

Peyton rubbed the sharp pain on her nose and faced Horace. She placed a hand on his black sleeve. "Yes, it's me. We have to go home now."

Bertha Mae grabbed Peyton's arm and stopped her. "He's

the photographer, my dear. Does some of my tintypes for me. Unfortunately, he's going to make a tintype of my beloved girl's funeral. I don't know what I'll do without her." Bertha Mae's mouth tightened like she thought about crying. "Bad things keep happening. I try to be strong." She glanced at Horace and her soft brown eyes returned, like she posed.

"I think we should make a tintype of the kitchen, Horace. We don't have one with the lovely Miss Peyton, do we?"

Horace assembled the tripod and camera without question.

Bertha Mae's expression was the same one Peyton had seen the first night she arrived—a gracious smile, celebrity-quality. Only now Peyton saw it for what it was: manufactured. She gasped slightly at remembering something from that first brief trip to the manor's memories, the first night she saw Beau.

"Maybe Horace knows how to get to the holiday photos where Ruby is?" Beau whispered to Peyton. He raised his eyebrows in question.

"Beau, I think I may know—"

"Come with me while I make you some tea," Bertha Mae interrupted and guided Peyton away from Beau. She jingled a set of keys that hung from her waist. She spooned white powder into the hot water and talked about not knowing how she could live without her daughter, her precious Rachel. She glanced at Horace, watched while he got organized for the next tintype.

Beau looked into the hallway.

Peyton stared at the camera that was aimed in her direction and stepped away.

"I received this camera as a gift from my husband," she

offered. "You know Alcott Manor is going to go down in history. It will be famous for its beauty, for the fact that my husband is a senator. So, I have lots of tintypes made. Even on horrible days like today."

Bertha Mae stood ramrod straight, her smile fading when she watched Peyton back away from her. Her long-sleeved black dress garnished with ruffles did nothing to soften the sharp angles of her mood. She whispered something to Hasseltine.

Peyton sidled up to Horace. "Is Ruby Lee here?"

His forehead turned into a roadmap of worry lines and wrinkles. "She's here?"

Peyton nodded and glanced at Bertha Mae, who poured water into the iron pot. "She's usually in the holiday scenes. I hoped she might be in this tintype today."

"You know how to get us home?" he asked.

"I'm working on it," she whispered.

Bertha Mae served the tea, called Peyton to the table.

Peyton spied Hasseltine in the back corner of the room. She waved a white tea towel at her from behind Bertha Mae's back. She shook her head furiously.

Peyton gave a subtle nod, backed away from the table.

Hasseltine calmed, though her eyes remained wide. She shook her head once more.

"What's the matter, dear? Don't want your tea?" Bertha Mae's tone was syrupy sweet, and yet there was a hardness to the edges. Like she dared Peyton to defy her.

"I'm going to let it cool a little, first," Peyton smiled her most accommodating smile.

Bertha Mae pressed the front of her dress. "Drink up. It will make you feel better."

Peyton thought she remembered Bertha Mae saying

something similar to her daughter when she gave her the oily medicine. "Excuse me, please," she said to Bertha Mae.

She made her way to Beau, who said nothing but pointed down the long hallway. The area slowly folded in on itself, its edges turning dark and crumpling like burnt paper trash. "We have to get out of here," he said. "The whole house is going to go away."

Peyton tapped her hands against the outside of her thighs. "What we do to one side we have to do to the other —" she said distractedly, remembering her yoga teacher's words. "I have an idea."

"What?" Beau slipped his arm around her and pulled her away from the memories that rolled toward them like a giant boulder, destroying everything in its path.

"Maybe we have to achieve some sort of balance in order to get out of here."

"What balance?" Beau's questioning look was wide with panic. "Like justice?"

She stopped. "Maybe justice. I was thinking more about the tintypes. What if getting home has to do with the number of photos that were taken beforehand? Mrs. Miller only made one tintype of me that day and that landed me here. Then I got caught in one here and that got me home, put me back where I started. How many did Mrs. Miller make of you that night?"

"I was drunk," he rubbed his forehead, trying to remember.

"Make a guess, it's important." Peyton waved Horace over.

Time moved too slowly.

The disintegrating memories burned too fast.

She showed Horace the hallway, how the scenes were

dying, and quickly explained why they wanted to figure out how many tintypes they had been in.

Beau's eyes looked past her. "There were five different suits and six or seven tintypes each. So, thirty-five. Maybe more."

"How many tintypes have you been in since you got here?"

He shook his head as if the answer wasn't an easy one. "I've avoided them for the most part. No more than five a year, I'd say."

"So maybe you have five or so left before it evens out," she said. "Hopefully not more than that."

"How many did she make of you this last time?" he asked.

She tried to remember. "Five? Or Seven?" They had been talking during the process and she wore the same outfit. She counted the poses. "Five," she finally said.

"You've been in two tintypes so far, so you have three left. Horace, what about you?"

"Two," he said without reservation. "Two left. I haven't been in that many tintypes, mostly I make them."

A horrible crackling noise sounded from the hallway.

"We have to hurry," Peyton said. "Horace, how quickly can you make more tintypes?"

"A few minutes per piece. Less if I have help with the developing."

"I'll help, I've done developing like this before," she said.

"How does that work with just the three of us? Someone will get left behind."

Peyton knew this. She also knew she would put herself last. If this worked, she wouldn't ask Beau or Horace to endure one more day in this place. Horace didn't look like he would physically survive the time. Beau had figured out how to get fed, but being left behind would push him beyond his mental and emotional limits. "I don't know. Let's just get started. How long do we have in this memory?"

"Not long. Everything shifts soon."

Peyton wondered. When the memory shifted, would there be another one to step into? Or had they all disappeared?

21

J ayne Ella propped her camera phone on the edge of one of the stairs. The lens pointed toward the floor at an angle so she could record the entire process. When she finally broke through the flooring and the cement, she wanted the camera to see Austin's watch. She needed that recorded proof.

She'd called the security company and told them she was hosting a private gathering at the manor, that the cameras would be off for the evening. Then she unplugged each of the cameras. They made her sign a paper relieving them of any liability. If the board found out she did that, she would have a hard time explaining her actions.

Talking the police out of patrolling the manor for the night had taken more doing. She was pretty sure she raised too much suspicion by her insistence that they not show up tonight. But it had to be done. She'd lied and told them she was hosting a small gathering, that some politicians were in attendance and they didn't want to be seen. The police finally agreed, albeit reluctantly.

Using four metal ladders, she created a partial dome

with extra long sheets of plastic. If she set it up right, the plastic would catch all of the wood and cement dust that would fly once the buzz saw began. She'd never used a buzz saw before and the man at the hardware store cautioned her, saying it was dangerous. "Knew a man once who lost control of the dang thing and sawed his foot right off. I recommend you hire someone to do whatever it is you need done."

She would have hired someone, but she couldn't have anyone knowing about the gold. She didn't need another Mrs. Miller in her life, blackmailing her for yet something else that she shouldn't have done, or worse, turning her into the police. Or maybe even taking the gold for themselves. She picked up a pair of heavy-duty steel-toe work boots, instead.

She unfolded a king-sized plastic sheet and placed it over the surrounding area. She checked her watch. She had no idea where Peyton was but she would wring her neck when she found her. Taking off like that and leaving her to manage the bankers on her own, it was unthinkable.

Jayne Ella shook the folds out of another sheet. Now that she thought about it, she needed Peyton gone tonight anyway. Jayne Ella had managed to get rid of all the volunteers for the night by giving them much needed time off.

She got Mrs. Miller to leave by telling her that she had just remembered a box of tintypes she had in a storage unit where some other Alcott belongings were held. Mrs. Miller loved those old photographs. She had kept them at the museum for months after Jayne Ella insisted they be moved to the manor.

The only wrinkle in the plan was Ira. Peyton's absence was driving him insane. As well it would any man. He had told her Peyton postponed the wedding, that she needed time to think things through. But he hoped to talk with her again. He checked in three times a day, wanting to know where Peyton was. He didn't say it aloud, but she knew he thought she had left him. Bailed on their engagement.

"I've sent her on errands," she told him when she found him on the back porch looking in windows. "She's meeting with our financiers," she said another time when he knocked on the front door.

For all she knew Peyton had gone for one last fling. Jayne Ella had been worried that Peyton was going to screw this one up. Too many memories of Beau. She didn't think her girl ever completely got over that boy. Now Peyton wasn't answering her phone or texts or email.

Jayne Ella refused to cancel the ceremony. She would find a stand-in and have the photographers make good use of the flowers, the tent, the chairs. Someone Peyton's size. Someone who could wear her wedding dress.

She wouldn't let Peyton ruin the perfect publicity opportunity. She tucked her hair into a black knit hat and slipped on a pair of safety glasses. Checked her watch. Five o'clock. If she worked nonstop, she could get through the layers of flooring and relocate all of the gold well before morning. Problem was, she wasn't one hundred percent certain where they had left the gold. Not precisely, anyway.

The great hall was a large space and if she were a few feet off here or there, she would have to keep cutting to find what she needed. That meant there would be a gaping hole in the floor, she couldn't worry about that. Keeping her back to the camera, she plugged in the round saw and turned on the power.

22

Like an earthquake, the manor's memories shifted and with such an abrupt force that Peyton lost her balance. She fell to the ground, her face hitting the cold tile floor. The cavernous black line slid toward her. She struggled to get to her feet and her heart jackhammered.

The camera slipped from Horace's grasp and tumbled toward the floor.

"Stay with us!" she shouted to Horace. "Hang on to the camera!" The kitchen walls shifted, their shape and definition morphing into different colors, a different scene. Beau slid his arm around her waist, helped lift her over and on to the other side.

Everything stopped.

They had arrived in the living room, the large area at the front of the house with two fireplaces and three sitting areas. Peyton looked toward the foyer. It was missing. Not empty, but gone. In its place was a beige nothingness, a blank screen.

"Have to find Ruby." Horace's voice was raspy and harsh. A white substance had gathered at the corners of his mouth.

He leaned on a nearby chair, lifted himself upright. He smoothed his gray hair to the side, ran a hand over his tired, drawn face.

Peyton wanted to help him, she wanted to ask Hasseltine to get him water and a meal. But there was no time. "Where's the camera?"

Beau pointed across the room. Bertha Mae stood at the head of the table that held flowers in vases and tintypes of Rachel. She finger-combed a long, thick lock of her daughter's brown hair, tied with a blue silk ribbon. The camera sat on its tripod, aimed at the display.

Bertha Mae placed the hair on the table, walked behind the camera and hovered low, like she tried to see what the lens would see.

"Not exactly the grieving mother," Beau said.

"We have to get that camera away from her, and get our tintypes made. We need to stay close together so we don't get separated." She tried to exhale relief that the camera hadn't been destroyed. But Bertha Mae's presence took all the oxygen from the room. Her softest expression, the one she saved for the camera, was gone. In its place was the hard shell that let nothing and no one inside.

Like she knew she was being watched, Bertha Mae jerked upright. "What are you two doing in here?"

"I'm here to help, ma'am." Horace limped toward her with practiced servitude, unmoved by her sharp tone. "Find Ruby," he whispered to Peyton.

She looked in the kitchen and found Hasseltine but no one else. There weren't any other rooms, and at the far end of the living room, the corners turned black and curled inward. This room was disappearing, too.

Peyton leaned close to Beau. "Ruby's not here and the other tintypes might not exist anymore. I don't want to leave her behind, but we have to go. We don't have a choice. I'll distract Bertha Mae for as long as I can. You and Horace take the camera, start making tintypes of each other."

"What about you?"

"You and Horace go first. He knows how to develop the tintypes, and you have more to do than any of us."

"I'm not leaving without you." Beau clasped his hand around hers and squeezed. "I won't lose you again."

She squeezed his hand in return. "Don't worry."

Peyton walked toward Bertha Mae like she approached a client. Someone whose image was a wreck.

Peyton remembered her grandmother's words. "The truth shall set you free, sweetheart. Confess it, stand on it, cling to it. It will always give you a way forward."

It was the first step with any client. Get them to tell the truth about what they'd done. Once she had their honesty, once she knew the real story, she had a chance at creating something new. She wondered if the manor needed Bertha Mae's honesty to help pave their way home.

Bertha Mae appeared as Peyton had always pictured her —an ideal representation of a loving mother, a gracious hostess, an esteemed senator's wife. Her hair was perfectly coiffed, with soft, brown, spiral curls that tumbled in the back. Two smudges of pink color dotted her cheeks, like she'd grabbed both of them at the same angle with a firm pinch. A single strand of pearls glistened at the neck of her frilled black collar.

"May I see you for a brief moment, Mrs. Alcott?" Peyton asked.

Bertha Mae quickly affixed her smile. "Horace, take care of making this tintype, please. I've already made one of the room, so I only need the display. This is the most precious one you'll ever make."

"I'll take care of it, ma'am." Horace took the camera under his arm, hope and fear in his eyes.

Peyton followed Bertha Mae to the far end of the room. She stood directly across from Bertha Mae and watched Horace carry the camera to the other side of the room.

Bertha Mae exhaled heavily, her floral perfume only thinly masking her sour breath. She talked about the service, the guests and the house. Peyton encouraged the conversation. The more time she wasted, the more time Beau and Horace had to use the camera.

"Now, what is it you need, dear?"

Peyton commented on Bertha Mae's composure, the elegant appearance of the manor, how sorry she was about Rachel's passing. Bertha Mae patted Peyton on the arm and turned to walk away. It was clear that she wasn't going to talk any further. Peyton screwed up her courage and said, "I saw Rachel's body in the basement."

Bertha Mae stilled herself mid-step. There was a subtle shift in her eyes, turning the soft brown to something mean and hard.

"That's a cruel thing to say to a mother who just lost her child," Bertha Mae said. "I think you should leave."

"I would love nothing more than to leave. But I think you need to tell the truth first about what you did. Just to me," she whispered. "No one else."

Peyton recognized the flicker of temptation in Bertha Mae's eyes. Every client she'd known so far showed the same sign at this moment of opportunity. The chance to release the secret.

Peyton leaned forward just slightly and whispered, "It will set you free. It could set all of us free."

Bertha Mae's mouth opened, her bottom lip quivered. The rest of her body was still.

It was coming. Peyton felt it in the hush between them. That moment before the secrets spilled, before the opening of one's conscience. A delicate, tranquil moment. An almost holy connection, that moment of confession.

Peyton breathed it in, tilted her head up. It would happen now, Bertha Mae would tell what she had done and how. She would cleanse her soul, the manor would release its tortured past, and she and Horace and Beau would return home.

Bit by bit the moment faded. The confession didn't come.

Peyton felt her world slipping away and she wasn't about to let that happen. "Mrs. Alcott. Tell me what really happened to Rachel. You and I both know she didn't drown."

Bertha Mae didn't move. Her mouth became thin and small and mean, like she sealed the secrets inside of herself.

"From the first moment I met Rachel there was a noticeable scent of garlic on her breath and skin, like an aura. A scent of garlic that strong, that often, it's a sign of arsenic poisoning." Peyton was leaning so close to Bertha Mae she nearly tipped forward. If she didn't confess soon Peyton was prepared to circle her ancestor's neck with her hands and choke it out of her.

She tried not to look at Beau and Horace. She didn't want to draw Bertha Mae's attention to them. She prayed they made progress with the tintypes.

Bertha Mae's eyes narrowed. "Are you accusing me of—"

"You put arsenic in that oil you gave her, didn't you? You poured poison onto a spoon and shoved it in her mouth."

"Rachel has always had that scent on her breath. It was the medicine. Not me." Hatred bled through Bertha Mae's words, she turned toward the window and crossed her arms.

Peyton's eyes shifted to the corner where Horace made another tintype of Beau. Horace stood beneath the cover of the portable dark room, developed the tintype quickly, carelessly. Chemicals splashed onto the floor.

"Why is her body lying in the basement when you've told everyone that she was lost in the ocean?"

"I'm a senator's wife." Bertha Mae spun around, and spat the words at Peyton.

That's when Peyton knew. There was no justice to be had here. She couldn't change Bertha Mae. Or what happened to Rachel, or whatever had happened to herself when she had been captive in the manor when she was ten.

She couldn't change a memory. She couldn't change another person. She could only embrace the truth.

Horace stood in front of Bertha Mae's camera now. Beau removed the cap, then, after a few seconds, replaced it. Horace went beneath the cover, she knew, to apply the chemicals to develop the image. She squeezed her hands into fists, this had to work.

Bertha Mae leaned toward Peyton, pointed her thin finger close to her face. "If you won't leave, I'll have you thrown out."

Peyton looked up and toward the end of the room that was curling, rolling toward them, eating everything in its path. "I don't think it's your house anymore," she said.

Bertha Mae cocked her head, confused. She eyed Peyton from top to bottom in a way that made Peyton's blood turn to ice. She opened her mouth to speak but looked toward Horace and Beau instead.

"What are you doing with my camera?!" Bertha Mae shouted to Horace.

Peyton gasped.

"Making a few tintypes of the room, ma'am." Horace's voice broke.

"I told you I only wanted the display." Bertha Mae stormed in his direction.

Peyton chased after her, tried to get in her path. Bertha Mae pushed her aside with surprising strength.

Bertha Mae snatched a tintype away from him. "What are these? You? Oh! This is a waste of material!" She tucked the camera into her arms like a baby. Walked it into the kitchen.

Horace groaned and grabbed his stomach.

Peyton remembered there hadn't been much time between the tintype she had been caught in and the first time she went back. She also remembered the stomach pain.

Beau grabbed his stomach, fell to his knees. He reached out to her and she kneeled beside him. "We needed fewer tintypes than we thought. Get the camera from her!" He reached after Bertha Mae.

Horace disappeared in a slow fade.

Beau's solid strength dissolved beneath her touch.

She sat alone on what was left of the living room floor, inched her way back to the doorway that led to the kitchen. The room crumpled in on itself, the manor's collected memories from that day were being crushed. They were about six feet away from her and getting closer.

23

Clouds of cement dust billowed inside the plastic tent. Jayne Ella turned off the circular saw. The last chunk of cement landed in the hole with a dull thud.

The entire process had taken too long. Her first few attempts at breaking through had not been the right location. She was on her fourth attempt and had carved a hole that was far bigger than what she originally planned. She waved at the tiny particles that flooded the air.

She should have been excited to see the gold again, but she wasn't. For some reason that she couldn't explain, she felt uncomfortable. Dread, even. Sick. Chills coated her arms. Fear swirled around her, the same fright she usually felt in this area of the manor.

She took off the dirt-covered protective glasses. She looked in the hole. Her heart dropped. It took only a few seconds for her to put all the pieces together, and she knew what he had done.

"Oh, Austin. *No.*"

The powdery dust irritated her eyes. She rubbed them,

forgetting that dust and grit covered her fingers. The dirt hit her contacts. She squeezed her eyes shut, stepped away from the hole. She lost her footing, fell back. Her tailbone cracked against something hard and she screamed.

Salty tears and dust clouded her contact lenses, made her blind. She tried to open her eyes and couldn't, grit effectively sealing the lids. She tasted the ground layers of Alcott Manor in her mouth. Her ears rang to the tune of the buzz saw, and she was in so much pain. She thought she had broken her tailbone.

She didn't know what time it was, but she had seen bits of early morning light through the heavy red curtains. The cameras would be back on soon. Mrs. Miller and the volunteers would be in before long. She needed to call them and tell them not to come.

She wished the hardware store clerk had suggested earplugs, she wished she had been more careful. She wished she'd never let Austin talk her into moving the gold to the manor in the first place.

Crawling on all fours, she navigated her way around the hole, trying not to imagine herself falling in and landing on the saw that was somewhere down below. Her face hit one side of the plastic and she lifted it over her, walked to the outside of the tent. She stood. "Ow!" She pressed her hand against her backside.

Tears poured down her face. Eyes shut and arms extended, she shuffled and fumbled her way to the kitchen. She pulled eye drops from her purse and squirted the liquid into each eye. No use. The pain was unbearable. She pulled the lenses from her eyes and flicked them. More eyedrops to flush out the dirt.

Her glasses were four prescriptions too old, their thickness kept her from wearing them in public. She was a vain woman, she made no apologies for that. But she carried them in her purse just in case. She couldn't see past the end of her nose without corrective lenses. She wiped the mascara and eyeliner from her eyes and cheeks with a damp paper towel.

A rapping on the back door sent her heart to her throat.

"It's me." Ira waved from the back porch.

She pressed her hand to her chest, tried to steady her heart rate.

"It's just me." His dark hair was a windblown mess, and his eyes were bleary like he hadn't yet slept in days.

Jayne Ella smoothed her hair, feeling dry dust and tiny chips of wood and cement. She unlocked and opened the back door. "Well, Ira? What are you doing here at this hour?" She kept her tone nonchalant.

"I couldn't sleep so I went for a walk. Saw the lights on and I thought Peyton might have come back. Everything okay?" He waved a finger at the area beneath her eyes. "You look like you've been crying."

"Oh. Eye drops smudged my makeup is all." She wiped at her cheeks with the paper towel again.

"Is she here?" He walked toward the great hall.

Jayne Ella quickly limped in front of him, placed her hands on his chest and stopped him just past the doorway. "I've got some construction going on in there, I wouldn't want you to get hurt. And Peyton's not here, sweetheart. I think she went home to get some rest. Her childhood home. My home. She probably didn't want to wake you. She'll be up in a few hours, you can see her then." Jayne Ella encouraged him to move out of the house quickly, but he walked slowly, mesmerized by the towering display of plastic sheeting.

"You've seen her? You've talked with her? Was she here?"

he looked around the room, pushed ahead, removing Jayne Ella's hands from his chest in the process.

"I think she's in and out, honey. Why don't you get some rest and we'll meet for lunch. Okay? You look tired." She headed him off again, tried to turn him toward the kitchen, but he was stronger than he appeared.

Ira gestured to the ladders and the giant sheets of plastic. "You know, if she changes her mind, the wedding could still be tomorrow, and the reception guests are expecting to have full access to the manor. Can this be fixed in time?"

Jayne Ella stopped. Chills crawled across her back and down her arms. A slight breeze blew, like someone passed by.

Ira didn't look at Jayne Ella. But his eyes searched the rest of the area. He crossed his arms, uncomfortable. He must have sensed it, too.

There was the feeling that they weren't alone in the room, that someone was circling them, saying things, yelling, maybe, in a way that was felt and not heard.

Jayne Ella wanted to tell it to leave, but there was no way to do that and sound sane. "Honey, I don't even know what's going through Peyton's head right now—"

The screen door squeaked and slammed.

"Peyton?" Ira called.

"Jayne Ella?" a voice called from the kitchen.

She turned and saw Austin coming toward her like the lead bull in a stampede. His rumpled navy blue golf shirt and wrinkled khakis told her he'd dashed out of the house quickly. She knew he must have grabbed yesterday's outfit off of the chair in his custom-made cherry closet, shoved his bare feet into boat shoes and sped to the manor.

He stopped short, his eyes narrowed at the ladders, the plastic sheets, and the white dust scattered on the hardwoods. He turned to her. Fury and paranoia glimmering in his eye, his face a mottled red and tan. All of her leaned away from him, even her vital organs seemed to cower.

He pointed a finger in her direction. "I knew you were going to pull something like this. I knew it. Told myself you weren't that stupid to do this behind my back—Who the heck are you?" Austin pointed at Ira.

Ira's chest swelled and he stepped toward Austin like he welcomed the fight. "Dr. Ira Byrne. Who are you?"

"This is Peyton's fiancé and he doesn't know anything about the—" Jayne Ella nodded toward the area where they had buried the gold. "Repairs I worked on last night." She placed a hand on Austin's chest and backed him a step away from where Ira stood.

Austin resisted.

"He's not involved," she whispered.

"Is he bothering you?" Ira asked Jayne Ella.

"No, honey. You go on. I'll call you in a few hours. Alright?"

Ira reluctantly stepped away, eyeing Austin like the unwelcome guest he was.

Austin studied her with a side-eye stare, sharp and mean.

Another noise, like chairs crashing to the floor in the dining room. Low voices this time. Male voices.

She gave Ira a little push and a pat and shut the door behind him.

She didn't stop to wonder if the noises in the house were burglars or volunteers that had snuck into the house. She didn't care who they were. She just didn't want anyone near the hole in the floor. But when she rounded the grand staircase she found Austin with a gun drawn and heading for the dining room.

"What are you doing?" she shout-whispered, hobbled after him.

He pointed toward the dining room. "You brought in help to do this, didn't you? They know, right?"

"Put that thing away before you hurt somebody!" she said.

Austin walked toward the dining room, arms extended, his gun leading the way.

Two people walked toward them, two men that she thought were long gone and dead.

Beau Spencer and Horace Miller extended their hands in front like they could stop bullets.

Austin gasped.

He stared at his son for a long moment, unbelieving.

"Beau?" he asked.

Beau nodded.

Austin dropped the gun, it clattered on the hardwood floor.

The two men held one another.

Father and son.

Austin wailed like a baby.

Jayne Ella pressed both hands to her chest.

"Where have you been?" Austin finally asked. He held him at arm's length. "And what are you wearing?"

"I don't even know how to explain."

Jayne Ella guided Horace away from the hole in the floor. No one else should know. Definitely not Horace because then Mrs. Miller would know.

"Horace?" Jayne Ella asked gently. "Where did you come from, honey? Where have you been?"

His head shook, maybe not intentionally.

Glass shattered in a loud crash. Everyone gasped. Horace grabbed his chest.

"Horace!" Mrs. Miller stood in the doorway with a collection of broken tintypes around her feet. Her two bony hands barely covering her open mouth. Her eyes filled with tears. "My Horace!"

They staggered toward one another with outstretched arms.

All Jayne Ella could think was that this was bad. So very bad. Too many of the wrong people in this area.

She waved her arms to Austin, gesturing for him to help move everyone out of the area.

He gave her a wide-eyed stare, the sudden return of his son was too much to comprehend. She waved her hands wildly, pointed to the hole she'd made in the floor. He snapped into action.

"Everyone, let's step into the kitchen. Get something to eat and talk. I want to know everything." Austin had his professional voice on. The one he used when he needed to coax someone into doing something.

"Beau—" Peyton stood at the entry to the dining room, her face flushed, her hair falling around her shoulders. She appeared fresh from a dream.

"Peyton!" Beau left his father's side and gathered her in his arms. He twirled her, held her close, kissed and kissed and kissed her until even Jayne Ella found tears on her cheeks.

"How did you get back?" he whispered.

She smiled, touched his face. "Hasseltine helped me."

"Peyton?" A voice called from across the room.

Beau released her, held her hand to his chest.

"Ira," Peyton said.

Ira Byrne stood at the doorway.

"It's—not what it looks like."

"You were kissing him."

Peyton looked at Beau and released his hand.

"Ira," Peyton said.

"Who is this?"

She squeezed her eyes shut, opened them a moment later. "This is Beau."

"*This* is Beau?

She nodded.

"The one who got away? That Beau?"

Jayne Ella remained still. Ira was more perceptive than she had given him credit.

"Have you been with *him* for the last two days?"

Peyton was quiet. She visibly swallowed hard.

Whatever her daughter had done while she had been gone, Jayne Ella could tell it was something she couldn't talk about. Not publicly.

Peyton walked to him, glanced at the ladders and plastic and the hole in the floor.

"I've been worried sick about you. And this is what you've been doing?" Ira's tone was sharp and condemning. His brown eyes were searing, searching her face.

Jayne Ella knew he questioned the promises that had been so certain and sure between them just a few days ago.. She knew what it was like to discover that the love of your life had left you for someone else. She looked at Austin.

His head turned from Beau to Peyton and then to his son again.

"Beau," he said. "We need to leave. Everyone, needs to leave."

"No, Dad," Beau said.

"I don't know what this is about." Ira gestured to Beau. "But he's your past, you realize that, right? This thing, this fling—"

Jayne Ella kept moving toward the hole she'd cut in the

floor, trying to block everyone's view. "Y'all need to take this outside. I have to finish these repairs. Plumbing issues are no small concern. Especially in a house this old. I have a wedding to host tomorrow—"

She glanced at Beau. The fierce look on his face was like a punch. It made her close her mouth.

"What do you mean you couldn't find her?" Mrs. Miller shouted to her husband. She tugged at her hair. "I saw her! She's there!"

Horace Miller tried to hold his wife but she pulled away from him. "I'm sorry. I'm sorry!" his voice choked with tears.

Mrs. Miller grabbed him by the lapels of his jacket. "You have to go back. You have to get her and bring her back. You were so close! Maybe only one or two tintypes away from her!" Her voice screeched.

What little life Horace had left seemed to drain from his body. "I can't go back, Martha." His eyes rolled back, his head lolled.

Jayne Ella ran to him, reached for his arm.

She missed.

Horace passed out, fell hard against the plastic sheeting that Jayne Ella had so carefully hung on the ladders. The plastic veil came down, as did two of the thirteen-foot ladders. They crashed with an unbearable echo in the great hall.

PEYTON RAN TO HELP. She and Beau and Ira pulled at the plastic to unravel Horace from his cocoon.

Mrs. Miller screamed.

She screamed once when her husband fell—a short

piercing noise that was mostly her husband's name. "Horace!"

But when she saw what lay hidden in the hole in the floor, she screamed long and hard. A deep, soul-wrenching wail.

Peyton had not seen that matching floral top and pants outfit in twenty years, but when she saw it on the skeletal remains buried in the depths of Alcott Manor, she recognized it immediately. The sleeves had ruffles at the shoulders and the pants were slim fitting. Light from the overhead chandelier caught the diamond pendant Ruby wore on the end of her necklace, the one she was so proud of, the one her father had given her.

Mrs. Miller's third scream was cut short by a low groan. She winced like she was in excruciating pain. She grabbed her chest, and toppled forward.

Peyton and Ira reached for her, tried to hold her up.

But she was dead weight.

24

P eyton fell forward when Mrs. Miller did and she lost her balance. She landed hard on the sawed, raggedy edge of the opening and a sharp piece of wood poked her belly. She screamed.

"Peyton!" her mother yelled.

She called her name in the same way she used to when Peyton lived at home. When Peyton was a child.

The sound of Jayne Ella's voice had an upward pitch at the end, like a hook. It pierced a memory deep inside of her.

It was buried deep in her subconscious. Dark and slippery.

But her mother's voice hooked it clean through, and dislodged it from its hiding place.

Peyton's world fell dark. Her breath came fast.

"Peyton!" She heard Beau call her name and felt his arms around her, catching her.

He carried her to the bottom of the grand staircase. A dark circle of blood spread across the front of her dress. It wasn't the first time.

Beau's arms wrapped around her and gave her a sense of safety.

Her fractured memory floated together like pieces of a forgotten puzzle.

She looked across the hallway, remembered Ruby twirling in the red dress that was too big for her, Mrs. Miller making the tintype. Much later, riding in the pillowy backseat of a car that Peyton didn't recognize, her dress still clean and white, feeling so sleepy in the dark. The windows were low, the scent of jasmine so heavy she could taste it on her tongue.

A man drove—she thought it was her father. He extended his arm around Jayne Ella, who leaned close to him. His watch had a dark blue face and diamonds that sparkled in the low light—not her father. Beau's father. She knew that sparkly watch.

The car stopped at her mother's salon. Jayne Ella opened the back door, gave her a kiss good-night, and explained that Mr. Spencer would drive her home. She told Peyton to go straight to bed, she said she would be home soon.

The car moved again, and for a long while. The dark and the motion made her drowsy.

Tires squealed.

Something heavy hit the windshield.

Peyton screamed.

They must have hit a dog or a deer.

That's what Mr. Spencer said.

He made her sit still in the backseat, made her promise not to move.

When the back door opened, Peyton braced herself to see the hurt dog. He must have been a big animal to have made such a loud noise. Mr. Spencer leaned in and, to her horror, placed the wounded, bloody dog in the back seat next to her.

Except it wasn't a dog at all.

It was Ruby Lee.

Blood covered her face and the floral print top with the ruffles.

Austin Spencer drove the car. He turned right too quickly.

Ruby fell onto Peyton.

She tried to scream, but the noise lodged in her chest, held there by the horror of it all.

Her mouth open, her body shaking.

Ruby's blood soaking into Peyton's white dress.

Next, she sat on the bottom step of the grand staircase. The sickly sweet stench of blood on her dress turned her stomach, the gelatinous feel between her fingers and its stain on her skin made her vomit. Mr. Spencer, covered in dirt and sweat, shook his finger in her face. Made her promise not to tell. "You wouldn't want your mother to get in trouble, would you? That's exactly what will happen if you say anything. So, we're going to pretend this never happened."

Peyton wrapped her arms around herself. She decided it was best if no one found out what had happened that night. Her father was leaving, he had told her that just a few days ago. She needed her mother to stay and take care of her and her sister. She would do better than not telling. She would make herself forget.

Numbness filtered into her brain like static, and she let it happen. Everything she had seen that night was too much to think about, anyway. Too frightening to remember.

The room came back into clear focus. Peyton blinked. Beau was at her side. Her mother knelt at her feet. Ira talked on his cell phone and hovered over Horace, who was coming around.

She turned to Beau. "It was your dad. He hit Ruby Lee with his car after the bank party that was here that night."

Jayne Ella shook her head like she didn't remember. "What bank par—" Her lips closed into a seal.

Beau rose slowly, started across the room.

Austin stood in the dirt pit, the Miller family grave, plastic sheeting fallen behind him, one arm full of gold bars.

Mrs. Miller lay belly first in the dirt. Her arm stretched over the diminutive skeleton.

"Dad. Stop," Beau said.

Austin raised one finger as if Beau made a wrong assumption. "It was an accident, son."

Beau shook his head, walked closer to his father.

"She was walking on the side of the road in the pitch black dark, no one could have seen her!"

Austin climbed out of the hole, his forehead dotted with sweat in the cool air. One of the gold bars slipped from his arms and clanged on the hard floor. He stooped to pick it up. "I didn't mean to do it—"

Austin moved toward the kitchen door. "It could have happened to anyone!"

Beau followed his father, his steps deliberate. He pointed to Mrs. Miller's body in the hole. "You should have admitted what you did. Then Mrs. Miller wouldn't have blamed Peyton for Ruby's disappearance and she wouldn't have sent me away."

Austin shook his head, continued backing to the door. "Mrs. Miller sent you away?"

Jayne Ella and Peyton stood to the side and slightly behind Beau.

Ira spoke in a low voice on what sounded like a 911 call.

Austin looked at Ira. He nodded to Jayne Ella. "You'd better put a stop to this. Because if I go down, you're going with me."

Jayne Ella looked at the bodies and the gold in the hole, then she turned her attention back to Austin. She slipped her arm around Peyton's waist, slowly shook her head. "No, Austin."

Austin stared at his son for a long moment, his eyes wide and panicked. He turned and ran.

Beau was no more than one second behind him.

Peyton and Jayne Ella followed.

When they found them, Austin was face down on the sidewalk, Beau held him down.

Gold bars were scattered beside the two of them.

Police and ambulance sirens screamed in the distance.

25

Peyton tilted her face to the sun and drank the heat into her skin. She dug her bare toes into the sand and listened closely to the music of the waves pounding the beach.

"Thought I'd never make it back here again," Beau said.

He wore his 1850s white shirt, unbuttoned, and suit pants, rolled up at the ankles. The jacket, tie, socks and shoes were inside the manor someplace.

His hand rested on hers, and he gave it a gentle squeeze.

Time seemed to slow with him there, as if every wave, every noise were being noticed, captured by the photographer's eye. She wanted to hear him sing, hear him play his guitar, hear his thoughts on all things big and small.

He released her hand. "Where's Ira?"

Her heart sank.

Last thing she wanted to do was discuss one man with the other. "He went back to his condo to change clothes and make some calls. I think he doesn't quite know what to make of all this." She opened her eyes and found Beau looking at her. "I don't know what to make of all of this. I know that I've really hurt him."

His lips flattened into a line. He turned toward the ocean.

She couldn't read his thoughts. She couldn't predict what he would say next.

He might have been wondering about Horace and how he was faring at the hospital. Or he might have been thinking about his father and what was next for him. He probably never expected to see his father led away in hand-cuffs by police, screaming all the while at the top of his lungs.

Peyton didn't turn around but she knew the yellow police tape was still around the manor, flapping in the gentle breeze. Because of the gold and Ruby Lee, police and investigators would be in and out for some time.

Jayne Ella spent the morning talking with the investigators. She had also called her attorney to be present. Before they arrived and before Austin was carted away, Peyton watched Jayne Ella climb in the hole she had dug. She ran her fingers through her hair and then she touched several bars of the gold. She picked up the saw and touched the plastic and the ladders. She appeared to be leaving traces of herself everywhere she could.

Peyton assumed this was to ruin any evidence she might have left behind years before. Any fingerprints or hair or fibers found could be attributed to the fact that Jayne Ella was in the hole today. She could claim that she just didn't stop and think that she might contaminate any evidence at the scene.

Peyton didn't know to what extent Jayne Ella was involved with Ruby Lee's death or the theft of the gold. To the best of her ability she would find out.

But she knew two things for certain.

One, the past could not be changed.

And two, the manor would remember whatever had happened.

Beau might also have been thinking about her and what their future held, if anything.

"What's up with your plans for today?" He thumbed toward the rows of white chairs and the reception tent.

"Ira and Jayne Ella called everyone a few days ago, told them I was sick, I think." She tried to make a smile.

He winced.

A wave built in height and crashed hard. Seagulls squawked and fluttered into the air like they were angry at the interruption.

"Everything got so messed up for us," she said.

He nodded slowly. "Thanks to my dad. And Mrs. Miller. But I think we proved to one another that we're not over."

She faced the ocean, her stomach queasy.

No matter the move she made, hearts would be broken. Including hers. There were no easy answers. "I still have things to work out. I made a commitment to Ira and here at the eleventh hour he discovers that I've betrayed that. And you don't know me anymore, Beau. I had to completely reinvent my life when you left."

"I know that I love you. And I think you still love me."

Her eyes burned with tears.

"You, your love, that's the only thing that kept me going all these years. It's the only thing that kept me fighting to get home."

"I've built an entire life without you, Beau. I have a future laid out. I have a home you've never even seen. I have another family that is waiting to welcome me into their lives forever." She stood, brushed the sand from her black leggings. "I have a career now, one that I really enjoy. You don't know that side of me, and work is a big part of my life."

"Okay. Okay." He ran his hand over his jaw, stood and faced her. "What do you want, Peyton?"

After a moment, she realized her mouth was open and she closed it. She had been so tied up with trying to figure out what she should do that she hadn't really asked herself that question.

"Honestly?"

"Yeah. Honestly. I'm not going to talk you into being with me."

"I don't know where I belong," she said. "That's as honest as I can get right now. Last week my entire life was planned out. I knew who my mother was, what this manor was about. My career was set. My future was set. Now everything has changed. My family could lose the manor. Your father has literally been hiding a dead body under the floorboards for the last twenty years, my wedding plans have been disrupted by the man I was supposed to spend the rest of my life with, the man I thought I would never see again."

"And that means?" He reached for her, and she stepped away.

"What if you get settled here and you realize that whatever you felt for me isn't there anymore?" she asked.

"I know what I feel for you. That's never changed."

"You don't know that."

"I do know that, actually. Let me ask you something. If you married Ira, could you honestly say that you would never look back? That I would just be some distant memory? Because if you could, then you should marry him. You should go on with your life the way you planned it without me, and I would wish you well. But if you meant what you told me when we were in the barn last night, that this wasn't over for you, then you can't marry him."

Beau pulled a small leather book from his back pocket. Tattered and worn. He handed it to her. "This is the book I told you about, the one I wrote in until you arrived. There's an entry for almost every day. Sometimes just a sentence. Sometimes a paragraph. I was going to give it to you sooner, but there wasn't really a chance."

Peyton held the book, afraid to open it for fear that the memories Beau had documented might swallow her whole.

The wind ruffled his blond hair, his blue eyes sparkled in the morning light. An openness, a softness that she thought was a new wrinkle to his personality. It emanated from him like a fragrance.

"Whatever you choose, whoever you choose, I want you to know that I've never stopped loving you. You're right about one thing. I don't entirely know who you are, but I hope I get the chance to know who you've grown into. Because I know that on the inside, you're the same beautiful girl I fell in love with over twenty years ago.

"I've had a lot of time to think about you and us, what we had and what we might have again. Although I don't know much about your career or your life in Boston, I do know one thing. I never tried to hem you in when we were together. The life we had planned was what we both wanted at the time. If you had said that you wanted something else, you know I would have supported that," he said.

She shook her head. "Beau. You've been cooped up in a tiny space for years. Before you left, you wanted to travel the world more than anything else because the whole town was too small for you. You can't tell me that you're not itching to leave and never come back."

"I've changed, Pey, and I've grown up. I wouldn't want to

leave you for any reason. Not travel or work or anything else." He looked out at the ocean, ran his fingers through his hair. "I have been gone for a long time. But the simple freedoms I'm about to enjoy are pretty sweet. I'm about to get in my dad's car, drive down the road and nothing is going to stop me. Least of all some stupid tintype." He chuckled. "Heck, just walking across the floor without fear of falling through a crack is reason enough to celebrate. My point is that I'm happy with a lot less than I was before." He held the side of her face with his hand, stroked her cheek with his thumb. "I'm just grateful.

"So, promise me this, Pey. Whatever you decide, don't make this about me and what you think I want. Or what anyone else wants. This is about you and deciding what's right for you. If you don't get that figured out, you're never going to be happy. No matter which direction you choose."

He kissed her.

He pulled away. His eyes remained closed for a moment. Like it was a final kiss.

A dark-haired man caught her attention and he walked toward them—more police, she suspected. Bad timing.

As he got closer she recognized that it was Ira.

He was wearing sunglasses she'd never seen before and clothes she didn't recognize.

He had showered and changed. His hair was wet and combed close to his head. It had been a quick shower, she guessed. The kind he took after surgery and when he had somewhere else to be.

"I'll leave y'all to talk," Beau said with a slight wave.

Ira took off his sunglasses. His eyes were red and bleary, like he hadn't slept in a while.

When Beau was well in the distance, Ira nodded to him. "Where has he been all this time?"

"It's a long story," she said.

"What, he was kidnapped or something?" He shoved his hands in his pockets, perhaps for comfort, never taking his eyes off of her.

"Kind of. Yes."

He stopped. "Actually?"

"It's a bizarre story."

They faced the water, their wedding site behind them. Too many things not being said.

"Shall we go inside and talk?" he asked.

"I've been cooped up in there too much lately. Fresh air is probably a better idea."

"How about we walk on the beach, then?"

They walked to the right, away from the white tent and the rows of folding chairs. Fat clouds the color of ash gathered overhead. She thought of running through the rain with Beau and the night they spent in the horse barn that wasn't there anymore. Guilt flooded her insides and her stomach staged a rebellion. She pressed her hand to her abdomen.

"Stomach okay, where you got scratched?"

"Yeah. I bandaged it." She stopped and took him by the hand. "Listen, you need to know—"

He shook his head and placed two fingers over her lips. "Don't." He swallowed hard. "Just—whatever it is, don't. I've given this a lot of thought over the last couple of days, even more so in the last few hours, and I've decided that I don't need to know."

"Ira, I'm so tired of secrets. My entire life I've lived with secrets. I want to be honest with you. If we don't discuss this, I think there will always be this shadow—"

"I don't *want* to know," he said quickly. "Whatever happened, we'll chalk it up to a very unusual situation. I'm guessing emotions ran high when he reappeared and—" He stepped away. He stared at the ocean and drew in a deep breath. "Whatever happened has happened. Today is supposed to be the day that we start our new life together. What happens from today onward is what matters most. I love you. More than life itself, I love you."

"I love you, too," she said. And she knew that she did.

Tears welled up in his eyes. "I haven't been around as much as I should have been."

"Ira— This is not your fault."

He brought her hands to his lips and kissed them. "You've had a lot going on. A lot of stress with the wedding and this house and your mother. You told me you wanted a small wedding and I should have listened. I should have told my parents no when they started inviting more guests and high profile people. We'll take our marriage vows today. On the beach. Just you and me and a minister. Maybe a couple of witnesses." His smile was soft and full of love. He kissed her hands. "Let's just—not mention the other again. Okay?"

She nodded.

"You love me, right?"

"I do," she said.

With puffy cheeks, he exhaled a sigh of relief.

She understood he didn't want specifics. He didn't want to hear her confess her feelings about Beau, how events unfolded, or how she ended up in his arms. He didn't want details. She could honor that.

So they walked along the beach and instead she told him what was on her mind and in her heart. Because a lot had happened in these last few days, and she was through with secrets.

———

26

P eyton drove the rental car back from Mrs. Miller's
house with the windows down. She hadn't realized
how much she missed fresh air until she had been
trapped inside the manor's memories.

She looked at Bertha Mae's 1850s camera that she had
strapped into the passenger seat as if it were a small child. It
was an evil thing, she thought. If only because Bertha Mae
had used it as such. Peyton remembered the tripod in the
basement near Rachel's body and the countless tintypes of
Rachel when she was sick.

She stopped at the intersection just before the Alcott
property line. The manor looked majestic and peaceful in
the distance, like it had been cleansed somehow. Emptied.

She knew the feeling.

Hidden toxic memories had been flushed up and out
of her.

She and the manor both had clean slates now.

She watched her mother's car pull into the front drive
and she followed her, parked her car right behind Jayne

Ella's. When she got out, Peyton's phone buzzed with a text message alert. Amanda:

Know you're almost on your honeymoon (lucky dog). No need to respond. Just letting you know we got the Sweet Chocolate deal! Great job and Congrats, my new Exec VP!! Promotion is yours!!

"Everything okay?" Jayne Ella forced a smile. She wore an Atlanta Braves baseball cap pulled low and her prescription glasses. No makeup. Not even lipstick.

"Yeah. I got the Sweet Chocolate account. And the promotion."

Jayne Ella's weak smile slipped. "That's wonderful. I know that's what you wanted. And you deserve it. More than anyone, I'm proud of you." Something was off center about Jayne Ella's tone.

"Thanks," Peyton said.

"Layla called and said they're keeping Horace in the hospital for another few nights. She said he was dehydrated, his blood pressure was low. I don't know where he's been all this time, but she also said he was malnourished."

They were silent for a moment.

Jayne Ella looked at the ground. "You put the keys back under the flower pot at Mrs. Miller's house? And you got what you needed?"

Peyton nodded, slipped her hands into her back pockets.

Jayne Ella stepped closer to Peyton, rubbed her arm. "I'm sorry," she whispered. "I'm really so very sorry about everything."

"He put her in the backseat with me," Peyton said.

Jayne Ella closed her eyes for a long moment. "The whole thing is just horrifying. Never did I think he would do something like that. I wish I'd known, I would have done something."

"I did tell you what little bit I remembered from that night. You told me it never happened."

"I thought you were referring to something else."

"What something else?" Peyton asked.

"I never knew Ruby Lee was buried here. I promise. You have to believe me."

Peyton watched Jayne Ella closely for any signs that she might be lying. Her mouth was still. No lips twisted to the side, and she didn't chew on her cheek.

"I thought you were starting to remember the gold and I didn't want you to."

"You knew about the gold," Peyton said.

Jayne Ella nodded. "It was a stupid thing to do." She told her about the night at the bank, her spur of the moment decision to do what she thought would end her financial problems.

"Your father and I were arguing a lot in those days. In large part because I was involved with Austin. He didn't know for sure, not initially, but he suspected. I thought Austin and I were meant to be together, and he often told me that we were.

"The night when we moved the gold here, your father suspected that I was out with Austin. I told him I was working at the salon. I guess he drove by and I wasn't there. It was late, and he went out looking for me. He finally found me here, with Austin.

"We had already moved the gold inside when I heard a car pull up. I came outside and found him here, with both you and Layla asleep in the back seat. He saw Austin's car and said he knew what was going on, that I was having an affair. He moved the two of you to the backseat of my car and told me he was leaving us.

"After your father drove away, I told you to stay in the back seat and to watch your sister, that I would be out in a few minutes. I went inside to tell Austin that I had to leave, when I turned around I found you standing in the great hall. We had gold bars on the floor, next to a big hole. You saw everything, including Austin.

"You said you were wearing a white dress and that threw me. The only time I knew you were at the manor at night when you were ten, you weren't wearing a white dress. It was dark blue."

Like a wriggling fish yanked from dark depths to land, that childhood moment found light. Standing in the great hall: her mother, Austin, stacks of gold, a hole in the floor. *"Mama? What are you doing?"*

Jayne Ella had run toward her, guided her out of the front door of the manor.

Peyton rubbed her forehead. She had forgotten that memory until just then. Apparently her perfect recall wasn't always perfect.

"But the night he hit and buried Ruby was the night of his bank's Christmas party. I wore a white dress that night." Peyton said.

"The night of the party was several days after we'd buried the gold. I guess he needed a hiding place for her body, remembered the hole we made in the manor and made use of it. I think he would have dug her up and moved her a long time ago. But I had cement poured over the subflooring, then we installed cameras and extra security. There was no way for him to get to her. I thought I was preventing him from taking the gold. I didn't realize I was sealing Ruby's body into the manor." Jayne Ella's lips remained still. Tears slid down her cheeks. She was telling the truth.

"Are you going to jail?" Peyton asked.

Her mother exhaled hard. "I don't think so. At least the attorney I spoke with says there isn't enough hard evidence. I hope he's right."

"Then what's going on?"

Jayne Ella studied her daughter carefully. "One of the bankers I met with this week has called. They've offered us a deal, but it's not a workable one. So, they're calling the loan."

"What's the deal?"

"They said they did some research on your credentials. They were impressed with your firm in Boston, the clientele and your reputation. They said we could keep the loan if you ran the manor." Jayne Ella adjusted her cap.

Peyton felt her mouth ease open. "But I don't live here."

"That's what I told them."

"I could design the plans from a distance and we could hire someone to implement them locally. We have lots of clients who do that."

"I told them that, too. But apparently we are one of the larger loans that they've inherited. They aren't comfortable sticking their financial neck out with us unless we can show that we have local and professional management. Someone of your caliber."

"Maybe if I talk with them, convince them that I would be hands on—"

"That would be great." Jayne Ella's lips drew into a flat line and Peyton knew she didn't hold out much hope.

"I'm sorry, for everything. I really am." Jayne Ella held her daughter close for a long time, kissed her cheek, then stood back. "I love you, Peyton."

Peyton noticed that her mother's mouth remained calm and peaceful.

"Thank you," Jayne Ella said.

Peyton's guard dropped, for what she thought might be the first time in twenty years. At least where her mother was concerned.

"I was going to go inside and see what kind of mess the police left behind. But I'm just going to go home." Jayne Ella took a final glance at the manor, then got in her car and left.

Peyton unbuckled the camera from the passenger seat and saw the black book Beau had given her. She tucked it into her waistband, went inside and tried to figure out what to do with Bertha Mae's camera.

She could smash it, then she wondered if she should burn it. For the time being, she decided to park it on a display shelf in the ballroom. She stared at it, wondering if it still held the power it once did.

Yellow tape at the bottom of the grand staircase caught her attention and she walked into the great hall. The giant hole in the floor was empty, no bodies, no gold. Even the presence she had felt in the area, the one she thought was Bertha Mae, was quiet.

No screaming, no fury or unexplained drafts.

She pulled the black book from her waistband and headed toward the porch.

She opened the front cover and drew in a sharp breath.

There was hardly any white on the pages, Beau's small print filled nearly every space, left to right, top to bottom. Many of the items he wrote about were the same memories that had reached to her through the walls since she had arrived. How he had proposed, how they met. There even a mention of the rose quartz bracelet he gave her and the way the pink stone appeared against her skin.

She ran her fingertips along the wall of the manor, seeing the house differently now, wondering if it had played a role in sending her Beau's thoughts. To let her know that he was nearby, that he needed help, or to remind her of what had once been.

She walked toward the front of the house, looked again at the hole in the floor, inexplicably knowing. The spirit that screamed with such fury hadn't been Bertha Mae's spirit at all. That wasn't her style.

The spirit that tried to make itself known, that knocked things over and howled and screeched, the one that had finally found peace—that had been Ruby Lee.

27

P eyton walked onto the back porch of Alcott Manor and flipped the switch on the ceiling fans to stir up the breeze. She picked up a couple of wadded paper towels that someone left behind and brushed errant dirt from the wicker couch cushions. The sun was just past its height for the day, edging toward the front of the manor. Magnolia shadows stretched wide across the short grass, white foam from calm waves bubbled onto the sand and left their trail. The tent and the chairs and the arbor had been removed from the great lawn, leaving another blank slate.

She walked inside, strolled along the main hallway, let her attention run through the house. It was empty. Nothing reaching from the walls. Nothing emanating from the furniture, no stories circulating or needing to be heard.

The rooms were at peace. The manor had let go of the many stories that once kept it too alive. With Mrs. Miller gone, Peyton was the only one left who knew all the history about Alcott Manor.

She ambled into the ballroom and studied several of the tintypes that Mrs. Miller had left on the table. One was a holiday celebration, maybe Thanksgiving. She looked closely at the guests pictured at the gathering. There was one young woman with what looked to be red hair, auburn. She stood in the background and her features were fuzzy.

She could have passed for a Ruby-lookalike, if guesswork were involved to imagine how she would have grown up. And if you were a grieving mother who desperately wanted to see her daughter again, to believe she could come back.

The tintype clacked against the table when she put it down, and Peyton turned her attention to the exhibit featuring some of Bertha Mae's belongings. She took down her tiara and her diary, her fan and white gloves, and placed them on one of the side tables. She would not allow Bertha Mae to be celebrated, or to be the center of anyone's admiration.

She thought about the museum that Mrs. Miller used to run and how it featured so many of Bertha Mae's personal items. She would make certain that those came down as well. She would find more of Rachel's personal belongings, she would feature those instead. The images started to flow and form.

Since her life had been ripped apart nine years ago, she had struggled to figure out where she belonged. When she was young, she thought she belonged in Charleston with her mother, later she thought it had been with Beau. Then, she thought it was with her career in Boston, along with Ira.

Now, for the first time in a long while, she wasn't blaming herself for anything—not for Ruby's disappearance, or Mrs. Miller's heartache. With the mysteries of her childhood and Beau's disappearance solved, she felt a calmness, an inner peace that she suspected the manor also embraced.

The belonging she had searched for strengthened inside of her. Fortified her. Not in the way she thought it would, but far better. She belonged everywhere, and yet nowhere, all at once. She was at home within herself.

Then, with typical mystifying manor-like style, she knew. Simply. Clearly.

She hopped into the rental car, sped down the white pebble driveway, then down the long road that lead to the beach. She drove all the way to where he was staying and parked her car in the public drive. She couldn't explain how she knew where he would be, she just did.

It was true what Beau had said. That once you knew what you wanted, everything else was easy.

She saw him standing on the pier, holding his camera. Her heart did a triple beat, caused her to catch her breath.

If she had made any other choice, she would have been like the manor—some part of her going over and over the secret she kept within. One day, that secret would have eaten her alive and it would have destroyed others in the process, too.

He turned as if he had heard her and he studied her. When she smiled, a genuine one that came from her heart, he walked toward her. It was then that the deepest part of her heart—the place where Beau had always lived—broke free. There was no more hiding any part of what she felt, least of all from herself.

"How did you know where I was?" he asked.

"This is where you proposed to me," she said.

He gathered her into his arms. "I love you," he whispered.

"I love you, too," she said.

They walked arm and arm, barefoot on the sand.

She explained that she had already spoken to Ira, that

he was on his way back to Boston without her. "I felt terrible about hurting him and breaking the engagement. But I would have felt worse if I had chosen to live a lie. He would have, too. And I have a feeling that as soon as my boss finds out he's available, she'll probably give him a call."

She thought about one of the last things Ira had said before he left, that he needed to figure out why he chose women who were unavailable. She knew he would work that out.

"Won't that be odd?" he asked. "Working with her if she's pursuing him? By the way, am I moving to Boston? Because you realize I would follow you anywhere."

She picked up a perfect sand dollar, ran her thumb over its fragile surface. "Actually, I've been offered a new opportunity, a local one, and I'm going to accept. This will give me the chance to have my own consulting business, and the client is a big one. I'm already getting some really good ideas on how to help them."

"Local?" he asked.

"Yeah. I'm excited about it. They need me and helping them is the right thing to do. Being here is the right move for me as well."

He lifted her chin and gazed into her eyes. He kissed her gently on the lips.

They started walking again. "What about you?" she asked.

"What about me what?" His smile was sly, and she nudged him.

"How does local work for you?"

"Local works just fine for me, as long as you're here. As long as we're together."

She wrapped both arms around him and studied his brilliant blue eyes that always had too much gypsy in them.

The fire was back, fueled by a bright happiness, but his need to roam had settled.

"My split-apart," he said.

She thought that was about right, and she laid her head on his chest. "Mine, too."

They walked to the pier and looked at the deep water glistening in the afternoon light.

"What will you do while you're living local?" she asked.

"My mother is setting up a fund for Horace. She feels awful about what my dad did to Ruby and their family. So, I'm going to help Horace get back on his feet, make sure he has whatever he needs. Then I'm going to get back to my first love—well, both of my first loves." He kissed her hand. "And I'm going to open that photography business."

"My new client needs a good photographer. When I pick up other clients, I'm sure they will, too."

"If your new client is who I think it is, I won't be shooting with any antique cameras."

"I appreciate that, actually."

He stood behind her and she leaned against him, his solid strength supporting her. "This feels really good, not to be running from anything."

"Yeah, it really does." He squeezed her in a firm hug.

She had the sense that they would be doing the exact same thing fifty years from then—holding one another, looking at the ocean and making plans for the future. The tide forced the waves against the shore, one after the other.

Gently, he turned her around, lowered himself to one knee, and held both of her hands in his. "Peyton, I knew from the first moment I saw you that I loved you, that I would always love you. Nine years later, you are still the most beautiful, brilliant woman I've ever known. And that will never change. Marry me. Be my wife, my partner, my soul mate. Forever."

She looked at him for a long time, cherishing the moment. "Yes. Absolutely, yes."

He stood and pulled her close. "Promise me this."

"Anything," she said.

"That we'll never have to spend another day apart."

She snuggled closer to him. "I promise."

The special place in her heart where she had always kept him near solidified within her, creating a permanent home. Because of the connection they shared, she knew they had never been fully separated, not really. And she knew, with a love this strong, that they never could be.

ALSO BY ALYSSA RICHARDS

THE FINE ART OF DECEPTION SERIES

THE FINE ART OF DECEPTION, UNDOING TIME

SOMEWHERE IN TIME

LOST IN TIME

THE FINE ART OF DECEPTION, BOXED SET

THE ALCOTT MANOR SERIES

THE HAUNTING AT ALCOTT MANOR

A MURDER AT ALCOTT MANOR

A STRANGER AT ALCOTT MANOR

THE CHASING SECRETS SERIES

CHASING SECRETS

FORCED PERSPECTIVE

Be the first to know about Alyssa Richards' next novel, sign up here: www.AlyssaRichards.com

and follow her on Amazon or BookBub to receive a new release alert!

ABOUT THE AUTHOR

ALYSSA RICHARDS is the USA TODAY BESTSELLING AUTHOR of romantic suspense and mystery thriller novels. She loves living in the South with her husband and two children. She also loves good espresso, her rescue dogs, magnolias and gardenias, and, of course, reading a great book. She grew up running barefoot in the Blue Ridge Mountains of North Carolina, where her favorite weekly adventure was a trip to the library with her mom.

Sign up for Alyssa's newsletter at www.alyssarichards.com to receive special offers, and news about her latest releases.

For More information
www.AlyssaRichards.com
Contact Alyssa at:
authoralyssarichards@protonmail.com

- instagram.com/alyssaauthor
- amazon.com/Alyssa-Richards/e/B00S1IGJ9O
- bookbub.com/authors/alyssa-richards
- goodreads.com/alyssarichards

CHASING SECRETS - A THRILLER

"Y ou're lying." Barbara narrowed her eyes at her husband.

David raised his glass of champagne and broadcast his perfectly white, nearly electric smile that could have won an election. "Everything's fine."

She raised an eyebrow to scold him; he was evading. "I didn't say things weren't fine. I said you were lying."

He cleared his throat and gestured with his glass. "To our second anniversary, to yet another clean health report, and to the baby we weren't supposed to conceive."

He placed his hand over his jacket pocket. It was an unconscious move. She knew that's where he kept a photo of himself at the age of eight, his head resting across his mother's chest, her head wrapped in a colorful scarf, her skin pale and drawn against the white sheets of the hospital bed.

Barbara survived the cancer, his mother hadn't.

She ran her hand through her hair, grateful to have hair again. Grateful that it came in twice as thick as she once had, grateful that it didn't come back gray as she had been told that it might.

The ring of their champagne toast sounded clear in the quiet outdoor restaurant. She took only a tiny sip. A few cars drove by slowly, their engines relatively soft. A man whizzed by, standing on an electric-powered scooter, which hummed like the motor of a sewing machine.

David kissed her hand.

She studied his assuring smile and his soft expression. He was full of love and secrets. She never could read him clearly when his lips were on her skin or when he smiled at her in that way. In fact, she couldn't read him well at all. Not in the way she read other people.

"I saw another stack of medical bills come in this week," she said.

He looked at her hand and gave it a squeeze. "I'm making all the money we'll ever need to overcome whatever life throws at us. Don't you worry."

"I don't know how you do it." She cast him her most scrutinizing stare, the one she planned to use when their child was a teenager.

"I can do anything, when it comes to you." David tucked his napkin in his lap, his smile widening like he was pleased with himself. "And as far as not being able to read me the way you want, you're just going to have to trust me instead."

"I'd rather be able to read you." She arched her eyebrow again.

She'd never been able to figure out that little glitch with her talent. With anyone else, she got a gut feeling and would know quite a bit about that person. It was a skill she really appreciated because, oddly enough, she didn't trust people all that much otherwise.

When she realized she couldn't read David, her first

instinct had been to stay away from him. But she fell in love with him. She couldn't help herself. He treated her like a queen, never gave her any reason not to trust him.

Problem was, the more she overrode her instincts so that she could trust her husband, the less she trusted herself.

"One day soon I'll tell you why," he said.

"*You know* why I can't read you?" she asked.

"I have a theory." David sipped his champagne, kept his eyes on hers, like he was prepared for her question. Knew what she was going to ask and when. Everything he did was deliberate and full of care.

"Then tell me, because this has been driving me nuts for years."

"I will," he said. "Soon."

"Now. Please."

David was a planner. He always had a plan A and a plan B. Sometimes a plan C. Always thinking ahead. "Soon enough."

"Fine. Then you should know that I've been hiding something, too."

"You're not capable of keeping secrets from me."

"Actually, I am."

"Are you feeling okay? Is the baby alright?"

She pressed her hand to her still-flat stomach. "We're fine. Perfectly fine."

He gave a little exhale. "You're carrying my heart, you know. Our heart, actually."

She smiled and nodded. "I know."

"I've been thinking about something..."

"Wait, David, what I have to say is really important." She heard a whine in her voice she hadn't expected. He had spoiled her over the years and now she whined. She would have to break herself of that.

"Just real quick. Then I want to hear your secret. Okay?"

She wanted his undivided attention later, so she cleared her throat to make sure the whine was gone. "Fine. Shoot."

"Does the name Elias mean anything to you?"

"Elias...Elias..." Barb repeated the name in her mind and felt a swell of guilt in her chest. She wasn't supposed to know their baby's gender, yet. But the nurse had slipped and told her during the last ultrasound. David would flip when he found out they were having a girl if he was already thinking of boys' names. "No, I don't think so. Why do you want to know?"

"He works with one of my customers. I think there's something off about him."

She and David often discussed their impressions of other people, especially when they didn't know them that well. People had tells, signs they unwittingly shared that gave insight into who they were. Barbara picked up on those little signs better than most. She had a bizarrely keen radar when it came to reading people. It was probably genetic, her dad was the same way.

That knack had always come in handy. In college she could tell which boys were genuine and which ones were looking for meaningless hookups. Within a few moments of meeting new sorority sisters she knew who would be a loyal friend, and who wouldn't be trustworthy.

David had good instincts about people, too, but hers were better.

She couldn't remember anyone named Elias. "Why would you think I know him? Did he ask about me?"

"No, but my customer warned me that he has a history of making moves on other men's wives. Friendly and non-threatening at first, then crossing the line from professional to inappropriate. Seems he might be a little...unbalanced. I got the sense he could be dangerous." Intensity flashed in David's eyes, just for a moment.

She recognized the sign. It was an unconscious thing he did when he wasn't comfortable with what he was saying. Some people rubbed their nose when they weren't telling the truth. Others spoke rapidly, blinked too much or even broke into a sweat. For David, his eyes flared. Just slightly.

Deliberately, she'd never told him that he did this, it was one of the very few tells he had.

She exhaled hard to help clear her mind and focused on the cars that drove by as a distraction. Barbara didn't believe David's story about Elias. But she knew David was warning her off of him for a reason. Probably something more serious than he wanted to share. He was always protecting her.

"Then you need to stay away from him as well," she said. "Keep him away from your business."

He raised his glass of champagne. "I will. Another toast. Then I want to hear your secret. To your continued good health. And a wish on this, our second anniversary: May our next fifty years of marriage be as wonderful as our first two."

"And a lot healthier."

"They will be." He pressed his hand against the breast pocket of his blazer again. "I'll make sure of it." Their glasses clinked in a toast. "Now that you're healthy, I want to reopen the conversation about shutting the business down for a while so we can travel. We need to see the world while we can, just like we always wanted."

"Oh, David." They had talked about traveling the world together almost from their first date. But now that her mother had passed and her father had had his second heart attack, things had changed. "I can't leave Pop alone for that long. You know he depends on me."

"Then we'll plan a long vacation, to celebrate your recovery. Just a few months. I'll explain it all to you once we're away, but it's important." His eyes were wide and intense. His hands were tucked into tight fists on the table, the skin stretched taut over his white knuckles.

"A few months, David, that's—does this have something to do with that Elias person you just told me about?"

The brown sedan that drove toward them slowed down enough to catch her attention. The driver wore a trucker's hat and aviator sunglasses, and he stared straight at them.

"David—" She pointed to the driver. At the last second, he raised his arm level and straight and pointed a gun at them.

David turned, then quickly stood to hover over her.

"I love you, Barb! Go to the—" David's words were cut short by several loud pops. Blood spattered across her face and covered her glasses. Her husband's body jerked violently, then fell to the ground.

"NO!" she screamed.

Restaurant guests shrieked, dishes crashed.

Searing pain ripped through her shoulder and knocked her to the floor. Barbara crawled beneath the table, yanked her husband's arm and tried to pull him to her.

But he was heavy, unmoving.

Blood poured from the back of his head, his eyes wide open and unseeing.

To Continue the Adventure...Click here!

>>>>Chasing Secrets Book 1

ACKNOWLEDGMENTS

With deepest gratitude...

    to my husband for his undying enthusiasm,
    to G & G for their love,
    to Peter Senftleben, my amazing editor,
    and to Lucinda for her loving support.

www.ingramcontent.com/pod-product-compliance
Lightning Source LLC
Chambersburg PA
CBHW061019120726
47910CB00006B/2018